THE ORANGE MISTRESS

Alice Wingard tells the story of how Nell Gwyn saves her from destitution when she is orphaned. Nell takes her to live in a bawdy house in Coal Yard Alley. The well-educated Alice finds her new surroundings shocking. Yet the girls' friendship deepens as, together, they move on from the theatre in Drury Lane, to Pall Mall and then to the court of the lascivious Charles II. Sharing happiness and sorrow, they encounter bloodshed, passion and political intrigue . . .

SARA JUDGE

THE ORANGE MISTRESS

Complete and Unabridged

LINFORD
Leicester

First published in Great Britain in 1989 by
Robert Hale Limited, London

First Linford Edition
published 2009
by arrangement with
Robert Hale Limited, London

British Library CIP Data

Judge, Sara.
    The orange mistress.- -(Linford romance library)
    1. Gwyn, Nell, *1650-1687*- -Fiction.
    2. Charles II, King of England, *1630-1685*- -
    Fiction. 3. Brothels- -England- -London- -
    Fiction. 4. Great Britain- -History- -Charles II,
    1660-1665- -Fiction. 5. Love stories.
    6. Large type books.
    I. Title II. Series
    823.9'14–dc22

    ISBN 978–1–84782–906–1

Published by
F. A. Thorpe (Publishing)
Anstey, Leicestershire

Set by Words & Graphics Ltd.
Anstey, Leicestershire
Printed and bound in Great Britain by
T. J. International Ltd., Padstow, Cornwall

This book is printed on acid-free paper

To Hazel Brown

1

This is the story of Nell Gwyn, my dearest friend and companion for many a year.

Soon after she took me in and gave me a home after that dreadful year of 1665, Nelly asked me to stay with her always. She could neither read nor write, and when she found out that I was a clergyman's daughter, and thus well educated until my fifteenth year, she begged me to become her amanuensis and read to her, or write for her, whenever such duties were required of me.

Even at that time Nelly was ambitious, determined to rise up from her poor surroundings and make her way in the world; and she realised that my knowledge of words could prove of value to her, apart from the strength of our friendship.

Gladly I agreed to remain, and never was to rue the day I first fell into the company of Nell Gwyn. For Nelly lifted me from being a penniless orphan in the most squalid alley off Drury Lane, to the theatre, to better living, and finally to Pall Mall and Whitehall and into the very presence of King Charles.

She asked me long ago to write her story, so that her sons would know the whole and rightful truth about their mother, and this I promised to do.

So, the words set down hereafter are the true adventures of Nell Gwyn, told to me by her, and some of them experienced by me, Alice Wingard.

This story will also be about me, for we have shared much together and my life has been so long a part of Nelly's, that I cannot refrain from putting down the thoughts and feelings of Alice — or Wiggins, as Nelly liked to call me — from time to time.

But the way that Nelly spoke, especially in those early days, is quite beyond my capability to put down correctly. So I have written all that she said using my own English but endeavouring, I hope, to show the intelligence, the courage, and the zest of my enchanting, illiterate friend.

We were of the same age, Nelly and I, when first we met, but very different girls in both looks and character. Nelly was pretty, light-boned and slender, and with the smallest feet in the whole of England, as she often liked to tell me. Although without education, she possessed a sharp tongue and quick wit even at the age of fifteen years.

Her hair was red-brown, with golden lights, and her eyes were hazel. Her nose turned up, there were enchanting dimples in her round cheeks, and when she laughed, which she did often, her eyes creased up until they almost disappeared.

Nelly was so alive and filled with energy, so ready with a jest and a quip, so warm-hearted, that I loved her and wanted to be near her from the first day we met.

I, in my turn, was thin, starving, miserable, and very plain.

'Gracious!' cried Nelly, when first perceiving me. 'What have we here? Is it a drowned rat left over from the Plague?'

She was carrying a bucket on her way to the pump and had almost fallen over my recumbent form as I lay in the gutter, no longer caring if I lived or died.

I remember that moment even now; the red warmth of her hair as she bent over me, her full lower lip caught between small white teeth, the compassion in her eyes. So many people had passed by uncaring, some giving me a kick, hoping that I would remove my wretched body from their sight. But not Nell Gwyn.

'What is the matter with you, dearie? And where is your home?' she asked.

I had difficulty in answering her, for I had not eaten for several days and had managed to sip but a few drops of the filthy water in the gutter beside me.

4

'No home,' I croaked, letting my eyes rest on her face, half believing that she was an angel from Heaven come to escort me to a better land.

'Lord save us!' cried Nelly. 'Not a rat but some poor sodden raven. Come home with me then, and get some food and drink into your belly.'

I heard the pail clatter down beside her and then strong little hands were around my shoulders and her insistent voice was commanding me to stand.

So weak was I from lack of sustenance, and so unprepared for such kindness, that I was of little use to my stoic rescuer.

'Hey, Tom — come here, lad, and give us a hand!' was shouted across the lane, then other hands and stronger arms enfolded me, and I was lifted high in a man's embrace and carried to Nelly's abode.

I remember little more of that first encounter, save that Nelly fed me some warm broth herself, before putting me to sleep in the bed I was to share with her and her sister, Rose. At first I was only able to feel gratitude for warmth, and comfort, and victuals, after so many weeks of misery. But soon I was to meet old Madam Gwyn and learn to my shame that I was being cared for in a bawdy-house.

This knowledge was to prove one of the biggest differences between Nelly and myself. For I had been brought up in an austere and God-fearing household, and both my parents had been followers of Lord Protector Cromwell, and staunch Puritans.

I remember my father working long hours amongst the poor in White Cross Street preaching of the evils of dancing, and the theatre, and all other pastimes. The entire family wore black garments, lightened only by white collars and cuffs, and the strictest religious observances were demanded of us, especially on Sundays.

There were three of us children; I was the eldest daughter, Charity was my little sister, and John, our brother, was two years younger than me.

Then the Lord Protector died and Charles Stuart returned from his exile on the Continent and was crowned King of England.

The London crowds rejoiced, theatres were reopened, and my father and other Nonconformists were filled with dread.

My parents struggled on, endeavouring to retain some part of their disciplined and orderly way of life. But with a fun-loving licentious King setting the example, people of both high and low birth followed his lead, and Sundays were treated the same as any other day.

Of course, being but a child at the time, I was not fully aware of all the difficulties my poor parents had to suffer but now, looking back over those years, I realise how terrible it must have been for them — seeing their safe, controlled, pious world crumble and become another Sodom and Gomorrah.

Suffice it to say that the first five years of the Restoration were, perhaps thankfully, ended for them by another more powerful enemy, the Bubonic Plague.

It was the most terrifying time of my young life, that summer of 1665, for I lost both my parents as well as my brother and sister, within a couple of weeks. I did not catch the dread disease, but was shut up in our small house in White Cross Street, watching my family die one by one, and unable to move away even when their corpses had finally been removed, because of the red cross upon our door.

Night after night I heard the doleful, haunting cry echoing through the dark streets — 'Bring out your dead.'

Women searchers came and took away the foul, stinking bodies of my once beloved family, but I was told to remain in the house. Then the doors and windows were boarded up, and bread and water were handed in through a gap in the boards when somebody remembered that I was still there, in case I, too, was carrying the infection.

By winter the heavy frosts froze the Plague germs out, and I was able to leave my home and wander the half-empty streets of the City, picking up what rinds and crumbs I could find, and begging for the rest.

It was in the spring of 1666 that I had dragged myself as far as Drury Lane and first met Nelly. Thank God I did, for there was little hope of life left in my shrunken heart, and I was praying most earnestly to die and be with my family again, when Nell Gwyn came to my rescue.

But a bawdy-house! What a place for a clergyman's daughter to find herself ensconced. And such noise and roistering at all hours of the day and night; with gallants, wearing strange and colourful garb, lounging and cursing and drinking too much in the company of Madam Gwyn's girls.

Dear me, how often my heart sank

during my time at old Madam Gwyn's abode in Coal Yard Alley, on the City side of the Lane.

I hated old Madam Gwyn — she was fat and waddling, with a red, coarse-featured face and a loud mouth, and she stunk of brandy.

'I will get us out of here, Ally-Wally Wiggins,' Nelly would say, having given me that name soon after she learnt of my second name of Wingard, and it soon became simply Wiggins.

She knew that I was ill at ease in such an unrighteous atmosphere, yet unable to leave the place and the people, for I had nowhere else to go.

'I will get us out of here,' said Nelly, 'and have such plans for our future, do not despair, dearest Wiggins. Bear with it all for the present, and stay with me and I shall take you with me when I go. For we will leave here one day, you and I, and I shall rise from this dung-hill and take my place in the great world outside, and you will come with me. Just see if it don't happen, Wiggins, and sooner than you may think!'

At this time Nelly was a fish hawker in the streets around Drury Lane, and I would go with her every morning to the Fish Market in Lewkenor's Lane, and help her to carry the baskets of fresh herrings, which we sold for ten a groat.

It was smelly, tiring work tramping the streets, crying out our wares, and I was always thankful to get back in the evenings, even if it was to the noisy, immoral bawdy-house. There I would retire to our shared room and try to sleep, despite the din downstairs. But Nelly possessed amazing energy and would help her mother and sister in selling strong waters to the gentlemen visitors until late into the night.

'How do you manage it, Nelly?' I asked her once, looking at her bright hazel eyes and ready smile. 'Are you not tired after a day on your feet?'

'Sometimes I am, specially in winter with the cold winds freezing me very bones when they rush up from the river.' She lay beside me on the bed and stretched out her slender legs, admiring her neat ankles and tiny feet. 'But bein' so small I ain't heavy and I'm *good* on me feet, Wiggins. One day I'm gonna prance and dance with them on the stage. I'm quite determined, Ally-Wally, and it's that thought wot keeps me going.'

'On the stage?' I asked, astounded by such a remark. 'But how do you get taken on at the theatre, Nelly? And it's very immoral,' I added primly, remembering my father's views on that subject. It was the work of the Devil, he used to say, and the theatre a most wicked and sinful place.

'It ain't more immoral than Ma's bawdy-house,' she answered quickly, 'an' you was glad enough to be taken *here*, Wiggins, so don't you start preaching at me!'

'I am sorry,' I said hastily, realising that she was right and it was stupid of me to condemn a place I knew little about, and also wrong to criticise the kindest and most generous person I had ever known. 'You are pretty and bright, Nelly, and your voice is good and strong from shouting out your wares. But how does a seller of fish become an actress?'

'I knows a few people and I listens to them gallants, wot think they knows everything. And the theatres are opening again soon, now that the Plague is safely gone, and I'll be trying right *here*, Wiggins, in Drury Lane. Orange Moll will be needing some more girls for them oranges, and I'll get me foot in the door that way.'

Before Nelly was taken on by Orange Moll there was another disaster in London and I shall always remember the Great Fire, for although it was a most exciting event for us, it was a tragedy for thousands of City dwellers.

Nelly and I went down to the Strand and walked along Fleet Street towards Ludgate Hill. We could see the height of the flames as they engulfed the City and we heard, even from that distance, the crashing and splintering of timbers as house after house was destroyed. We could smell the burning, and the smoke, and feel heat in the parched air above us.

There were hundreds of people in the streets, poor refugees running from their homes, pulling carts behind them piled high with possessions; some with but a few belongings in their arms which they had managed to salvage from the burning heat.

I saw the King and his brother, the Duke of York, for the very first time that day and wished that my father had been alive to see them, for the Stuarts looked like caring men in that tumult. They also showed great courage and forcefulness of character, for they had ridden over from Whitehall and stayed all day near the engulfed City, giving commands, ordering buildings to be blown up, hoping that a space could be made to stop the approaching flames.

It was a day of new beginnings for me, for I also met Luke Markham, although I did not know his name until later, and despite his muddied and dishevelled state, I felt that he, also, was a kind and caring gentleman.

Nelly and I had moved away from the Fleet Bridge down on to the river bank, and were watching the wooden wharves being removed on the opposite bank, and fire posts being established by soldiers. It was then that we first noticed the stranger.

It was obvious from his full breeches with the ribbon trim, his silk stockings and high-tongued shoes, the gold braid on his jacket and lace-bordered cravat, that he had started the day well dressed and was obviously a gentleman. He, and a young lad beside him were helping the poor, distraught people to clamber up the river bank away from the boats, which were ferrying refugees from the far City bank. Men, women, and children were filling the small craft, carrying bundles in their arms. The Fleet Bridge was jammed with escaping inhabitants, so many had taken to the boats.

'Do not stand there!' shouted the man. 'You are in the way and it is dangerous in this mud.'

'How did the fire begin?' cried Nelly, ignoring the man's words and lifting her face to shout back at him, above the screams and wailing and the crashing of timber in the distance.

'Rumours are spreading almost as quickly as the flames,' he answered, straightening his back and resting for a moment before the next boat arrived. 'You will be told by many that it is a plot, and that the fire was started by Catholics.'

'Oh, no!' cried Nelly, placing her hands on her mouth.

And I felt a surge of hatred at his words, fanned by memories of my father, and his loathing for the Papists.

'But 'tis not so,' said the man firmly. 'Do not believe such rumours and stamp them out, as we must try to suffocate the flames. It was a normal fire, begun in a bakery in Pudding Lane, and the wind has been strong and blown the fire further and further forwards. It has not helped that all the buildings are made of timber,' he added.

He lifted his hand to his sweating, dirty face, and the river mud showed clearly on his once fine stockings, and on the lace at his wrists. Then he turned to look at me.

I believe, even then, I found him attractive for, despite his weariness and the despair of so many unfortunate people all around, humour seemed to lurk behind his troubled grey eyes, and I noticed how long-fingered and graceful his hands were though now engrimed with mud and slime.

The man was studying me with equal interest once he had turned his attention away from Nelly, and then he lifted one eyebrow and said, half-jesting, half-brusquely,

'Back, mistress, from whence you have come. This is no place for you and the flames may not stop at the Fleet River. 'Tis said that Cornhill and all of

Cheapside is destroyed, and the fire has now reached St Paul's. Go home,' he insisted, his voice softening, 'and start packing your belongings in case you, like these poor wretches, will be forced to leave your abode.'

I nodded, grateful for the chance to escape such an intense gaze.

'Come Nelly,' I said, taking her hand and trying to lead her away from the riverside.

But she was exhilarated and pulled her hand free from mine. The fire was still some distance away and had not harmed us, not like the terrible Plague which had enveloped the whole of London, and taken so many people in its ravenous embrace. In fact, we were told later, the fire did not take one life, it only destroyed thousands of houses in the four days and nights it raged.

'Come, Nelly,' I said again, but she was moving forward up towards the bridge again.

'There is so much to see — I want to

stay for a while,' she called back over her shoulder.

For a moment we were separated by the jolting, shoving crowd and I lost sight of her.

The man's hand touched my arm. 'Let her be,' he murmured. 'Your Nelly looks to be a survivor and will come to no harm. But you seem of more frail stock. Where is your home, mistress? And what is your name?'

'Alice Wingard, sir, and I live with Nell Gwyn in Coal Yard Alley.'

He gave a courteous bow but his handsome face had tightened. 'Then, Mistress Wingard, I beg you to return to your alley. There is enough work to be done for the homeless this day, and if you have a safe abode return to it now and leave this scene of devastation. Hey, Will!' he called to the young man who had been working beside him. 'Will, lad, take this lady back to Drury Lane and do not leave her until she is safely within her house in Coal Yard Alley.'

Will nodded and grinned at me; a lovely fresh complexioned boy, he looked, not bearing the pinched white features of the normal City youth.

'I can manage alone,' I said hastily, not wanting to take the lad away from his labours. 'Thank you for your advice, sir, and if you should see Nelly again, please tell her where I've gone.'

He nodded and turned abruptly as another boat came lurching, overburdened, towards the slippery bank. I smiled at Will, then made my way slowly up to the street and joined the throng in their steady flight away from Ludgate and towards the safety of the Strand.

2

Once the Great Fire was over and life around us returned to normal, Nelly was true to her word that autumn and I found myself accompanying her to the King's House quite near us in Drury Lane.

'I'm going to be an orange-girl and sell 'em for sixpence each,' Nelly told me excitedly. 'Orange Moll, who has charge of the girls, wants another at the theatre and says I will do nicely. I can talk and laugh and jest as much as I like, and oh, I shall love it, Wiggins! *And* seeing all them gallants from Court — maybe I shall find meself a gentleman of me own.'

'Be careful, Nelly.'

I knew that she was very attractive to men — had seen how she flirted and joked whilst selling strong waters to her mother's customers. But up until now

Nelly had refused to be bedded by any of them, and old Madam Gwyn had not demanded it of her, perhaps hoping that her pretty and lively daughter would do better for herself outside the bawdy-house.

Rose, who was taller and quieter and darker than Nelly, had already been ensnared by one gentleman, who often came and called for her services. I had been shocked when first realising this, wondering how any mother could allow her daughter to behave in such degraded fashion.

'Rose is different from me,' Nelly had said, shrugging her shoulders. 'She is not ambitious and will take life as it comes, so long as her belly is full and she has money enough for ribbons, and slippers, and new petticoats.'

'And you, Nelly?' I asked, wondering how she could avoid going the same way and, if she did, what would become of me? For I could never, ever, bed with a man I did not love, and to whom I was not married. Fortunately, my looks were not impressive and my body was still very thin and angular, and nobody had asked for me.

'Me,' answered Nelly, grinning at me, 'me is going higher than this old lane, Ally-Wally, and don't look so worried 'cos I told you that you will always come with me. You're gonna be my amanuensis when I'm rich and famous, remember? And write me letters and do all wot a clerk does for important men.

'Now, how about selling oranges, too? No? Didn't think you would. Then you must come with me to the theatre and go round the back, and help actresses put on their stage attire, and help them powder and paint their faces. You can do that, can't you, Wiggins?'

I nodded. I was not going to remain at old Madam Gwyn's bawdy-house without Nelly, and the rear of the theatre should not be too frightening. There was no way at all that I could have forced myself to stand in front of the stage, selling oranges to the noisy, jostling throng, like Nelly did.

The first time I went with Nelly had been a terrible shock and I was thankful to retreat and find the tiring-rooms behind the stage. We had arrived just before noon because, Nelly had informed me, the doors opened then and anyone who wanted a good seat made sure to get to the theatre early.

The performance did not start until half-past three, but the long wait did not worry the audience. Music was played, which pleased some, I suppose, if they could hear it. The orange-girls shouted out their wares, and the people crowded in, all talking and laughing and calling greetings to friends.

There was so much chat and laughter — even whilst the actors and actresses were performing — that I wondered why people bothered to spend money on what was really just a social gathering.

The atmosphere became extremely hot as the hours passed, because of the hundreds of candles, but Nelly did not mind either the heat, or the din.

'It's all such fun, Wiggins, seeing and hearing all them fancy folk, and one day I'm gonna be an actress, too. I'm gonna stand up on stage and have 'em all shutting up and listening to me 'cos I'll be so *good*!' she declared, once we were home again, and lifted her skirts and danced a little jig across the floorboards of the room we shared.

'Look at me legs — splendid, ain't they? And you can hear me voice, can't you, Ally-Wally? When I'm shouting out, 'Oranges — will you have any oranges?' You can hear me better than the rest, can't you?'

I nodded. Nelly's voice was always clear to me above the other girls', but maybe it was because I knew her.

'You need good legs for some of them parts. Oh, I look and learn all the time, Wiggins, and me voice is strong and I can make 'em laugh, I *know* I can!'

'But how do you get a part?' I asked slowly. 'It seems to me that Mr Killigrew has enough actresses as it is.'

'Pooh,' said Nelly, pouting her lips.

'He may have many females but none as good as me. I just need to show Mr Killigrew once — just once — and he'll want me for every part there is!'

'That's big talk,' I answered soberly, 'and how can you learn your lines when you can't read?'

'That's why I want you, Wiggins.' She grabbed my hands and spun me around the room with her. 'Ah, no,' she went on, panting slightly, 'you're heavy on your feet for such a slim girl, and definitely not a dancer! But that is good — wouldn't do for me to be jealous of you, would it now? What I want from you is what I ain't got meself, and that's words, Wiggins, *words*. You must read me lines out loud and I'll say 'em after you, and you must hear me and hear me until I *know*. See? That's why I need you always with me, Ally-Wally. You are going to teach me lines and then I'll be a proper actress.'

As always with Nelly in those early years, she got what she wanted, and was taken into the King's Players which was the company that performed at the King's House — or the Theatre Royal as it came to be called — in Drury Lane.

I, of course, went with her and was useful behind the scenes, helping her to dress, assisting with her face-paint, and hearing her say her lines over and over again.

It was a strange new world for us both, with a scene-room behind the stage where properties were kept, and where the actors and actresses waited for their cues.

Leading players were provided with their own rooms, and Nelly was to have her small private room later on, but at first she had to use the women's tiring-room up the stairs, with the other females in the company, and the actors had their men's tiring-room beyond.

To me, the most instant feeling was a sense of smell — not the aroma of face-paint, or candle-wax, or the many hot, unwashed, perfumed bodies, but the smell of sweet, strong oranges which filled my nostrils every day at the King's House, and even now, when I smell an orange, I am immediately transported back in time to the Theatre Royal, Drury Lane, and see the small, excited figure of Nelly as she began her new life selling that luscious fruit to the audience.

Nelly's first part was in a comedy called *The English Monsieur* and the play was written by the Honourable James Howard, who was married to John Dryden's sister.

There began for me a most interesting time for I was brought out of my pious and sober thoughts with surprising speed.

Always, at old Madam Gwyn's bawdy-house, I had held myself back from the ugly, sordid surroundings and looked at life with 'a stench beneath my nostrils,' as Nelly used to say. I was too good for that place, and showed my feelings; seldom laughing, or finding any joy in the life there, although grateful to Nelly for giving me sanctuary, and her friendship. But I was never happy there and could not pretend otherwise; nor had the selling of fish been an attractive form of employment.

Once Nelly became involved with the theatre, however, and had raised herself from the lowly state of orange-girl to being one of Mr Killigrew's actresses, my life changed again and I found interest in my surroundings, in the people I saw, and most of all in the continual gossip about Court life and the goings-on of the rich and famous.

Perhaps it was inevitable, but soon I put my austere puritanical upbringing behind me and began listening to the talk around me, becoming as intrigued as Nelly in the lives of the courtiers and gallants, and their various mistresses.

The behaviour of these people was little different to that of the gentlemen and sluts of old Madam Gwyn's bawdy-house, which so disgusted me. But because the chat was now about the wealthy and high-born, because the people I saw were magnificently attired and bejewelled, because their behaviour stemmed from the example of the King, himself, it made everything seem more acceptable and less vulgar. At least so I explained my changed attitude to myself.

And England was tired, weary of the Puritan Government under Lord Protector Cromwell; bored with plain dark garb and no laughter; hungry for amusement and gaiety and beautiful clothes and some lustre in life, I thought.

When Charles Stuart was crowned King of England and announced that he, too, was bored with poverty and endless travelling and lack of pleasure, and intended making his Court at Whitehall a place of enjoyment and beauty, it was understandable that all England should go wild with delight.

The theatres had been closed for twenty-three years, Nelly informed me, and King Charles not only allowed two to open as soon as he returned from exile, but he also made the decision to allow women to perform on stage, as was allowed on the Continent, and which had never been done before in this country.

'But then His Majesty likes and admires women,' Nelly said, patting at her red-brown curls and smoothing down her skirts, 'and when he sees me on stage he'll admire me so much that he'll ask for me, Wiggins.'

'You set your sights very high, Nell Gwyn,' I answered, smiling at her enthusiastic little face. 'I suppose the next thing will be a crown upon your head and me having to curtsey to you as the Queen of England!'

I was joking, but Nelly took my words quite seriously.

'The King is married to that Portuguese Princess, and although her English is not good 'tis said she is learning fast and will no doubt soon speak it better than me. So no, dear Wiggins, I don't expect to become Queen, but I do hear that His Majesty is a great one for having mistresses, and who knows *what* my future may be if I keep on performing and being *seen*, Ally-Wally!'

At this time I saw John Dryden, the famous poet and writer, who was later to become the King's Poet Laureate.

I met Mr Samuel Pepys, who, like the King, was interested in an actress, or two, and who worked as Clerk of the Acts to the Navy Board.

I saw the Duke of York and his wife, both interested in the theatre, and the Duke had a theatre named after him, and his own players, under the management of Sir William Davenant. When Nelly was not working we often went to the Duke's House and watched performances there.

I saw the Countess of Castlemaine, the King's mistress renowned for her beauty, and I met again the only man I was ever to love — Luke Markham.

Luke liked to visit both theatres whenever he was in London, and one evening he saw Nelly and me walking home after a performance, and he stopped to talk to us.

'Why, you're the gentleman we saw at the Fire,' cried Nelly, looking up into his handsome face.

I recognised him also, though this time so freshly attired, so gracious and charming, that it was hard to remember him as the tired man whose clothes had been ruined by the slime from the Fleet River.

'Yes, Mistress Gwyn,' he said, bowing over her outstretched hand, 'my name is Luke Markham, and I wanted to tell you how much I enjoyed your performance this afternoon.'

I believed, at first, that he was more interested in Nelly than he was in me. But she, although always attracted to the opposite sex, and Luke was an exceptionally handsome man, was already enamoured of Charles Hart, a good-looking actor at the Theatre Royal. And Nelly was always loyal to her lovers — even if she managed to have several of them. It was always one at a time with her, which was more than could be said for most of the attractive and desirable females I knew about.

Now I had best return to Nelly and her clever acting, for it must not be forgotten that this is her story, and my affairs will play but a small part on the stage of Nell Gwyn's dramatic life.

I remember some of her parts very well, and realised immediately Nelly began acting that the comic roles were ideal for her. She had sometimes to perform in serious dramas and tragedies, but she was never happy in such plays. The audiences, although loving her as she became more famous and applauding loudly whenever she appeared, obviously felt, like me, that Nelly was best suited to the humour which she bore within her, seemingly from birth.

Though where she got it from often puzzled me. Old Madam Gwyn was an ugly, fat and avaricious dame, whom I never saw so much as smile, and quiet, dark Rose did not sparkle, either. Maybe Nelly inherited her sense of humour from her father, but he was unknown to me, never spoken about by her family, and Nelly told me only once, and quite abruptly, that she knew little about him and that he had died in an Oxford gaol.

So, inherited or not, Nelly possessed a great wit, a love of life, and a merry laugh which grew louder and more raucous with the years, and her part as Lady Wealthy in *The English Monsier* really suited her.

She played the rich widow who knew the true importance of wealth and beauty. Lady Wealthy possessed a good heart and a fine sense of the ridiculous. In fact, so like Nelly that it was no wonder to me that Mr Killigrew had given her the chance to perform. In the play Nelly was the woman who teased, but who finally reformed and married her lover.

It was at this time that Nelly became greatly enamoured of the actor, Charles Hart, and he and Nelly were to perform superbly together, especially in comedies, and Hart was to partner her often at the Theatre Royal. He was a magnificent man — tall, handsome, and very charming, and I was most surprised when Nelly tired of him and found herself another lover.

Charles Hart was one of the most popular male actors of the day and the audience loved him as much as they did Nelly. When the two played opposite each other the theatre was always packed to the very doors. In one way only was Hart better than Nell Gwyn, and that was in serious and tragic parts.

Once she and Charles Hart fell in love she began spending more and more of her nights away from home, and it was then that my friendship with Luke Markham really began.

He would wait for me when I left the theatre, and walk with me up the lane to my lodgings at old Madam Gwyn's.

Luke was tall, lean and broad-shouldered; always elegantly attired and with his thick, dark brown hair cut just below his ears, not allowing it to flow loose upon his shoulders as was the fashion.

His fine eyes were a clear, light grey and very attractive, fringed as they were by black lashes beneath dark rather fiercely arched brows. His nose was long and straight above firm, well-shaped lips, and he sported neither beard nor moustache on his smooth brown skin.

His complexion was so healthy, his eyes so bright and piercing, that I asked him once if he enjoyed hunting. Luke Markham did not have the look of a man who spent his days indoors.

He smiled at my question.

'Yes, Mistress Wingard, I love the speed and excitement of the chase and hunt whenever I have the chance,' he said, his right eyebrow lifting as if in mockery at my words. 'I also travel a good deal and no doubt the fresh air keeps me healthy.'

We had stopped at the mouth of the narrow alley which led me to the rear of Madam Gwyn's abode. I never entered by the front but scuttled through the kitchen and up the stairs to our bedchamber, always hoping that I could get myself safely hidden away before anyone spotted me.

I hated the house more and more as the weeks passed, and with Nelly seldom accompanying me, I often wondered for how much longer such awful lodgings could be endured.

But Nelly knew of my feelings and begged me often to be patient.

'It will not be for long, dear Wiggins,' she used to say, 'bide just a while longer and then we'll move to a better place, I do *assure* you. You can keep it nice for me if I am away with my Charles Hart, and you'll be happy there, I know.'

Now I paused at the entrance to the alley as Luke Markham doffed his hat at me. He was wearing the new petticoat breeches, chestnut brown in colour, trimmed with yellow looped ribbons. His short jacket was also brown, with deep cuffs, worn over a mustard yellow shirt, and his wide-brimmed hat was decorated with feathers and more yellow ribbons.

There was a wide ornamental sword belt worn across his left shoulder and from which hung his sword, and Luke Markham looked, to my admiring eyes, like a very splendid gentleman.

'Before you run away like a frightened mouse, tell me something, Mistress Wingard,' he said. 'Why do you always make for the rear of this building instead of going in at the front? Is it only with me that you appear so reticent? For I am a man of the world, mistress, and would not condemn you for your place of abode, nor for your other activities when not at the theatre. God knows, we have a supreme example in our King's behaviour, and nothing either shocks me, or offends me, be assured of that.'

Heavens, I thought, he believes me to be one of old Madam Gwyn's whores, and thinks I have been trying to deceive him by going in at the rear.

'Mr Markham,' I replied quickly, 'do not imagine that I live in this wretched place because I like it, nor because my presence is required here as a service to gentlemen. I *hate* the house and inhabit it only because of Nelly.'

'All right, all right,' he answered, raising both eyebrows at the sharpness of my reply and stepping back a pace. 'It was natural to assume that you lived here for a purpose, but I see that I was mistaken in my assumption. Forgive me, Mistress Wingard, but do, I beg, explain why you became so friendly with little Nell Gwyn. Amusing and delightful she may be, but scarcely the companion I would expect of someone as well-spoken as yourself.'

'Nelly saved me from starvation and death,' I said. 'All my family perished last year in the Great Plague and I was lost and lonely and yes, *wanting* to die, when Nelly found me and took me in.'

'I see,' he said soberly, and his eyes were gentle as they looked down at me, all former mockery gone from his face.

'And I may be well spoken and better educated than Nelly — but what use is that if one has nowhere to go, no one to talk to? I was saved by Nelly and have been loved and comforted by her ever since. She, in turn, is grateful for my knowledge as I am able to read her parts to her, and she learns her lines from me.'

'A veritable amanuensis,' he remarked, smiling.

'I love that word and so does Nelly now that she knows what it means. Yes, I am her secretary, although I have not written a word for her yet. But she has such dreams and ambitions, Mr Markham, and is quite determined to rise from this dreadful place and prosper in life, and I will go with her.'

'You could learn from Nelly also,' he said slowly.

'Learn from her?'

He nodded. 'Nell Gwyn is a very pretty young girl. Ask her how to dress your hair properly, and how to put a little paint on your face and — '

'How dare you!' I cried, halting him before he could mention anything more about my faults.

The blood had rushed to my cheeks

as he spoke, and anger flared in my breast. How dared he speak to me in such a fashion! I knew that Nelly was lovely, knew also that I was thin and plain by comparison. But even if Mr Markham was a man of the world, even if he was a connoisseur of women like the King, there was still the matter of human courtesy, and he had no right to criticise my looks.

I gathered my skirts in both hands and swung away from his piercing eyes.

'Mistress Wingard, I only meant to help,' he called after me as I ran down the alley, but I did not look back and he did not follow me.

Suddenly I was filled with dislike for the man whom I had at first thought to be so handsome and charming. It was all right for the likes of him to dress fashionably and look a perfect gentleman; he had plenty of money to squander on laces and ribbons and silk stockings; he was often at Whitehall, he had told us, and thus mixing with the most extravagant and bejewelled of courtiers who were always to be found near the King. But if Luke Markham were any kind of gentleman, he should have realised that Nelly and I did not have a spare penny. She was fortunate in being naturally pretty and having the money from her theatre performances to help towards her petticoats and face-paints.

I had nothing, save for the few garments her sister Rose no longer required. Nelly's slippers and skirts were all too small for me.

But the next day at the theatre, when the tiring-room was emptied of bodies and I had a moment to myself before the actresses came back after the first Act, I sat in front of the small mirror and gazed at my face in the flickering candle-light. With Luke Markham's words still burning in my ears, I saw at once what he had meant.

My hair was dull, light brown and totally without curl, hanging thin and lifeless to my shoulders. My brows and lashes were pale, scarcely noticeable in my equally pale face. My eyes were blue and pale, my nose was small and my mouth too big.

Looking down I saw that the old gown which Rose Gwyn had given me was worn and creased, a once blue cotton which had faded to a dirty grey. My petticoat was lank and dirty and my bare feet were thrust into worn clogs.

No wonder Luke Markham had urged me to improve my appearance. For the first time I was seeing myself as I really was — through another person's eyes. Although Nelly saw me continually, and would have spoken her mind had she considered me in need of improvement, my looks were a part of me, a part of her life, and something she accepted as readily as she did her fat, brandy-reeking mother, and the sordid surroundings of the bawdy-house.

Leaning forward I studied my face more carefully. My skin was unblemished and I always made sure to scrub my face and hands every day, but it was clear to me that some powder and paint would improve my features considerably, and if I learnt to curl my hair what a difference that would make to my appearance.

When I asked Nelly to help me she laughed.

'Got yourself an admirer then, Wiggins — must be that handsome gentleman, Mr Markham!'

'I do not have an admirer, and wish only to improve myself for my *own* satisfaction,' I replied.

I could see from the saucy expression on Nelly's face that she did not believe me, but she showed me how to smooth rouge upon my pale cheeks and salve on my lips, and a stick of kohl accentuated my eyes. She also taught me how to wind my hair around tongs, heated at the fireside, and once washed and curled my locks sprang into life, framing and enhancing my face.

'What is this salve?' I asked, running the tip of my tongue around my lips and finding it not unpleasant to taste,

45

but rather greasy in texture.

'Mrs Knipp says it is made by mixing cochineal, white of hard-boiled egg, milk of green figs, alum and gum arabic,' answered Nelly. 'Don't know what half them things are but it do taste good, don't it? And my! You look a different girl now, Wiggins.'

We were in our room in Coal Yard Alley that day, I remember, and being on my own with Nelly, and not surrounded by other actresses, gave me confidence to practise my new appearance.

'Now for some Belladonna for your eyes,' she declared. 'Just a few drops of this, Wiggins, and you'll have great velvety eyes. We *all* have this on stage and it works wonders.'

So drops were put into my eyes and when I finished blinking and squealing, I had to admit that they improved my normally uninteresting countenance.

But Lord, what a pother it all was! And how I cursed Luke Markham in my mind for making me want to spend so much time improving my looks.

'If you were really clever and attentive and *cared*, Wiggins, I believe you could make yourself almost as beautiful as Frances Stuart, and *she* is acclaimed by all as being the loveliest creature at Court.'

'Frances Stuart?' I said. 'Who is she?'

'Oh, you do annoy me with your lack of interest in things wot matter *most*,' replied Nelly, quite crossly for her. 'Wiggins, do pay attention and listen to me, and to all the gossip going on around you. Sometimes I think you live in a world of your own, my girl. You may be in love, but you must keep your eyes and ears open or you'll never progress!'

My cheeks reddened beneath the rouge and I pretended a great interest in the little pots of lotions before me.

'I am *not* in love, I tell you, and sometimes all those females chatter so much I cannot keep up with them. There are always numerous conversations going on in the tiring-room between the actresses and their admirers, everyone jabbering at once, and I try to concentrate on you, Nelly, and your lines and do not have time for other matters.'

'Sorry, Wiggins, you are wonderful to me and I shall always be grateful,' she answered swiftly, 'but you must try and be aware of what is going on at Court. Now then, lesson for today — Frances Stuart is a Maid of Honour to the Queen, and the King is besotted about her. She comes to the theatre sometimes and I'll point her out to you. She always dresses most elegantly, 'cos she was brought up in France and is very aware of the newest fashions from Paris. She is also very young and remains a virgin — so 'tis *said*.' Nelly did not sound as if she believed that.

'I like her,' she went on, ' 'cos she 'as taken the King's attention away from Castlemaine, and I have *never* liked that female.'

'You know more than I do, but then I was born a Puritan and cannot understand what is meant by much of the talk that goes on around me.'

'Poor, pious Ally-Wally,' she retorted mockingly. 'But if you are to stay with me, dear, you'd best change your Puritan ideas, and quick! I know Ma's brothel is not the best place for you — nor for me, neither — but if a girl wants to rise in this world, Wiggins, there is only one way that I know of, and that's in a man's arms, whether you like it, or not!'

I sighed. 'I don't like it, can never like it, or condone it, but I'll follow you, Nelly, wherever you go, do not doubt that. Now tell me why this Frances Stuart has taken the place of the Countess of Castlemaine in the King's affections.'

I, like Nelly, did not care for the Countess. She was very beautiful with auburn hair, a voluptuous figure, and dark blue eyes. I knew that she had been King Charles's mistress for many years and had borne him several children, but she was extremely arrogant and liked constant attention, all the time.

I had seen her at the theatre, sitting in one of the most expensive boxes in the lower gallery, talking and flirting through the entire performance with some of the young gallants in the pit below her. The young men were dressed in the latest fashions, all lace-frills and ribbon-trims, and many were holding long, silver-topped walking-canes. The Countess had been wearing a gown of scarlet taffeta, heavily boned at the bodice, with a low scooped neckline showing off her magnificent bosom, and great puffed lace sleeves.

Jewels had sparkled at her throat and in her ears, and on her deeply ringleted hair, and I knew at once why Luke Markham had found me plain. I looked as if I had come from the gutter. The Countess of Castlemaine looked as if she belonged at the Court of the King.

The seats in the boxes where she sat cost four shillings each, so it was obvious the Countess had money — probably paid for by King Charles, said Nelly. Yet Castlemaine did not come to see and enjoy the performance. She came to be seen, and to talk to whichever young man caught her fancy.

No wonder Nelly was annoyed by her and, apart from her conceit, I disliked the lady for the distress she had caused the Queen.

I remember Nelly telling me such a sad tale she had heard about the little Queen's first arrival in England. She was a foreigner, not knowing our language, or our way of life.

The King had long had the Countess of Castlemaine as his mistress and, once he was married, he continued to see her which I found a most un-Christian and wicked act.

'He not only had her in his own bed,' said Nelly, 'but he also insisted that his wife must take her as Lady of *her* Bedchamber.'

'How cruel!' I exclaimed. 'Does he not love Queen Catherine, then?'

'The King loves many women,' answered Nelly, 'and as he is King, all the females in his life must obey him.

The little Queen was very upset, of course, and refused to have Castlemaine as Lady of the Bedchamber, but the King insisted, and His Majesty got his own way.'

'I do not like him at all,' I said indignantly. 'My father never had a good word to say about the Stuarts, and now I realise why he disliked them.'

'Careful, Wiggins,' said Nelly, 'for the Puritans are out now and Charles Stuart is King of England whether you like him, or not. And, after all, Catherine is *Queen*, so that must make up for a lot.'

'But not for having your husband's mistress in your bedchamber!' I cried.

Nelly shrugged. 'I heard that the King was ashamed of how he had treated Castlemaine — her husband, Roger Palmer, had left her, not surprising, I say, and she was with child by the King and he wanted to console her. And she is a *very* strong-willed lady and often makes life miserable for those around her with her violent and wild rages. So His Majesty was worn out by her tantrums and gave in to her demands. Castlemaine was determined to take her place as Lady of the Bedchamber, so he granted her wish and made the Queen do likewise.'

'Then he is a weak man,' I said, 'and not a King to be proud of. What is this Frances Stuart like? Is she a gentle lady, and will she be kind to the little foreign Queen?'

Nelly smiled. 'You must not care too much about people, Wiggins. Life is often unfair and cruel, and there is seldom anything we ordinary folk can do about such matters. All I do know is that La Belle Stuart — that's French, ain't it?'

I nodded.

'Well, all I know is that La Belle Stuart has completely taken the King's heart and he can think of no one but her. If she is kind to the Queen I do not know, but she appears to have kept her virtue so far, so perhaps she has some good qualities — but her resistance is making the King ever more frantic and crazed with love.

'He has even ordered that she should pose for a new coin, Wiggins, so I've heard tell, and will be called Britannia and gaze out over the sea.' Nelly gave one of her coarse chuckles. 'Seems mighty peculiar to me, 'cos a coin should have a king or a queen's head on it, shouldn't it? But there — ' she shrugged, 'that just shows how mad King Charles is about this Frances, and poor Queen Catherine will just have to grin and bear it.'

3

In February of the following year Nelly played a part in one of John Dryden's new plays which I believed to be her best, and I was not the only person to admire and congratulate her.

Mr Samuel Pepys, who worked for the Duke of York, who was Lord High Admiral, was interested in an actress at the King's House and one day he came into the tiring-room and enthused over Nelly's portrayal of Florimel.

I was glad that the gentleman was interested in Mrs Knipp and not in Nelly, for he was not a handsome man — with nose too large, thick, full lips, and rather bulbous eyes. I also felt, watching him gaze lasciviously at the simpering Knipp, that Samuel Pepys was too full of his own masculine importance.

Charles Sackville Lord Buckhurst

also became a great admirer of Nelly's at this time, and I could understand her attraction to him, for he was as fine a figure of manhood as Charles Hart, but to Buckhurst the grace and charm were through breeding, whereas the actor had always to portray such qualities.

However, my opinions about Charles Sackville Lord Buckhurst had to change in the coming years; Luke told me tales about him, and a group of other titled gentlemen, which made my stomach churn with disgust. But more of them anon.

Nelly was suddenly famous, adored by the crowds and by several important people, and poor Charles Hart was seen less often in her company. We moved also that year, as she had always promised, away from old Madam Gwyn's bawdy-house to much more respectable lodgings to the south of Drury Lane. It was the fashionable part, near the Strand, and the Earl of Anglesey was one of our neighbours, as was the Earl of Craven.

Lord Buckhurst was very clever at writing songs and satires, and I often think of some of his lines, remembering Nelly and that delightful little house we shared, close to Craven's mansion. I know that Buckhurst's song was about his Bonny Black Bess, with hair the colour of coal, but nonetheless Nelly always comes to my mind when I say the words —

. . . 'All hearts fall a-leaping,
    wherever she comes,
And beat night and day like my
    Lord Craven's drums . . . '

She had followers and admirers galore, and we all loved her.

'This is nothing yet, Wiggins,' she exclaimed, when I showed my excitement at living in such august surroundings. 'I'm gonna rise and rise and take you with me — we are not finished yet, I tell you. And one day you and me will live in such state you'll not believe your eyes at our own coach, and footmen, and rich furnishings.'

I smiled but remained silent. I could believe anything of Nelly, and knew her to be ambitious. But this little cottage, near the gates of Craven House, was just perfect so far as I was concerned and well away from old Madam Gwyn and her hated bawdy-house.

From the doorway of our new abode we could see the Maypole in the Strand, which had been set up after Charles Stuart returned from exile. It was of a great height, rising high above the surrounding houses, and was surmounted by a crown and vane, with the Royal Arms richly gilded.

In the May of that eventful year we watched the milkmaids with their pails entwined by garlands, dancing down to the Maypole celebrations with a fiddler before them.

We also saw Samuel Pepys, very fine in his black cloth suit trimmed with scarlet ribbon, and a cloak lined with velvet. He doffed his hat at Nelly.

'I'm coming again to see you in

Secret Love,' he called to her across the lane. 'I enjoy it so much that I intend seeing it many times.'

Nelly thanked him, and as we went back into the house she told me that the King called the play his own.

'His Majesty suggested the plot to John Dryden,' she went on, 'and always takes a great interest in our performance.'

'Has the King spoken with you yet, Nelly?'

She shook her head, but did not appear put out by the lack of Royal interest.

I had seen King Charles several times now, once at the scene of the Great Fire, and again at the Theatre Royal, sometimes accompanied by the Queen. She looked small, dark, and very foreign to my eyes, and also rather nervous. His Majesty I did not find particularly attractive, although people said that he possessed great charm.

His figure was good, tall and with fine bearing, and his locks were thick, black and curly. But his face looked older than his thirty-seven years, and there were lines from nose to mouth which appeared etched into his skin. Charles Stuart had a very dark, swarthy look about him and I was to learn later that he was known as 'the black boy' in his youth. His eyes were good, but melancholy, and although renowned for his wit, he did not smile at all whilst I watched from my peep-hole in the scenery.

Both he and Queen Catherine were magnificently attired but I could not help feeling sorry for the little lady. Having watched the Countess of Castlemaine some time before, it was obvious that the Queen could in no way compare with Castlemaine's extraordinary beauty.

The Countess was once again Royal favourite, for La Belle Stuart had eloped with the Duke of Richmond that spring, and gossip had it that the King was furious. Maybe that was one of the reasons for his air of melancholy, I thought, and hoped that the play, and more especially Nelly, would make him laugh.

Nelly played Florimel opposite Charles Hart's Celadon, and their marriage in the play was more of a May Day mockery than a religious ceremony. Nelly was seldom off stage and I remember how much time and trouble she had spent on those lines, keeping us both up night after night until she was word-perfect.

And there had been a great many lines to learn.

I think it was in the fifth Act that Nelly really showed her great ability — having to dress in male garb, which showed off her excellent legs to advantage. She strutted and preened, and held herself as proudly as any young gallant, even though she was such a small girl. And when she danced her famous jig, the audience went wild with delight.

I shall always remember her saying, as Florimel — 'I am resolved to grow fat and look young till forty, and then slip out of the world with the first wrinkle, and the reputation of five and twenty'.'

It was as if Dryden had written the part especially for her — dear Nelly, how true were those words, spoken in jest so long ago.

I often wondered if the King noticed her then and would have liked to know her better? But Nelly had already been noticed by another Charles, Charles Sackville Lord Buckhurst, and it was not long before poor Charles Hart was left alone and Nelly went off with the gentleman of rank and breeding.

King Charles, meanwhile, was said to be interested in an actress at the Duke's House, named Moll Davis.

'Mrs Knipp says the King has taken a house for her in Suffolk Street and given her a ring worth £600,' said Nelly, with a little grimace. 'Well, *I* don't think that Moll Davis can act nearly as well as me though it must be admitted that her singing is quite fine.'

'And how does the Countess of

Castlemaine feel about this new mistress?' I asked, wondering what such a tempestuous lady's reaction would be.

''Tis being said that Castlemaine's setting her sights on my old lover — Charles Hart. Well, much good may he do her. *I'm* off with Lord Buckhurst now and don't give a fig for Hart or Castlemaine. I suppose the Countess wants to pay the King back for taking an actress to his bed — we are ever so low, you see, Wiggins, us females from the theatre. Just common prostitutes in the eyes of most people. But I don't *care* what folk think no more 'cos Nelly from the alley is now beddin' with a real live lord!' And she gave a triumphant crow of delight.

'Mind my ears, Nelly,' I cried, clapping my hands to my head. 'I don't want to be deafened.'

'Sorry, Wiggins.' She lowered her voice, but her hazel eyes were still sparkling with excitement. 'Now listen to me, 'cos I got news for you. I'm giving up the theatre and going to keep house with Charles Sackville Lord Buckhurst, in Epsom.'

'Oh, Nelly, you're not!' I had been so happy with her in our little cottage in Drury Lane, her words came as a great shock.

'You must come with me, Wiggins,' she said firmly, 'and see how the aristocracy live. I said I'd always take you with me and so I shall. Tidy up here and once all is sorted to your satisfaction, let me know and I'll send for you and the rest of our belongings.'

In fact, I never moved to Epsom for in a few short weeks Nelly was back, vowing that Buckhurst did not know how to treat a female properly; she had been both maltreated and abused, and would never see the man again.

I believe, from some of the things Nelly told me, that she had probably been over-generous with Lord Buckhurst's money and had used his name in order to purchase clothing and jewels for herself. It was naughty of her, because he had already given her £100 to spend on herself and I was not surprised by his anger. But Nelly, in all the years we were together, was always bad with finances and in a way I could not blame her. She had known such poverty in her youth, it was a great joy for her to spend and spend once gold was within her reach.

She also told me that Buckhurst had invited his friend, Sir Charles Sedley, to join them at Epsom.

'They are both most witty and intelligent gentlemen,' she said, 'and very clever with writing verse. But they do not know how to treat a female properly, Wiggins, and I was used like a common prostitute and am *thankful* to be home again, even if me money's run out.'

I was overjoyed to have her back with me in the lane, but meanwhile had had a strange adventure of my own.

It must have been about a week after Nelly had departed for Epsom, when I was awakened by a strange tapping noise against my window one night. Pulling my shawl about my shoulders I opened the casement and saw young Will standing below; the young lad with the fresh country face who had been with Luke Markham at the Great Fire, and who always accompanied his master to London.

'Will?' I called down, in great surprise. 'Is that you? What are you doing here so late at night?' Fortunately it was a clear night, with the moon shining into the lane and showing me the boy's upturned countenance.

'Let me in, Mistress Wingard,' he said hoarsely, 'but be silent about it. I have something to ask you.'

Very puzzled, I lit a candle and went down the narrow staircase to the front door. Once inside, Will leaned his back against the closed door and looked fiercely at me.

'Can you be trusted, mistress? I need your help but only if you swear to hold your tongue and not breathe a word to anyone. Where is Mistress Nelly?' He looked behind me into the dark chamber.

'She is not here and we have only one maid who is asleep in the loft. What do you want, Will? And where is Mr Markham?'

'The Master has been hurt in a duel and needs peace and quiet and warm water for his wound. But nobody must see him, or know about this night's visit. 'Tis only for the night, to get rest and cleaning of his wound, then we'll be away.'

The lad looked exhausted and worried and my heart went out to him.

'Bring Mr Markham in — of course I can hold my tongue, silly boy. I am not one to gossip. Hurry now, we must not allow him to bleed to death whilst we stand here prattling. Fetch your master and I'll put water on to boil and look out some clean cloths for you.'

When he departed I left the door on the latch and hurried to set the pot on the fire. Within a few minutes Will and Luke Markham appeared and we settled the man on a stool before the hearth. Then I left them and went to slide the bolts across the door and make sure that all the shutters were tightly closed. Even as I was checking the windows I heard the night-watchman doing his rounds, and reckoned my two visitors had had a narrow escape.

'Two o'clock of a fine windy night — take heed of your fire and your light!' called out the man's voice, before I scurried back to the fireside.

Will had taken off Luke Markham's cloak and jacket, and freed his left shoulder from the shirt which hung in bloody, torn tatters down his arm. Will was bathing the wound gently with warm water, but the basin I had given him was dark with blood.

'Quickly, help me with this cloth,' he said, and we bound the nasty gash tightly with strips of linen.

I could see by Mr Markham's white face that he was in considerable pain, and had probably lost a good deal of blood already that night. When Will had told me it was a duel, I had imagined it to be a quarrel with swords, but this wound looked to me both singed and blackened around the edges, as if from a pistol shot. If so, no bullet was embedded in his flesh and, fortunately, the gash was not deep.

'Are you sure it is clean?' I whispered. Luke Markham's head had fallen forward on to his chest and I believed him to be unconscious.

'Clean enough,' answered the lad abruptly. 'Once I get him home Mother will take care of him. But I've got to get him safely away from London, Mistress Wingard, and dare not make a move until he has recovered somewhat.'

'The horses?'

'They are stabled at the inn yonder — I can collect them tomorrow — but we got to make sure Mr Markham's well enough to travel.'

In fact they stayed two days and two nights with me, and for some of that time Luke Markham was delirious. Will hated leaving me alone with him, but the lad had to sleep, so we took it in turns to watch beside the wounded man, who had ended up sleeping in Nelly's and my bed whilst Will and I made do on the floor.

Mr Markham was safe in the chamber, for Peg, our little maid, took the stairs straight down to the kitchen from the loft above and spent her days there, cooking and washing and running errands for me. I told her only that I had a sick friend staying with me a while, and I would do all the feeding and caring, and Peg accepted that without question. She was very young, illiterate like Nelly, but with none of my friend's intelligence, and grateful to us for giving her food and lodgings in return for her service.

By the third day Luke Markham's fever had eased and he had regained his faculties, although still very weak.

'So,' he said, looking at me with faint humour as I leaned over his recumbent form, changing the soiled dressing on his arm, 'I am indebted to Mistress Wingard for a place of refuge in this unfortunate crisis. I thank you, mistress, and hope one day to repay my debt.'

'I could not deny Will entry,' I answered, 'even though it was so late at night. And it is fortunate that Nelly is away in Epsom and thus you are doubly certain of secrecy.'

'You could not deny *Will*,' he repeated, his tone mocking, 'but what of me, Mistress Wingard? Would you have refused Luke Markham had he come knocking at your door one late night? I seem to remember a time when you were most curt with me, and ran from my presence before we had finished our conversation.'

'Lord, sir, that was long ago!' I replied, pulling the cloth a little too tightly round his arm and making him flinch. 'Forgive me.' I loosened the linen somewhat before fixing it firmly into place on his warm skin. 'We know each other better now, and I would always help a friend in need, if it were within my power.'

'You look upon me as a friend, Mistress Wingard?' His light eyes were quizzical.

I nodded. 'I do, sir. Both you and Will are friends of mine, as too is Nelly.'

'Three friends!' he exclaimed. 'You are indeed a fortunate young lady, and looking remarkably more attractive, dare I say? No,' he went on quickly as I jerked my head at this response, 'do not take affront, I beg. If we are to remain friends you must learn to understand my sense of humour and, as friends, may I now call you Alice? And you, I hope, will call me Luke.'

I felt myself blushing at the gentleness of his voice, and busied myself with collecting the soiled rags and placing them in the basin beside the bed.

'Yes, I shall call you Luke, and Alice will be pleasing to my ears. I have not been called that since I was a child, living with my parents in White Cross Street.'

'What does Nell Gwyn call you then?'

'I am Ally-Wally, or just plain Wiggins with her,' I said.

Luke lifted his head and chuckled aloud. 'That sounds typical of your Nelly — but what ugly, unromantic labels for a pious puritanical maid!'

'I prefer them to the words pious and puritanical,' I answered sharply. 'I am neither of those, Mr Markham — '

'Luke,' he said.

'Luke — I am a normal female, with perhaps an over-severe upbringing, but since my time with Nelly I have learned much, and neither the gossip of Court life, nor the goings-on at the King's House have managed to shock me. So long as *I* am not expected to live my days immorally I see no reason to condemn others for what they choose to do.'

He clapped his hands together in applause and then let out a yelp as his arm hurt him.

'Careful, Markham,' he muttered,

'you're not healed yet.'

'How can you hope to get on a horse today,' I said anxiously, knowing that he was still far from well and definitely not able to ride any distance.

'I have a splendid steed, Alice, who is my best friend and who probably knows me better than I do myself. Thunder will be well rested by now, and will carry me as gently as he would a newborn babe, away from London. Do not worry, mistress, for Will rides with me and together we will reach safety and further loving care, I have no doubt of that.'

I pursed my lips, still not happy about the arrangement but feeling that it was probably safer for Luke to depart at once, rather than wait a few more days and perhaps meet a very curious Nelly.

As luck would have it, Will and Luke made a sedate and satisfactory departure from my door, and Nelly did not make her appearance at the lane until the end of August.

She went back to the King's House and was taken on at once, although some of the parts chosen for her were neither impressive, nor enjoyed by her. Perhaps it was Mr Killigrew's way of punishing her for leaving them all in her rush out to Epsom, and into the arms of Lord Buckhurst? Nelly was always at her best in comic roles and serious parts did not suit her and she hated having to act them.

She played Cydaria in Dryden's *Indian Emperor* and Valeria in his new tragedy *Tyrannick Love* — neither of which brought out the best in her. But she excelled as Mirida in the comedy *All Mistaken*, and as Donna Jacintha in Dryden's comedy *An Evening's Love, or the Mock Astrologer*.

Of course it had to happen, and I was really only surprised that it had not happened earlier — for with the audiences now clamouring for Nelly, with the handsome actor Charles Hart falling for her many charms, with Lord Buckhurst being enchanted by her, even for so short a time — it had to happen that the King would send for Nelly.

And what excitement and joy for her to obey the Royal command, and what things she had to tell me about the Palace of Whitehall, and the arrangements which were made to get her up the Privy Stairs and into the Royal bed.

'Will Chiffinch meets me and takes me up them stairs,' she said, her hazel eyes sparkling like firecrackers. 'Will Chiffinch has lately taken over from his brother Thomas, and is Page of His Majesty's Bedchamber and Keeper of the King's Private Closet.'

Suddenly our world expanded, and I found myself learning new things almost every day. Things that a girl, brought up in a God-fearing Puritan household and orphaned and friendless at the age of fifteen, would never have known but for the influence and companionship of Nell Gwyn, the Royal mistress.

But Nelly was only one of them. For Charles II, I had to accept, enjoyed the company of women not only for their seductive charms but also for their friendship. One female was never enough for the King and he chose them, many and often, for their looks, for their grace, and for their wit.

All the Royal mistresses were beautiful, at least all the ones we knew about. Who knows how many others there were, escorted up the Privy Stairs by loyal Will Chiffinch? But the known mistresses were all beauties and excelled at carrying themselves with grace, and dressing with both elegance and style. Where Nelly scored — and I do not believe there was another who possessed her special talent — was with her use of words, illiterate as she was, and with her wit.

The King was always amused by her and that was doubtless the reason that she remained with him until his death.

In the tiring-room, however, she had often been teased about her clothing.

'You seem to hang your clothes on you, Nelly, without a thought of what you look like,' said Mrs Knipp once.

77

'It's all slap-dash and hurry, hurry, and that-will-do-I-must-go, sort of thing.'

'But she looks wonderful despite that,' I put in quickly.

And the other actresses, and the gallants who were visiting that day, all turned to stare at Nelly.

She, unperturbed by such attention, shrugged her shoulders and then lifted her skirts to do a little twirl. And, regardless of her negligence, her lack of fussing and poking and patting, she did indeed look wonderful in her gown of deep green velvet, which darkened her eyes and which went most beautifully with her red-brown hair.

It was a fact that, whatever she wore, both then and later, became her.

Another truth about Nelly and the King was that she was always faithful to him, which could not be said of some of his female partners, and she made him laugh. And that laughter, during the difficult years ahead, was probably her strongest hold on the Royal heart.

Such stories she had to tell me about

the King, making him appear a most human and likeable figure to my prejudiced mind. He was always good-humoured, Nelly said, and possessed astonishing energy.

'And not only in the Royal bed!' she added, with a wicked glint in her eyes. 'No matter how late he retires, Wiggins, he is always up early, sometimes at five o'clock in the morning. And off he goes to St James's Park to saunter round and see his birds, then on for a game of tennis, or something he calls pell-mell which needs great strength with a mallet.'

'A mallet?'

'Yes,' said Nelly, looking wise. 'He hits a ball very hard with this mallet and the ball must pass through a ring hung six feet from the ground. The King is very good at that game,' she went on proudly, 'and he likes boating on the Thames, and swimming, and riding and hunting and dancing. He is a most splendid man, Wiggins, and my *only* complaint is about his dogs.'

'What dogs?' I asked, my brain whirling with all the information she had thrust at me.

'Them spaniels — that's what he calls 'em — and nasty, yapping things they are, too. He will have them with him *wherever* he goes, Wiggins, and I don't like them creatures sniffing about in the bed.'

'Not in bed with you and — ' I paused, not wanting to conjure up the picture in my astounded mind.

'Oh, yes,' said Nelly. 'They pup and suckle and do what they want all over the place, and he *loves* 'em, so we all have to put up with them. But I don't much like it, Wiggins, even with the bed curtains closed — I feel as if we're being watched, you know?'

I nodded, sniffed, and changed the subject. Such private details were not for me.

A satirist at this time wrote —

. . . 'There Hart's and Rowley's souls she did ensnare — And made a King a rival to a player . . . '

80

I felt sorry for poor Charles Hart, who had truly loved Nelly, but supposed that to have the King as a rival was almost a compliment to him. When I asked Nelly why the name Rowley was used, she laughed most heartily.

'Ally-Wally, you'll wish you'd never asked me that! But you'll need to know in the future so I'm the best one to tell you now. Charles Stuart is nicknamed Old Rowley because of one of his stallions which bears that name. And this horse is the most vigorous in the Royal stud. The King is known as Rowley because of his numerous sexual activities, dear Wiggins, and his many bastards.'

Her words did not shock me. After my time at old Madam Gwyn's bawdy-house, followed by the gossip at the Theatre Royal, I had become used to listening to tales of immorality and debauchery.

'Have he and the Queen no children?' I asked. 'And who are all these bastards? Oh, Nelly, is it right that you should go to Whitehall so frequently? No wonder the Queen is unhappy — her wicked husband is always with some other female!'

'Now, now, Wiggins, that's your Puritan spirit showing — and what you say is grossly unfair. The King beds often with his wife, I'll have you know, and the fault is *hers* that they have no children — not his for want of trying. She conceived this year in fact, but miscarried in May.'

'I am not surprised. She must be so upset by all his mistresses and his immoral behaviour — it is no wonder she remains childless, poor lady.'

'Wiggins, Royalty is not like us ordinary folk and King Charles can do exactly as he likes. He is ever so good to the Queen, and gives her masses of jewellery and gowns and — '

'And still beds with that Castlemaine female, and Moll Davis, and now with *you*, Nell Gwyn. You should be ashamed of yourself!'

'Well, I'm not!' Nelly tossed her

red-brown head at me. 'My Charles the third is a darling, loving man *and* he always speaks kindly of the Queen and says he admires her simplicity and prudence, even if she does resemble a bat.'

'A bat!' I cried. 'There — how can you admire him when he speaks in such cruel fashion about his wife?'

But to the forefront of my mind came the vision of Queen Catherine — small, dark-haired, and rather squat of figure, and I remembered seeing her in conversation with the Duke of York at the Theatre Royal, and noticing how her front teeth seemed to protrude. But a bat! What an unpleasant way to describe his wife. 'And why Charles the third?' I went on.

'Charles Hart was the first,' Nelly replied, 'Charles Sackville Lord Buckhurst was the second, and now Charles Stuart is my third and last.'

'Last Charles, or last man?' I asked belligerently.

'Charles the third is the only man for

me. I love him most dearly and will remain with him for as long as he wants me,' she said softly.

'Then be careful, Nelly. It does not seem to me that the King is a faithful lover.'

'No,' she murmured, 'he is not called Old Rowley for nothing, but I understand him and his ways and am not a jealous female, Wiggins. Fortunately, Castlemaine is out of favour now and my Charles is going to buy her a house of her own, and get her out of Whitehall. She is not faithful to him, Wiggins, and he likes his mistresses to remain true to him.'

'Until *he* tires of them!'

'Yes, maybe so, but she is a nasty, bad-tempered creature and getting old, anyway, so she must go. My poor Charles has told me many tales about Castlemaine, and how he has put up with her for so long I do *not* know. She used to scream and shout and stamp her feet if she didn't get her own way; she vowed more than once to set fire to his Palace, or dash out her baby's brains on the hearthstone; and if she played cards she had *always* to win, else Charles had to pay her losses.'

'Dear me, what a fool he was to put up with her for so long.'

'She was very, very beautiful,' said Nelly defensively, 'And her beauty delighted his eyes. I also think that her wild nature captivated him. But fortunately, they are both growing older and my Charles is probably finding Castlemaine's rages, and her numerous lovers, rather boring now. He does love her children,' she went on rather wistfully, 'and so will always go and visit wherever Castlemaine may be.'

'How many bastards has he by her?'

'Five, I think, though the eldest one, Anne, is thought to be by her husband, poor Roger Palmer, but nobody really knows. And there are lots more, Wiggins, just to shock your pious mind some more. There's the Duke of Monmouth, a handsome lad, from Charles's mistress in Holland. That was before he came back here as King — when he was in exile, you know? And silly old Moll Davis has given him a daughter, calling her Mary Tudor, so I've heard. Then there was others when he was abroad, I believe, and that's all we *know* about. Could be many more besides from Old Rowley!'

'Dearie me,' was all I could say. 'Poor, poor Queen.'

'Oh, do stop!' Nelly cried sharply. 'Do you want to go on living with me, or not? 'Cos I can't help telling you things about me and the King, but no more can I bear your continual moaning and groaning. Do you want to go back to Ma's bawdy-house in Coal Yard Alley?'

'No, I do not,' I retorted quickly.

'Then hush your mouth and stop wailing about the poor Queen. Charles is going to help me get better lodgings at Lincoln's Inn Fields and you're welcome there with me. Do you good to live in more luxury and I always said you'd come with me, Wiggins, wherever

I went — but you got to accept my way of life and not *grumble* so.'

'I'll stay with you, Nelly, you know that. And I'll try to hold my tongue but it won't be easy.'

'Then try extra hard. And I'll have letters for you to write for me 'cos I'll have money now, and want better clothes and nice furnishings. You must write to the silversmith for me, and to the needlewoman, and we'll have a great time together spending lots and lots of my Charles's money!'

4

Soon after Nelly and I moved to our new abode in Lincoln's Inn Fields, and she was seen more frequently in the King's company, I found myself being visited by Luke Markham.

It was pleasant for me to have a gentleman friend, and I found him both charming and amusing. It was also nice having someone intelligent to talk to and Luke told me a great many things which I would never have heard from Nelly.

She loved dining, and dancing the Bransle, the Coranto, and the new French dances, and meeting many of the King's witty and extravagant friends at Court. But she was not interested in the political scene which, when Luke explained matters to me, I found most fascinating.

He explained about the poor Earl of

Clarendon's departure from England, and about the Dutch war, and King Charles's terrible debts.

'I liked old Clarendon,' said Luke, 'but he and the Countess of Castlemaine never got on and I believe it was her influence which made the King dismiss him.'

'I may be stupid,' I said slowly, 'but can only explain it by saying that I have been too long in the company of theatre folk, who think only of their looks and their performances. Please tell me who Clarendon is, and what has happened to him.'

Luke smiled, sitting across the parlour from me, looking as handsome and debonair as ever with petticoat breeches of wine-red, decorated with pink ribbons; large red bows upon his square-toed shoes, and a long coat of red velvet buttoned to the waist.

I was thankful that he did not wear the fashionable periwig for his own hair was thick and shiny, and always looked clean. I had heard awful tales in the tiring-room at the Theatre Royal, of periwigs which had smelt like the gutter, and *some* which had been seen to have lice running in and out of their perfumed curls.

'Honest as ever, dear Alice,' he remarked, 'but at least you do not appear bored by my chat, nor pretend knowledge which you do not possess. The Earl of Clarendon was the Lord Chancellor of England, and had been with the King all through his exile, giving him excellent advice. He did well here, too, once Charles Stuart came back to take the throne.'

'Then why did the Countess of Castlemaine dislike him?'

'I suspect because Clarendon had been with Charles, and dominated him, for far longer than the fair lady had done, and he was also very watchful of the Privy Purse, which had been paying countless sums into Castlemaine's greedy hands.'

'And why did we have to fight the Dutch?' I asked.

Luke smiled. 'All rather foolish, I

fear, and Clarendon certainly hoped to avoid confrontation. But we are both seafaring nations, Alice, and very jealous of our trade abroad — and unfortunately neither the great oceans, nor our numerous colonies, were enough to keep us apart. So,' he shrugged his broad shoulders, 'we did battle which neither side was able to win, and peace was finally declared in July last year. But wars cost money, Alice, and the Royal debts are now enormous.'

'So Clarendon was blamed?'

'He was blamed for negligent administration, and his dismissal was popular because he had many enemies in Parliament.'

'As *well* as Castlemaine?' I cried.

'Yes, though she could vanquish an entire army on her own, I have no doubt. But the people hate Clarendon also, and blame him for producing a foreign Catholic Queen, who appears to be barren, and he is also disliked because his daughter married the King's brother.'

'The Duchess of York is Clarendon's daughter?' I asked in surprise.

I had seen her once or twice at the theatre, with the Duke, and had thought only that she appeared a rather plain lady, although always beautifully attired. Her husband I considered a more handsome man than his brother, King Charles. For the Duke of York possessed a thinner face, with a fairer complexion, and with his long red-brown hair — like Nelly's in colour — he was very pleasant to behold, bearing none of the King's swarthiness, or deep lines upon his skin.

Luke nodded. 'The Earl of Clarendon was much against the marriage,' he went on, 'but nobody believes that, thinking that he wanted his daughter to marry the Duke so if the King remains without a legitimate heir, his daughter will one day be Queen of England.'

'Oh,' I said, trying to sort out the facts in my bewildered mind. 'And have the Yorks any children?'

'They have two living girls — a

daughter, Mary, born in 1662 and Anne, born the year of the Great Plague. Unfortunately, the Duchess of York is a Catholic, again to her father's dismay, and 'tis said that her husband will soon be joining the Church of Rome.'

'How dreadful!' I exclaimed, remembering my own father's views on the Papists.

'Do not tell me that you are also an enemy of Popery?' His right eyebrow lifted in mock surprise. 'Ah, yes, I forgot for a moment — you are a pious Puritan, are you not, dear Alice? And would like to see all Catholics beheaded on Tower Hill.'

'No,' I answered quickly, for the little Queen was a Catholic and I had always felt sorry for her, 'I would not wish harm to any of them, but it is important that Protestantism remains the faith of England, Luke.'

'Why?' He looked serious for a moment.

I frowned. 'Do not tell me that *you*

are a Papist, Luke Markham?'

'You have not answered my question, Alice Wingard. Why must Protestantism be the only religion? Why can we not all worship as we wish?'

'Because,' I said, and swallowed, wondering what to say next.

What did it really matter how people worshipped, how they prayed? There was only one God and both Catholics and Protestants believed in Him. What was it my father had always said about Popery? Why had he always been so adamant on the subject, so filled with hatred and anger about the Roman Church?

'Because we do not want to return to the days of Bloody Mary,' I said with relief, the words coming to me at last. 'We do not want poor innocents burnt in their thousands because the Church of Rome says they are heretics. And remember Guy Fawkes and that wicked Gunpowder Plot? All planned by Catholics. We are an island race and proud of our independence. We want to worship in *our* way, like our good Queen Bess did, and not become slaves to Popish tyranny.'

Luke clapped his hands together in loud applause.

'Well done, Mistress Wingard! I can see you performing at the Theatre Royal yet! Rise and take a bow, I beg. That was an excellent speech and spoken with great heart and fervour.'

'You are mocking me,' I said indignantly, 'and do not believe one word of what I have said.'

'No, indeed, I do not believe a word — but nor do I mock you, Alice. I understand what you are trying to say,' he went on more soberly, 'and can sympathise. But I do not *agree* and believe, like the King, that all should be allowed to worship as they wish. His mistress, Castlemaine, became a convert to the Church of Rome some years ago, and when members of her family begged him to make her change her mind, Charles said that he was only interested in the bodies of his ladies, he would never meddle with their souls.'

'Oh, well, if the *King* thinks it's all right no doubt you think the same. Just like Nelly — her Charles the third can do no wrong in her loving eyes.'

'But don't you see,' Luke said more gently, 'that there are too many people like you, Alice, who will not accept freedom of worship and will do anything to take away the honest man's right, commanding him to worship as they do? You are fiercely Protestant, but others are fiercely Catholic, and if we were all allowed to worship as we chose there would be no need for such hatred and ferocity.'

And he sighed, making me realise that he did care about people even though he treated life as a joke for most of the time.

I shrugged at his words. 'Maybe you are right, but I don't like the Roman Church and the way it tries to take over in another country. And I don't want it here in England, Luke, not ever!'

'Good Puritan lass, remain true to

your faith by all means, but do not attempt to force your religion on others, Alice, or you will be copying the ways of the church you abhor.'

Seeing so much of Luke Markham at this time, and having our interesting and stimulating discussions, made me wonder about him. It occurred to me that I knew nothing about him as a person, or about his family and upbringing.

He was a very handsome man with his splendid tall figure, graceful bearing, and unusual clear grey eyes. He always dressed in the latest fashions and with his talk of the Court, and of the various personalities in the Houses of Lords and Commons, I wondered if he was a minister of Parliament. But he had never told me where he lived, what he did for a living, or even if he had a family.

One evening Luke came to see me, after a pleasurable few hours at the theatre he informed me, and as Nelly was out seeing the King, I decided to ask him to stay and sup with me. I was a reasonable cook and little Peg was a great help to me, so when he accepted my invitation I hurried to the kitchen to tell Peg what to do with the carp and lobsters, which had been purchased from the street vendor that very morning. I also told her not to forget the flagon of wine, which I hoped would encourage Luke to sit over our repast and tell me the many things I wanted to know.

In fact, I not only gained knowledge about his work, but learned more about the man, and about his background.

He had been born in the year 1635 he told me, into a strong Royalist family.

'Like you, Alice, I possessed loving parents and a brother and sister. But being some years older my happy youth was shattered earlier than yours. My father was killed at the Battle of Naseby, in 1645, leaving me and my older brother to care for our family as best we could.'

'We managed well enough until the fateful year of '51 — when both my brother and I took up arms on behalf of Charles Stuart, and I saw my brother die on the sword of a Cromwellian soldier, at Worcester. My sister died of the smallpox the following year, and my mother soon after — worn out, I believe, by her family's disasters.'

His grey eyes had darkened as he spoke, and his expression was one of unusual sadness at the memories.

'Oh, Luke,' I said, sitting forward on my stool and clasping my hands tightly together. 'What terrible tragedies you have experienced in your life. I, in my despair, met Nelly and was befriended by her, but what could you do in your sorrow?'

He shrugged and his smile was twisted.

'I lost everything during the Commonwealth; our family estate in Hertfordshire was taken over by the Roundheads, and had it not been for Will's mother, I would have been totally bereft. But, like your Nelly, Mrs Brown comforted me, gave me a loving home and more than her fair share of patience.'

'Is she still alive, your Mrs Brown? And was she a servant to your family?'

He jerked his head in surprise at my question and it was clear to me that Luke had been far away in thought — no doubt reliving his troubled past.

'Mrs Brown a servant?' he repeated. 'No, Alice, the Browns were never employed by my family. Her husband was a soldier, I believe, but she has been widowed for some years now. I met young Will by chance, out in the country one day when he was being set upon by a group of ruffians. He had sold a cow at market, he told me, and the gang were after his money.'

'Anyway, I advanced upon them, seeing that this lad was alone and desperately trying to save his life — let alone his money — and we managed to break a few bones between us. Then I took Will back to his cottage and Mrs Brown and her son have been devoted to me ever since.'

He smiled and looked more cheerful.

'That is my country retreat now, Alice, the little cottage set on the edge of the Marybone Fields. I feel safe there, and loved, and am always well fed and cosseted whenever I visit.'

'And your London home?' I asked. 'Where is that?'

'I have no home in London,' he replied. 'Since the Restoration I have been trying to claim back my inheritance in Hertfordshire, but the King is not able to return all the stolen properties to their rightful owners, and I am one who has fared less well than others.

'At first I was both bitter and angry, hating Cromwell for what he had done to my family; hating Charles Stuart for not putting all the wrongs to right. But now I do not care so much, Alice, and the years have taught me to treat each new day as it comes and be thankful that I am alive, with enough money in my purse to afford the theatre, and fine clothes, and the wages for Will, and the keeping of my beautiful Thunder.'

His voice had become tender on mentioning his horse's name as it had been when he spoke of Will's mother. Those two, I thought, are the only things Luke Markham really loves. And deep in my heart I felt a small pang of longing, wishing that one day I might also cause him to feel the same tenderness for me.

Hastily I put the idea from me.

'What is this work which fills your purse? You have such knowledge about Court affairs — are you something to do with Parliament, Luke?'

He threw back his dark head and laughed.

'Nay, Alice, a Parliamentarian am I not! It is a tricky business for those men and I am gladly out of it. I am only a seeker of information for King Louis, an agent for the French. And in my rounds of coffee shops, and in the theatre audiences, and milling with the crowds at Whitehall, it is surprising what news can be gleaned from numerous conversations, if one knows the right people.'

'An agent for the French?' I did not understand the meaning of that at all. 'What do the French want to know?'

'Everything,' he replied. 'Everything about Charles Stuart, and what he really feels about them, and whether England would support them in their fight against the hated Hollanders. Oh, there is no end to their seeking for information, Alice, and I supply them with what knowledge I have.'

We had finished eating by then and Luke leaned forward, placing his elbows on the table. His long-fingered hands were propped beneath his chin and he looked irritatingly self-satisfied.

'Not more wars!' I exclaimed, helping little Peg to clear away our repast. 'I thought that after the peace of 1667 there would be no more fighting against the Dutch.'

Then I seated myself on the stool opposite my visitor and saw him shrug his broad shoulders again.

'The King's nephew, William of Orange, is here now on a visit,' Luke went on slowly, 'hoping to secure the money which Charles borrowed from the private coffers of the House of Orange when he was in exile. But His Majesty does not care for William, finding him too much a Hollander and too strong a Protestant to his liking.'

'But how do you *know* all this?' I cried. 'Do you often speak to King Charles? Does he whisper state secrets in your ears?'

Luke smiled, stretching out his legs beneath the table and still looking smug.

'I have my contacts at Court who tell me much, then it is for me to decide what is true and what is being grossly exaggerated. And it is not hard to *see* the King, Alice. You have only to go to St James's Park early one morning and you would see him for yourself. He is a most accessible monarch, as every petitioner knows — walking with his dogs, or studying his birds.

'I have seen His Majesty several times with his nephew, and his attitude towards the young man appears to be both patronising and critical. I do not believe that King Charles likes either William, or the Hollanders, Alice, and am fairly certain that he far prefers the French and will do anything they ask of him, provided they supply him with money.'

'And what do *you* think of this Prince of Orange?'

'I admire him,' said Luke. 'He never knew his father, who died before he was born, and his mother — sister to our King Charles — died when he was but a boy. But he has shown both intelligence and diligence in his country's fight against the French, and is already making a name for himself as a military commander.'

'No wonder the King dislikes him for one of them is all *for* France, and the other is totally against.'

Luke nodded. 'And, unfortunately for Charles, this William of Orange is very closely connected by family ties to England, and is in the Royal line of succession after the Duke of York and his children.'

'Maybe the King will have a legitimate heir yet,' I said hopefully.

'Unlikely, Alice.'

'Then perhaps he will make the Duke of Monmouth his rightful heir? He is the King's son, at any rate, and a Protestant, so Nelly says, and I would think he has more right to the throne than this Orange William.'

Luke laughed. 'You should be all *for* oranges since your beloved Nelly began her rise to success with that fruit. But no,' he said more seriously, 'I cannot see Charles Stuart allowing his bastard to overthrow his brother York's rightful inheritance. Moreover, he is planning great things for his empty coffers with King Louis of France.'

'Nelly says King Charles is in great financial troubles,' I said, 'and Parliament will not give him the money he so desperately needs.'

'But the French will give him much, if he agrees to their demands.'

'And what are those demands?' I asked.

'Time will tell, and I have the feeling that much will happen this summer. The King's sister, the Duchess of Orleans, is coming over from France and there is to be a meeting at Dover between her and her brother. King Louis is determined to gain control over Charles in his fight against the Dutch, and the Duchess of Orleans has always been a favourite of Charles's and they correspond frequently. It will be interesting to know for what reason Madame is travelling to Dover.'

It is difficult to remember what I knew at that time, for the year 1670 is so long ago and I have learned a great deal since then. But I am sure that Luke went on to explain to me that evening all about Charles's obsession for Louis of France, or the Sun King, as he was known because of his sumptuous and glittering Court, and absolute monarchy.

King Charles's youngest sister, Henriette-Anne, had married the brother of the French King shortly before Charles's Coronation in 1661, and brother and sister had not met since her marriage. Thus making this meeting at Dover of supreme importance to them both. The Duchess had for her husband Philippe, Duc d'Orleans, a most wicked and per-verted man, who did not love his wife but adored his favourite, the Chevalier de Lorraine.

Luke also told me that he was sure King Charles would like an alliance with France.

'But you cannot know that,' I cried, 'unless you open the private letters of the King and read the contents?'

'My dear Alice, I would not dream of doing such a thing, and it is quite impossible, anyway. But people talk, and it is surprising how much news leaks out if one has money to spread around.'

'And you receive money from the French for all the secrets you find out here? Then you are a spy, Luke Markham, and I find that most dishonest and unpatriotic!'

'Not a spy — an agent,' he answered calmly. 'And the Dutch also have their agents here. It is politics, Alice. Information is vital if a country is to survive in these troublesome times.'

'Then why can you not be an agent for *us* and find out things for England?' I cried.

'Because we are in desperate financial straits and the payment would not suffice,' he said. 'I have been poor for many years, Alice, and vowed long ago that I would not suffer poverty again. A cousin of mine is married to a French lady, and if he is to rise in the French Court, he must provide information which is of value to King Louis. I tell my cousin what he wants to know and he gives me the money I need. So we are both satisfied.'

I did not like the idea at all, but as the political scene was outside my little world it did not seem prudent to argue further.

'Cromwell and his Commonwealth ruined my family,' went on Luke, 'and the Restoration has done nothing to relieve my problems. So I have taken my life, and my future, into my own hands and will work for whoever pays me best.'

He stood up and moved across to where I sat.

'You look more beautiful every time I see you, Alice Wingard. You must have been taking tuition from pretty Nell Gwyn.'

He bent towards me, his eyes warm with approval on the kohl which darkened my eyes, the fresh rose of my lip salve, and the soft, shining ringlets which now caressed my shoulders and hung in dainty curls across my brow.

'You told me that my appearance was plain and needed attention, and you were right,' I said, tilting my chin at him. 'All this face painting and hair curling takes a great deal of time and sometimes I wonder why I bother with so much fuss. But the finished result is worth the effort, and Nelly likes it.'

'Nelly likes it!' he exclaimed, straightening his tall form and pulling me to stand before him. 'What about *me*, Alice? I find you quite enchanting now, so does my opinion not matter to you?'

'Of course,' I answered, very aware of his strong, powerful body close to mine. 'I always find you well-dressed and pleasing to the eye, Luke Markham, so am naturally satisfied if my appearance commends itself to you.'

'So cool, so composed, my Puritan lass! Have you ever been kissed by a man, Alice?'

Blushing, I shook my head, trying to remove my hands from his firm clasp.

'No, Luke Markham, and I thought you were a friend of mine,' I said, looking up into his amused face.

'I am your friend, Mistress Wingard. And can one not kiss a friend farewell?'

'Not against her will, not like those horrid young gallants and rakes at the theatre whom Nelly was always telling me about.'

'So you have never been kissed?'

'Never.'

'And would not care to feel my lips touch yours?'

I shook my head, staring at the gold buttons on his jacket. It was too soon for such embraces and I was not ready — not sure of my own trembling feelings, uncertain of the desire which my improved looks had aroused in the man.

'I thought we were just friends, enjoying each other's company and conversation,' I said, feeling my heart beginning to pound beneath my tight bodice. I did not want anything more from Luke Markham, not yet.

'Very well,' he said quietly, and let go of my hands allowing me to step back from him. 'I will leave you as a chaste and virginal friend, Alice Wingard, and look forward to our next meeting. I may come again and visit you? You will not deny me these excellent meals and fireside chats when I am in London?'

His grey eyes were serious as they gazed down at me.

'You may always come and see me, Luke, and be most welcome. But do not ask for more than I am prepared to give,' I added hastily.

Even as I spoke the words I felt them to be too self-righteous, too Puritan, and knew that, in truth, I would like to feel his arms about me and his warm mouth on mine. But foolishly I played the prim maiden, and Luke Markham was a gentleman of honour and did not force me.

'Then we shall remain friends, dear Alice, until such a time as you desire more from me. Then, sweetheart, you will know what love is all about and I can assure you 'tis one hundredfold more interesting and enjoyable than mere friendship.'

He bowed low before me, then walked to the door.

'You did not tell me where you lived,' I called out, following him and feeling strangely bereft by his departure. 'Where do you go to now?'

'You should never ask a man where he is off to when you have been so cruel as to refuse his advances,' he replied, turning to face me, his tone once again light and mocking. 'But have no fear, sweet Alice, I am not off to seek comfort at old Madam Gwyn's bawdy-house. I have lodgings in Maiden Lane, not far from here. So if ever you should want Luke Markham, for friendship or for more, you will know where to find me if I am in town. Ask at the King's Head Tavern — it is not a home, but somewhere to rest my body when I need repose.'

He lifted his hand and then strode out and away down the cobbled street.

5

Nelly, meanwhile, was becoming more and more enamoured of her Charles the third, and the group of witty, clever and talented men he had around him, and she mentioned the names of Sir Charles Sedley, who had been at Epsom with her and Lord Buckhurst, the Earl of Rochester, and the Duke of Buckingham. She was most taken with the last named, I remember, and told me how the common folk loved him for his humour, and the way in which he spoke to rich and poor alike, without conceit.

King Charles loved him almost as a brother, for Buckingham had been taken into the household of Charles I, when he and his younger brother were but children, and they had grown up with the Royal Family.

'The Duke of Bucks is the finest

gentleman I have ever seen,' said Nelly rapturously. 'His conversation is so easy and charming, he dresses most beautifully, and has a strong, tall and active body. Best of all is his way of turning all things to ridicule and making us laugh by his mimicry. Truly, he was born for gallantry and magnificence.'

My mouth fell open with surprise at her words, although I had noticed previously that her way of talking was improving daily now that she was so often in the King's company.

'Nelly, you must have learned such speech from this very man. I have never heard you talk so eloquently before! Are you sure that you do not mean King Charles by that description?'

'No.' Nelly shook her head firmly. 'I mean George Villiers, second Duke of Buckingham, and I hope one day that you will meet him, Wiggins. Though I rather wonder if your strait-laced mind will appreciate his humour.'

She went on to tell me that Buckingham had been in exile with

Charles for many of the years that he had been on the Continent, but whereas Charles Stuart had been greatly under the influence of the Earl of Clarendon, Buckingham had not liked the old adviser, and the feeling had been mutual.

'Clarendon never ceased trying to poison the King's mind against his friend, Bucks, so it was a very good thing when the old man was forced to leave England. His departure was due mainly to my clever Duke of Bucks.'

'But I thought it was the Countess of Castlemaine who persuaded the King to get rid of Clarendon,' I said. Surely that was what Luke had told me?

'Ah, but Bucks and Castlemaine are related,' answered Nelly. 'They are both Villiers, and although I dislike her I do like the Duke very much indeed.'

I wondered if I would ever be able to understand the interweaving of the political scene, and all the characters involved in it.

'Is the Duke of Buckingham married?' I asked, and then wished that I had not, for Nelly broke into further details about her Duke and my poor brain became even more muddled.

'Yes, Ally-Wally, the Duke of Bucks was clever and married the only daughter of Lord Fairfax, and *he*, I'll have you know, was one of Cromwell's best generals. In fact, Fairfax was given the Villiers estates in Yorkshire by Parliament when the war ended.'

How strange, I thought, to marry the daughter of a man who was your enemy. Or by so doing, did Buckingham hope to retrieve his family fortunes? It was a similar story to Luke Markham's for he, too, had lost everything during the Civil War but he had not married a daughter of the enemy. At least, I thought not. There was still much I did not know about Luke Markham.

'It seems an ill-assorted marriage to me,' I said slowly. 'Are they happy together?'

Nelly smiled at me and then leaned forward and patted my cheek.

'Dear Wiggins, you are like a little girl sometimes and want happiness for everyone. Let me tell you now, dearest friend, that marriage seldom makes for happiness. I am convinced that being a mistress to a great man is far better than being his wife.'

'So they are not happy together.'

And I thought of the King and his little barren Queen, who was wife to His Majesty but continually aware of the stream of mistresses led up the Privy Stairs by Will Chiffinch.

'They say the Duchess of Buckingham is a little round, crumpled woman, very fond of finery, but without the least idea of how to adorn her body with elegance. But she is no fool, and remains the first lady in the land after the Queen, and the Duchess of York.'

'That is indeed a high position,' I said. 'So why are they not happy together?'

'Bucks is so clever — he writes verse

and plays and dialogues — oh, there is no end to his talents! And he said one thing, Wiggins, which I have never forgotten. And you remember it also, if you ever wish to wed a man. Bucks said — 'Wives we choose for our posterity, mistresses for ourselves' — '

'So your dear Duke has found himself a mistress? No wonder the marriage is not a success.'

Like all the others, I thought bitterly. Like all the rakes Nelly had known previously at the theatre. Was it not possible to find a truly happy, faithful husband in this world?

'My dear Bucks found himself the wickedest and most vicious of females, and I am sure that one day he will regret it. But Lady Shrewsbury possesses some quality unknown to me, which enslaves men and drives them wild with passion. There are many at Court today who wear a yard of her tresses by way of a bracelet, and I believe she would have a man killed for her every day and only hold her head up higher on account of it.'

'Dear heavens!' I cried. 'What a vixen! And has *she* a husband?'

'She did have,' answered Nelly, 'but when Lord Shrewsbury grew tired of being a cuckold he sent a challenge to Buckingham. They fought a duel in the January of 1668, and Buck's sword pierced Shrewsbury's right breast and came out at the shoulder.'

'That is horrible!' I cried. 'Did he die at once?'

'No.' Nelly shook her head and her bright little face sobered. 'I do not blame the Duke of Buckingham,' she went on stoutly, 'for he had to accept the challenge, and it was all that Shrew's fault, anyway. But her poor husband took some time to die and it wasn't till March that he finally passed away. There was great public outcry at his death, but of course it did not mean anything to me then, Wiggins, 'cos I didn't know Bucks at that time.'

'How *can* you like the man, Nelly?'

'I told you,' she snapped, ''twas all

121

that Shrew lady's fault. She had been cleverly out of the country when it happened, over in France, but some months later she returned to England and took up with Bucks again. Then he did a foolish thing and took her back with him to his home at Wallingford House, which is at the far end of Whitehall.'

'And?' I prompted, for Nelly had paused in some distress.

'And then his Duchess protested for the first time, and I do believe that I would have done the same, Wiggins. The Duchess said that she and that other creature could not live together in the same house, and Bucks replied he realised that, and he had therefore ordered the coach to take her back to her father's.'

'Well, I think he is an intolerable man and cannot understand you at *all*, Nelly. He should have been sent to the Tower for such cruelty!'

'There are times when I do not admire what he does,' she admitted, 'but he makes me laugh, Wiggins, and Charles loves him, despite his faults, and he is ever so clever. Now great arguments are building up between him and the Duke of York — for Bucks is a believer in the Protestant faith and 'tis said by many that the Duke of York is a secret Catholic.'

'Of course Bucks always wins any argument because he is so much sharper than the poor Duke! In fact he often says that the King could do things if he *would*, and the Duke would do things if he *could*.'

'Meaning King Charles is lazy and his brother stupid?'

'My Charles is not lazy,' said Nelly quickly, 'but perhaps a bit slow in making decisions — he has so many interests in life, Wiggins, he cannot be busy with Parliament and that dreary Privy Council *all* the time. As for York, Bucks has no admiration for 'dismal Jimmy', as he calls him, and says it worries him dreadfully to think that he may one day become King of England.'

'Well, that has really nothing to do with the Duke of Buckingham, and it will be up to King Charles to decide on his successor when the time is right.'

I did not like the sound of this Bucks at all, and wondered for how long such a reckless and outspoken man could exist in the turbulent world of politics and intrigue.

The year 1670 was a most exciting one for us as Nelly began the climb to fame and fortune, which she had dreamed about.

That spring, John Dryden had written a new tragedy and wanted Nelly to play opposite Charles Hart, as Almahide. She would gladly have taken the part even though *The Conquest of Granada* was a tragedy, but she could not.

'Because I am expecting the King's child,' she told me, her eyes sparkling with joy. 'Let us pray most fervently that it is a boy, for then I will make Charles give him a title, and little Nelly from the alley will be the mother of a Royal Duke!'

'Oh, Nelly, I shall be so proud of you!' I threw my arms about her and held her close. 'When will it be born? And have you thought of a name? Can you choose it, or must you ask the King? And this house is too small for a family — will he not give you a bigger place — like he did Castlemaine? For you will need more servants. And will he give you money to keep yourself and the child in proper fashion?'

The King had bought the Countess of Castlemaine a fine building called Berkshire House, at the bottom of St James's Street, with beautiful gardens backing on to the Park. And it was said that he had settled a pension of over £4,000 on her.

'So many questions, Ally-Wally, and yes, to most of them,' Nelly replied smiling. 'I'm pesterin' for a bigger house and we'll likely get it, but Charles has first to meet his sister again, for they have not met since her marriage ten years ago, and he has always loved her most dearly.

'So *first* I'll have me baby, Wiggins, then Charles can give us a better place to live. But I gotta wait till the summer 'cos he's meeting his sister in May, or June, I believe.'

Whilst the Court was away from London, meeting and entertaining the Duchess of Orleans at Dover, my dearest friend gave birth to her first son on the 8th May, at our lodgings in Lincoln's Inn Fields. He was named Charles Beauclerk.

I was sad for Nelly that she did not have the proud father by her at that time, but she was wonderfully patient and overjoyed to have given birth to a healthy boy-child.

'Wait till Charles sees him — ain't he a honey? Look at his fingers, Wiggins, and his little rose-mouth.'

Her mother came waddling up to view her grandson, and her sister Rose came, but I kept myself out of sight at such times. Much as I loved Nelly, I could not feel affection for her family who, I always felt, came to see Nelly because of what they hoped to get from her now that she was an acknowledged mistress of the King.

However, I was determined to be around when Charles Stuart arrived to look at his son, for I had never seen him at close quarters before, Nelly having always gone to him at Whitehall on all previous occasions. But now that she was the mother of his child, and confined to the house for the next few weeks, I had every hope of seeing His Majesty properly.

And I wanted to see him very much, to know what the man possessed, apart from majesty, which made him so very attractive to many different kinds of women.

At the same time as I was wondering about the King, I thought also of Luke Markham. I had not seen him for some time and hoped that all was well with him. I missed the man, and the conversations we had had together, and although Nelly was full of chat about the people at Court, and their numerous amours and quarrels, she had little idea of the political scene. I longed to talk to Luke again and find out more about King Louis of France, and who had taken the Earl of Clarendon's place, and whether there was still a likelihood of war with the Dutch. I hoped that he was at Dover also, and would come back to London when the Court returned, and then call on me and bring me up to date with all the important news.

That autumn Nelly performed on stage for the last time, and pleased both Dryden and the King by playing the part of Almahide opposite Charles Hart's Almanzor.

I shall never forget her as she spoke the Prologue, wearing a broad-brimmed hat and wide waist-belt, which emphasised her slim figure. Although it was but a few months since she had borne little Charles Beauclerk, she had regained her slenderness and looked quite ravishing. The audience was delighted to see her again and the applause was deafening. But the part of Almahide was Nelly's last.

'I'm gonna be a good mother and a good mistress now, Wiggins, and there ain't no time for prancin' about on stage no more,' she told me.

I saw the King when the Court returned to Whitehall and, as Nelly had expected, His Majesty was delighted with little Charles Beauclerk and informed Nelly that he would find a residence for her nearer Whitehall, in Pall Mall.

He called frequently at that time, and after we moved from Lincoln's Inn Fields, and I was at once aware of how tall he was, tall, and with very dark hair and complexion. He was not at all handsome, with a large fleshy nose and an ugly mouth. But he possessed great charm, as I had heard, and was surrounded by a mass of barking, snuffling, wagging little dogs.

King Charles had not been long in the chamber where Nelly was reclining with her son, when he turned his head and spoke to me, and his voice was musical and soft, his dark eyes most kind, as he asked my name, and how long I had been with Nelly, and who my parents were.

When I told him about the Great Plague, and how I had lost my family at that time, a most compassionate expression appeared on his lined face and for that moment he made me feel as if I really mattered to him, as if he and I were alone in the room together, and that he had the time to stand and listen to my entire history, for hours, if need be.

No wonder the common folk loved him when he walked in the park each day, and they were free to go up to him, and talk to him of their problems if they felt so inclined. And if they could keep up with him. For Nelly had told me that her Charles walked most rapidly, and with his long legs and great strides he could usually outwalk anybody else.

'Odd's fish! But you have had a terrible early life, Mistress Wingard,' he said gently, when I had finished answering his questions. 'Methinks you and I must have more talk together for I, too, have suffered much. One day I must tell you of my escape from Worcester, and the many adventures which befell me before I set foot in the safety of France.'

'Worcester?' I repeated, for that name had sunk into my brain since hearing it from Luke.

The King nodded grimly. 'When Cromwell destroyed my army and almost captured me, there was a price on my head, Mistress Wingard, and the description of 'A tall, black man upwards of two yards high' was posted everywhere. But loyal Catholics helped me, you know. The Penderell brothers, and the good priest Father John Huddleston, and we made for Bristol with me dressed as a servant.'

He smiled, his melancholy face

lighting up with amusement as he remembered his flight.

'And you departed from there by boat?' I asked, looking at his fine figure in its satin, ribbon-trimmed breeches, long jacket with deep flared cuffs, and the frothing lace cravat at his throat, trying to visualise Charles Stuart in threadbare clothing, his face blackened in disguise, and his feet ill-shod and bleeding.

'Impossible to get a boat at Bristol,' answered the King, 'so I went first to Trent House in Somerset, then on to Dorset, and ended up in Sussex where I found a Captain Tattersall willing to take me across the Channel.'

He picked up one of his dogs as he was talking, and held it against his chest gently fondling its ears.

'Lord sakes, Your Majesty!' cried out Nelly. 'You have not found *another* captive listener! I beg you not to bore my Wiggins with your adventures just now, or she'll be yawning her way off to bed when I most need her.'

I was astounded by Nelly's impudence and quickly said that I was in no way bored by His Majesty's story, and found his adventures most enthralling.

The King smiled again as he moved away from me and back to Nelly, still carrying his dog.

'I came to see you and my son,' he said gently, 'and will leave your Wiggins alone now. But wait until little Charles is older, me dear, and then he will be glad to hear the tales his father has to relate.'

'Maybe,' said Nelly, 'but do not bore *him*, either, Sire, else he'll be bawlin' each time you come to the house.'

'He won't bawl at me.' The King dropped the dog on to the couch beside Nelly and lifted the baby in his splendid velvet-clad arms, swinging it high above his head. 'A glorious boy, Nelly and one to be proud of. Odd's fish! I have me a pack of healthy sons now, but methinks it strange that God does not see fit to grant the same joy to my dear wife.'

His voice had dropped to a near

whisper as he ended and I felt my heart lurch at the sadness in his tone. So, despite his many mistresses he did love Queen Catherine, I thought, and wanted most desperately to have a legitimate child by her.

'No more signs — no hope?' asked Nelly quietly.

The King shook his mass of thick black curls. 'No hope now, I fear. And what will happen to England when I'm gone, eh? But there — ' he placed the baby back in its mother's arms and straightened his tall body. 'Let us not think too much about the future but dwell instead upon the present. Get you well, Nelly, and back to the stage for Dryden must be satisfied and has written this part especially for you, so he tells me. Then I'll find a nice pretty house for you, me dear, so that you and my son can live close by me.'

Nelly nodded and blew him a kiss as he left her side and walked from the room, followed by a stream of dogs.

I did see Luke later that year, soon

after we moved from Lincoln's Inn Fields into a new residence at the north end of Pall Mall.

'Great heavens, I had trouble finding you, Alice,' he said, when he and I had time to talk in the Common Parlour to which I had led him.

'If you had called more often these past months you would have been aware of our movements,' I retorted primly. 'I suppose you have heard about Nelly's son?'

'Yes, indeed, another bastard for the King.'

'Let us not talk of Nelly and the King, for I do not know how long you will be staying, nor when Nelly may call for me,' I said hastily. 'So tell me please, all the things you have learnt these past months, and what has been happening abroad. I have missed our interesting conversations and look for you to keep me informed as to what Parliament is doing. I have met and talked with the King now,' I added, 'and find him a most charming and gentle man.'

Luke smiled. 'Every female does,' he replied. 'But then they do not have to govern, or make decisions. Lord, Alice, if you were but to know what has been going on down at Dover, it would shake your Puritan mind, I can assure you.'

'Tell me.'

'You will promise to keep hold of your tongue, as you have in the past? No word to your friend Nelly? Or to anyone else for that matter?'

'You know you can trust me, Luke, and I have told you before that I am not a blabbermouth, and Nelly is only interested in *people*, not in politics. What was so important at Dover?'

He sighed, leaning his head back against the tapestried chair of which Nelly was so proud. We had only possessed stools before in our different lodgings, and this chair was one of the first things she had purchased with the King's money.

There were even finer pieces of furniture in the Withdrawing-Room and Hall, but these were not private places to sit and talk quietly together. Nelly so often had visitors, people wanting her attention for some plea or worry, knowing of her kind heart and close friendship with the King, always hoping that she would pass on their problems to the Royal ear.

So I had taken Luke into the Common Parlour, which was where Nelly and I would sit together of an evening if she were not engaged in any social activity, and where little Charles Beauclerk would be brought to see his mother for a cuddle before bedtime.

It was very pleasant to be able to entertain Luke in a more elegant fashion now that we had the King's money to spend, and I had asked Peg to bring us a dish of chocolate each, enriched with eggs, sack and spices.

'I do not know everything,' Luke began slowly, 'but have gleaned much during my stay in Dover, and it is good to talk to somebody about it all — somebody I can trust — for speaking my thoughts out loud helps me to adjust matters more clearly in my own mind.'

He took a satisfying sip at his dish of chocolate.

'And you have discovered much that will interest your cousin in France?'

He smiled. 'I think my cousin will not be the first to tell King Louis the news. The French King had his own agent, Alice, and that was none other than the Duchess of Orleans. Madame played her allotted part to perfection, whilst she was with her brother.'

'She was not an agent for King Louis!' I exclaimed. 'Why, she was an English Princess — a Stuart — sister to the King of England! We heard of her death soon after she returned to France, and Nelly said the King was distraught with grief and shut himself away in his bedchamber for days. Do you think she was poisoned, Luke?'

He shook his head.

'Rumours such as that always follow the unexpected death of a public figure,' he answered. 'Although many suspected her unpleasant husband, there is no proof that he had a hand in her death. Madame was a fragile, pale creature, Alice, and I believe she died from the bursting of a stomach ulcer.'

'But she was a friend of France,' he went on, 'as is her brother, and King Louis sent her as the ideal person to carry out the secret dealings which were so important to both monarchs. Two treaties have now been concluded, Alice, and one will be made known to all.'

He paused, and his grey eyes had darkened, I noticed, as they did when he was troubled about something. But Luke was so often mocking, or making jests about people and events, that I had not often seen that grey turn to the colour of rain clouds gathering before a storm.

'Go on,' I said.

'The other may only be known on the death of King Charles, or when he sees fit to make it known publicly. But this second is a dangerous document, and few know of its existence as yet.'

'But *you* know,' I cried. 'So how many others may know, also? And what is so dangerous about it? Tell me, Luke, I do assure you that your words will go no further than my ears, and these four walls.'

'So discreet, my Alice, and so very intrigued. I will make an agent of you yet, my dear.' His words were light but his face remained troubled.

'Not me.' I shook my head firmly. 'I find these matters fascinating to hear, and there is much I want to know about the state of this country and the future of this realm. But I am a female, Luke, and glad of it. As you so rightly said, we have no say in government and thus no need to make decisions, sign documents, cause unrest or disappointment, or hatred in others. I want only to know what is happening. The rest I leave to the menfolk, and God help them and the King, is all I can say. I like listening but not *doing*.'

'You sound like our beloved King

then,' he said shortly, 'who is by nature most slothful and will listen to everybody, but has great difficulty in making decisions.'

'Yet this important document has been signed by him?'

Luke nodded. 'Negotiations have been going on for a long time, you realise, and the King corresponded frequently with Madame, his sister, and she had long been in favour of this treaty.'

'Then what is so dangerous about it, Luke?'

'The second part. The first is of an alliance with the French, and their co-operation against the Hollanders, and this will be made known and signed by all five members of the Cabal. But the second part would mean civil war in England if the truth came out.'

'Not another war in this poor country! Go on, Luke, tell me what you mean.'

'I mean that in the secret part of this treaty, known to but a handful of people at present, King Charles gives his undertaking to declare himself a Catholic, and thereby reconcile this country with Rome.'

'The people will never accept that!' I cried. 'And Parliament will not either.'

'The King has a great deal of work to do if he wants to put this idea into the minds of his ministers, but the document does say that he may declare himself at a time of his own choosing. So there is no hurry for him to speak out. And he will doubtless feel that the money he will receive for this secret treaty is worth everything else. There will be a subsidy of £200,000 for each year of war with the Dutch, and the promise of a further £140,000 for imposing his will on his people, using force of arms if necessary, and making this a Catholic country once more.'

I felt ill at the thought and knew that no one, not even King Charles himself, could make me believe in a faith I neither liked, nor admired.

'Who else knows of this dreadful

document?' I whispered.

'Officially it is known only to King Charles, King Louis, the Duchess of Orleans knew, of course, and Clifford and Arlington — the two ministers who signed it at Dover. But I know, and the clerk who told me knows, as do several of the French, I have no doubt.'

'But what about the Duke of Buckingham? Nelly is always talking about him and telling me how close he is to the King. He is clever and a strong Protestant — oh, I suppose he was not told because he would have fought against it?'

'Exactly that.' Luke smiled at my enraged expression. 'There are five leading ministers, Alice, and their names are linked to spell cabal — so they are always known as the Cabal.'

'The King was determined not to have one man in power, like the Earl of Clarendon who continually dominated him, so when the Chancellor departed from these shores, the Cabal appeared and His Majesty now has five men to try and control instead of one.'

'What are their names?'

'Clifford, who is a Roman Catholic and thus aware of the treaty. The Earl of Arlington, who is one of the King's closest companions and suspected of having Catholic sympathies. He also signed.

'The Duke of Buckingham, your Nelly's friend, who is the most arrogant and self-willed of men, but prides himself on representing the Puritan interest.'

'So he was not informed,' I said.

'Neither was Lord Ashley, an equally unscrupulous and ambitious man and a staunch Protestant, nor the Duke of Lauderdale, who is not greatly interested in politics but rules Scotland with an iron hand.'

'Dear me,' I stared at my companion. 'What an unattractive and unreliable group of men. And you mean to tell me that *they* are the Chief Ministers of State at present?'

'I am afraid they are. But do not

forget that the King has total power over Parliament, and can have it prorogued when he so wishes.'

'What does that mean?'

'It means that he can dismiss it at the end of a session without resorting to dissolution, which would mean new elections and new ministers, and Charles would not want that too often. He also holds resources of patronage, Alice, and members can always be bribed to support his Royal programmes. Above all, the business of government is still in the hands of the King, and the ministers whom he alone selects.'

'Well, I do not consider that he has selected good ministers in this Cabal of his. He may be able to bribe them — but only if he has the money, and it seems to me that Parliament is always keeping him short of finances. Nelly told me that her Charles had but three collar-bands in his wardrobe, and no ink or paper for his Council table. Just think of that — and he is the King of

England, Luke!'

'He will be able to call on Louis of France for financial support now, and if he had fewer mistresses and less greedy ones at that, Charles Stuart would be far better off. I believe there will be another mare in the Royal stables soon,' he went on thoughtfully, 'for the Duchess of Orleans brought a very beautiful Breton girl with her to Dover, and the King was most taken with her.

'Now, Buckingham has been sent to France to attend Madame's funeral, and it is expected that he will bring this young Louise de Kéroualle back with him for the King's attention.'

'Nelly is able to hold her own with King Charles,' I replied firmly. 'Now that she has produced a son for him her position is quite safe.'

'Castlemaine gave the King three sons but he tired of her, and she was far more beautiful than your Nelly.'

'Castlemaine was getting too old and she was not faithful to His Majesty,' I snapped. 'And Nelly really loves the

King and will never take another lover, I know that.'

'You and your Nelly,' Luke said, rising from his chair and smiling at me. 'Would that you would prove so loyal to me, Alice Wingard.'

He reached for my hands and pulled me up from my stool to stand before him.

'Have you thought more of that which I last told you? Do not pass your life without one amour, sweet Alice. For the years go by and age creeps upon one when it is least expected.'

He let go of my hands and placed his fingers beneath my chin, tilting my hot face up to meet his.

'You smell so delicious I could eat you!' he exclaimed. 'What a tease you are, Alice. One kiss, my heart, and then I shall leave you to your days of chastity. But I have not been scorned by a woman before, and will not readily accept dismissal now.'

Before I could step back from him, before I could push his hard, velvet-clad body away, his arms went round me and his admiring, smiling face came close to mine, his lips brushing gently against my mouth.

It was a swift, undemanding caress, then Luke was standing back and pulling on his gloves before my senses had fully recovered.

'You are going?' I asked in bewilderment.

'Yes, I am off — 'tis safer so whilst my courage lasts, Alice Wingard. But spare a thought for me tonight when you lie warm and snug in your lonely bed.'

It was the perfume, of course, which had tempted him and proved my undoing. The damask perfume, which Nelly had given me in the little casting bottle, with its perforated lid.

'Try it, Wiggins,' she had said artfully, doubtless knowing of its effect on the male sex. 'I have more than enough of me own now, and think you'll like the smell.'

I had sprinkled some of the liquid

onto my wrists, and on my bosom, and had found the aroma delightful.

'It is made of musk and ambergris, sugar, benjamin and aloes wood — all added to rose water,' Nelly said, smiling at my enraptured expression, 'and my Charles likes it ever so much.'

Luke Markham did also, I thought later, feeling myself go red at the memory of his body so close to mine, and his warm, firm lips brushing my mouth. Next time he visited I must make sure not to have any damask perfume on my skin, for I knew that the emotions he had aroused in me, even from so slight an embrace, were likely to become stronger the more I saw of him.

And he appeared to find me equally attractive. Dear heavens, where would it all end? To become his mistress was totally against all my beliefs and yet I knew, also, that Luke Markham was not the marrying kind.

6

Once Nelly had become a mother, and was known to all as the King's mistress, she was able to visit Whitehall publicly and I went with her on a few occasions.

The Palace was a great sprawling mass of buildings along the Thames, built by King Henry VIII, Luke had told me, and King Charles's father, the first King Charles, had intended building a new palace in its place, designed by Inigo Jones.

Inigo Jones was a very talented and enlightened architect, Luke also informed me, and it was he who had been responsible for the Piazzo at Covent Garden, and St Paul's Church there, with its fine pillars. But he had only managed to complete the Banqueting House at Whitehall before his death in 1652.

Mr Jones must have been fond of pillars, I decided, when first seeing the

Banqueting Hall. There were huge marble pillars holding up the galleries which ran all around the walls beneath the panelled ceiling, where musicians played and people could walk, and look down upon the King and courtiers below.

The ceiling impressed me very much with its magnificent panels, all painted, I learnt, by a Flemish painter, Sir Peter Paul Rubens, who had been knighted by the present King's father.

But there were so many people, officials, courtiers, servants and dogs at Court that the noise and confusion was dreadful. I saw a large table around which courtiers played at basset with piles of gold coins before them, and every doorway led off to another room, and then another, making me keep very close to Nelly for fear of losing myself.

Very soon the splendour and the depravity, the beautifully attired court-iers and their obscenities, the gaming, the debauchery and the drunkenness, revolted me, and I preferred to stay at

151

home unless Nelly particularly asked for me to go with her. Later, I heard tales from Luke about Buckingham's friends and the knowledge appalled me. He agreed that these men were intellectually brilliant; they could compose graceful verse and were renowned for their wit at Court; but they were also capable of vicious, bestial acts in pursuit of so-called pleasure.

'Rochester is consistently drunk,' Luke told me, 'Sir Charles Sedley ordered his servants to waylay and horsewhip an actor who caricatured him on stage, and Lord Buckhurst murdered a tanner by mistake, but made such a clever story of it that he was acquitted.

'They all have too much money,' he went on, 'and become easily bored, so take out their energy on raping young girls and attacking helpless citizens. Not long ago, Buckhurst and Sedley spent a night in gaol for running naked through the London streets.'

These exquisites were friends of the

Duke of Buckingham, and the King — yes, and my Nelly, too, and known as 'the merry gang'. They might have enjoyed their wild wicked pursuits, and amused people as depraved as themselves, but they angered me and I went to Whitehall as little as possible.

Nelly enjoyed the lewd jokes and the public display of fondling and kissing which went on all the time at Court, but I did not. I think she wanted to be near the King too, because she now had a rival, as Luke Markham had warned me.

It was the Breton girl, Louise de Kéroualle, and King Charles would not leave her alone.

In the August of that year the King created Castlemaine the Duchess of Cleveland, and she had her house, and the Palace of Nonsuch to keep her happy. His Majesty had Nell Gwyn, and was becoming very interested in the young French girl, so he pushed Castlemaine gently out of his way in the most charming fashion.

Nelly had never been worried about Castlemaine for she always said that the lady's bad temper and violent nature would be her undoing, but I rather wondered how my friend would react to the new French beauty.

I seldom saw the Queen, for Whitehall was considered not the right place for her, and she had been moved away to Somerset House in the Strand, poor lady. But the King visited her, Nelly informed me, and the Royal couple were to be seen together on ceremonial occasions, and at all the banquets and balls which were given for important visitors and foreign ambassadors.

'The Queen really adores Charles,' I remember Nelly saying once, 'and he is always at his most tender with her.'

And so he should be, I thought, when he has time for her and is away from his numerous mistresses for a while.

I saw Nelly's Duke of Buckingham and realised why she was so taken with him. He was magnificently dressed in full breeches of silver satin, which were gathered on to a black velvet band at the knee and decorated with pale blue ribbons. His long jacket was of mole-coloured velvet, with buttons of silver, his lace cravat was bordered with silver trim, and he paraded a long walking-cane trimmed with more pale blue ribbons.

The Duke moved with supreme grace and I noticed many people watching him as if they could not turn their eyes away from his strong, tall body and mass of light brown hair, so cleverly curled that I could not be sure if it was his own, or a periwig. All around him there was laughter at some jest he had made, and he looked a most courteous and affable gentleman.

Similar to Nelly, I thought. Although she did not have Buckingham's breeding, she had the same kind of wit and sense of fun, which made all those around her laugh and enjoy her use of words. It was no wonder she got on well with her Bucks.

I also saw Buckingham's amour, the

Shrew lady, as Nelly always called her, and was very surprised to see the infamous Lady Shrewsbury at Court.

'Look at that nasty creature,' Nelly whispered, as the lady in question moved in front of us surrounded by an admiring group of gallants. 'And ain't they stupid, panting after her like she's a bitch on heat. She really is a *horrid* whore!' And she spat out the words close to my ear.

'Why is she allowed here?' I whispered back. 'It does not seem right to have such a wicked female gallivanting at Whitehall.'

Lady Shrewsbury was also beautifully attired in gold satin, making the couple appear most regal with their silver and gold ensemble, but the lady wore a great deal more lace than her lover, trimmed around her petticoat, and at her waist, and in the numerous frills on her huge puffed sleeves.

Her hair was thick and brown, falling in loose ringlets over her wide brow and around her white neck. Her mouth was very red, but her eyes were frightening — I thought them insolent, bored, and goat-like as they stared out from her expressionless face. Her carriage was disdainful, as she moved slowly forward, paying little attention to her fawning companions.

'Oh, the Shrew is allowed,' said Nelly, 'because everyone's mistress is allowed here at Court. King Charles sets the example so they all follow his lead. And I'm glad of *that*, Wiggins, else you and me would be sitting at home right now.'

She gave a low chuckle, unusually subdued for my Nelly, with her normally loud laugh, but we were in the midst of a large crowd and she did not want to draw attention to herself that day.

'Bucks told me his Shrew is a Catholic,' she went on quietly, 'and she drives him mad with all her confessions and her priests. I suppose she has so many sins she can't help going so frequently to confess.'

'If Buckingham is such a strong

Protestant how *can* he have a Papist for a lover?'

'Because my poor Bucks is totally enthralled by that Shrew, Wiggins, and until the spell is broken he will be unable to leave her alone. He said once that love was like a game of chess and if both were cunning gamesters, they need never make an end of it.' Her face contorted with a sour grimace. 'I hope the Devil punishes that female one day, for I cannot see any man being able to control her.'

'I hope King Charles will avoid her allure,' I said, worried by Nelly's remarks.

'Oh, the King is far too busy to become entangled in the Shrew lady's web,' answered Nelly, more calmly. 'He has that French girl now to occupy his mind, and his hands. Look — there she is, next to Charles. What do you think of her, Wiggins?'

There were so many people present, all trying to get near the King and attract his attention, that I had difficulty in seeing Louise de Kéroualle that day. But I caught odd glimpses of her, and remember being surprised by her youthful appearance and her mass of tight black curls.

'Funny thing is that dear Bucks made an *awful* mess of the French girl's arrival here,' Nelly told me later, when we were home again. 'I am sure she must have been simply furious. Not that it matters — I don't believe anybody likes her at Court, Wiggins, 'cept perhaps that wishy-washy Lord Arlington.'

'What happened between her and Buckingham?'

'Bucks had quarrelled with his cousin Barbara — '

'Castlemaine?' I queried.

'The Duchess of Cleveland now, if you don't mind,' answered Nelly pertly. 'As I was saying, Bucks quarrelled with Cleveland so was determined to raise up a new mistress as her rival, and he said I was all right but not *dignified* enough. I was a bit cross at that, but know him so well that I couldn't be offended for long.'

'Why did the Duchess of Cleveland and your Bucks quarrel?'

'Oh, Wiggins, you do annoy me with all these interruptions when I am trying to get *on*,' cried Nelly. 'And I don't *know* why they fell out 'cept that Bucks always supported that Frances Stuart, who the King *really* loved, and she wouldn't have him, remember? And Cousin Barbara was mad with him for taking sides against her and she really *has* a temper! Now she is getting more and more friendly with the Duke of York — old dismal Jimmy — and Bucks don't like *that*. Can I go on now?'

'Yes,' I said.

'Well then. Bucks decided to introduce this French girl to Whitehall and Charles needed no persuading 'cos she'd caught his eye when she came over with Madame to Dover. Remember that?'

I nodded.

'So Bucks went over to France for

160

Madame's funeral, taking with him all the right invitations from Court, and the girl agreed to come. Bucks then sent her off with some of his suite to Dieppe, saying that he would join her at all convenient speed, and they would sail for England together.'

'And?' I prodded.

'And dear Bucks forgot all about her and came home by way of Calais, leaving Mistress Froggy kicking her heels in Dieppe!'

Nelly let out an uproarious burst of laughter.

'He didn't!' I cried. 'Whatever was he doing to make him forget such an important person? And he was bringing her back for the *King*. She must have been terribly angry at such an affront.'

'She was, and 'tis said that she will never forgive him for that,' Nelly roared again. 'He told me later that she bored him so much he could not abide another day with her, and anyway, he was in a great hurry to see his Shrew lady again. But it is a pity,' she went on

161

more soberly, 'cos Arlington does not like my Bucks and may well prove a dangerous enemy — he was the one who eventually met Froggy and placated her. Now if the King becomes ensnared by Froggy's charms, Bucks may find himself without Royal friendship, as well.'

'Is King Charles really intent on making this girl — what is her name, Nelly? I am not good with such foreign words.'

'Carwell,' replied Nelly. 'We all call her Mistress Carwell, or Froggy.'

'Well, this Louise Carwell — does the King really want to make her his mistress? Is he not content with you, Nelly?'

'Content with me?' She opened her hazel eyes very wide. 'Course he's content with me, Wiggins. But you should know Old Rowley by now — he likes lots of mares in his stable, and now that cross old Cleveland has gone he wants someone else. This Mistress Carwell will do nicely, thank you very much.'

'And you don't mind?'

'I said once that I wasn't jealous — well, I'm not really — but I've seen this girl, Wiggins, and I'm a *little* bit jealous of her.'

'Is she very beautiful? I only caught a glimpse of her at Court and thought she looked very young and quite different to the Duchess of Cleveland.'

'You'll see her properly one day, swanning around at Whitehall, and you'll know what I mean. She looks so young because of her simple, childish face. She's got lots of black curls and *I* think she'll get fat quite soon — specially if she has a baby. Ain't got the sort of figure which will keep thin for long. But I dislike her most because she's too full of herself, Wiggins. All high and mighty and better than anyone else, but if she becomes my Charles's mistress she'll be no better than the rest. We're all whores and she'll be one, too.'

'Is she not his mistress yet?'

'No, playin' hard to get, she is.

Though what good that will do her I
don't know. *Says* she's a virgin and
maybe hopes that Charles will divorce
Queen Catherine and marry her.
Imagine that! Be like old Harry Eight,
won't it?'

'But the King would never do that!' I
cried.

'No.' Nelly shook her head. 'I don't
believe he will ever get rid of the Queen
— tho' Bucks has some mad ideas of
popping her into a convent, or sending
her off to America so Charles can
divorce her and marry again.'

'But that's wicked! How can your
Duke think of such dreadful things!'

'Bucks hates dismal Jimmy, Wiggins,
and is terrified of having a Catholic
king. Now, it's not known for sure,
but Bucks tells me he is certain that
dismal Jimmy is a Catholic. His wife
was one for sure, before she died, and
they all say she had control of
everything about her husband except
for his codpiece. And Bucks says he
will do *anything* to stop York taking

over the throne when Charles dies.'

'It's always the same worry,' I said sadly, 'no legitimate heir to the throne, and who will take over on the King's death? What has happened to the little girls, Mary and Anne of York, now that their mother is dead? And are *they* being brought up in the Roman faith?'

'No,' said Nelly again, 'Charles has sent them away from St James's Palace and off to Richmond, where they are having a most sensible education under Lady Frances Villiers. The lady's husband is a cousin of my Bucks, and he says that the Lady Frances is a most reliable Protestant.'

'Will the Duke of York marry again? It must be sad for the family to be split up now, with no wife or mother at St James.'

'Oh, dismal Jimmy rides over to Richmond very often to visit his daughters, so they see enough of each other, and if he does marry again it had better be to a Protestant,' said Nelly, 'otherwise Bucks will be even more

165

unpleasant about poor old James. But my Charles is going to live for an awful long time yet,' she went on quickly, 'so let's hope Bucks keeps his head and acts more sensibly in future. Then we'll all have fun and a laugh at silly Mistress Froggy and her grand airs and graces.'

'I'm glad about one thing,' I said, 'and that is that this baby-faced Carwell is not a bad-tempered, violent female like Cleveland, or your Buckingham's Lady Shrewsbury. The King is probably hoping for a quieter life with the French girl, and I'm *sure* it's the reason he's fond of you, Nelly. You make him laugh and are always good-tempered and cheerful.'

'Sometimes I wish I weren't,' she replied sadly. 'Sometimes I wish *I* could rant and rage and scream at people. Those kind of females get what they want, Wiggins, all the time, it seems to me. 'Cos their lovers are scared of them, and excited by them, and men just don't seem able to control wild females, and that makes 'em all the more eager to hold on to them. Silly, if you ask me, but it's true, ain't it, Wiggins?'

'Well, true of King Charles and Cleveland,' I said slowly, 'and of the Duke of Buckingham and his Lady Shrew — but it can't be a pleasant life for them, can it, Nelly? And your Charles has now put the Duchess of Cleveland aside and is interested in this young, more gentle French girl. Maybe the Duke of Buckingham will also tire of his Shrew. Just wait,' I went on firmly, seeing that she still looked pensive, 'in the years to come I feel quite certain that pretty, witty Nelly will still be with her Charles the third, because she has such a loving nature.'

Nelly smiled. 'You do me good, Wiggins, and I'll remember your kind words. I can't change meself, that's for sure, but if I kin keep Charles laughing, and make him feel calm and happy in my company, that's all I'll ever want from life. And a title — ' she added quickly — 'a title for me and me son.

Then I'll die content.'

It must have been at about this time, when we first moved to Pall Mall and Nelly had borne her son, Charles Beauclerk, for the King, that I heard about The Sweep.

Perhaps it was because Nelly was now mixing with very wealthy people and listening to the sort of talk she would not have heard in the theatre, or maybe it was because she was beginning to travel more and thus the fear of highwaymen became more prevalent.

The King was mad about horse-racing, and made a regular pilgrimage to Newmarket every spring and autumn, taking with him ministers and mistresses alike. Such a large company of travellers had no fear of the 'gentlemen of the road' as they were called, for these robbers only attacked single horsemen and coaches, or very small groups of riders. They were cowardly criminals and would never stop a well-guarded, well-escorted number.

The Duke of Buckingham had told Nelly many tales about highwaymen who roamed the country after the Civil War.

'Many of them were Royalists who had their property taken from them by Parliament, in punishment for having supported the King, Bucks says. And he told me that *some* are real Cavaliers of the road, but others are horrid, Wiggins.' And she gave a little shiver.

'He has special knowledge of one, a Captain Zachary Howard, who set out to gain revenge on Protector Cromwell's men. This Howard heard that General Fairfax was sending some plate, and a letter, to his wife and so Howard stopped the coach and robbed it of all its contents.'

'Was that General Fairfax the father of Buckingham's wife?' I asked.

Nelly nodded. 'That's how my Bucks knows, Wiggins. Well then, this Captain Zachary Howard took the letter to Lady Fairfax, pretending to be a messenger from her husband, and as he was a well-spoken gentleman and very charming, the poor lady invited him in and gave him a bed for the night. When the household was asleep, Captain Howard tied up and gagged all the servants, then he raped Lady Fairfax and her daughter before riding off with the plate and many other things stolen from the house.'

'What a fiend!' I cried. 'Attacking innocent females in such barbarous fashion. I hope he was captured quickly. Was he, Nelly?'

'Yes,' replied Nelly. 'He was too clever one day and tried to hold up six Roundhead officers, and they overpowered him and took him to Maidstone Gaol. Bucks said he was hanged in 1652 and I was ever so glad to hear that, Wiggins.'

'I should think so, too. Such thieves and scoundrels should not be allowed to molest poor innocent people.'

'But some are not too bad,' answered Nelly, thoughtfully. 'There is a Frenchman, by name of Claud Duval, who is often seen in Holborn Fields, and he is supposed to be most charming and polite, and has many amorous conquests with the ladies. Bucks told me that this Duval has even been known to dance with a lady — inviting her out of her coach with utmost gallantry, and performing the Coranto with her on Hounslow Heath, in front of her husband.'

'Was the lady harmed?'

'No, Duval has never killed a victim, so far as is known; he only asked her husband to pay for their excellent performance together, which he did. And it all ended happily 'cos the husband was thankful that his life, and his lady's, were spared — Duval rode away with the money he wanted, and the lady was enchanted by the dancing highwayman and his courtesy and grace.

'I would not mind meeting *him* on me travels, Wiggins, or the one they call The Sweep, for he is also polite and never hurts his victims, so I've heard tell.'

'Nelly, don't be a fool!' I snapped.

171

'These men are dangerous no matter how well-mannered they are, or how handsome, and they are thieves who must be caught and punished. *Do* be careful if you travel out of London, and always stay close to the King's company — then you will be safe.'

That autumn I stayed behind to care for the house, and to keep an eye on little Charles Beauclerk when Nelly accompanied the King to Newmarket. She possessed servants enough these days, but I did not want to become caught up in the rowdy and debauched company at Newmarket, and told Nelly that I would remain quietly in Pall Mall until she returned. She quite understood my decision and took Mary with her, a young maid, to help with her hair, and with her dressing.

To be honest, I was probably hoping that Luke Markham might call. He was so unpredictable and difficult to pin down — sometimes calling frequently over a period of several weeks, and then off and out of sight for months on end.

This time I was disappointed and he did not put in an appearance, but Nelly arrived home earlier than expected, and filled with excitement about her adventure on the way back to London.

'I was missing little Charles most dreadfully,' she said, 'and had to return before the others to see my darlin' again.'

She held the baby in her arms, covering his head and face with kisses.

'The most exciting thing happened to me, Wiggins, and I do wish you had bin with me — it was quite scary, only he was ever so gallant and I'm sure wouldn't have harmed me.'

'What are you talking about?' I asked, staring at her in surprise.

'Well, I came back in the coach alone, just with Mary, 'cos Charles and the others were staying on longer at Newmarket, and they all *said* to be careful of highwaymen, and to take John as me escort.'

Her eyes were sparkling and she looked very bright and pretty, so I could tell she had not been hurt.

'Oh, Nelly, don't say your coach was stopped? Was it that Claud Duval? And what did you give him? Tell me quickly.'

'We had managed our journey very well up till then and John puts his head in my window and says — 'I reckon we can make it across the Fields by nightfall, Madam Gwyn, but we can stop at a tavern in Marybone overnight if you prefers.' And I says — 'Oh, John, who will be wantin' anything off me? Just tell George to drive on smartish and we'll get home safe and sound this night.' So we was doing that — going at a fair rate — then I hears John cry out and suddenly the coach slows down and there's the sound of a pistol shot.'

'Nelly!' I felt my heart beating faster at her words, and placed my hands on my breast to try and calm it. 'What happened then?'

'It was getting dark but the moon was out and I *saw* him, Wiggins, plain as could be! He was mounted on a great black horse, all booted and silver-spurred, dressed all in black wiv' a mask over his eyes. So black, everything about him, that's why it's certain he was The Sweep. But he was a real gentleman, lifting his hat to me, and asking for what money and jewels I had in a most courteous manner.'

'And how much did you give the villain?'

'Well, he said he was sorry to be troubling me but he had a wife, most poorly at home, and three young children to support, and would be ever so grateful for anything I could give him.'

'So you felt sorry for him and gave him everything you had?'

She nodded, pressing her mouth against little Charles Beauclerk's soft downy head, and gazing at me with reproachful eyes.

'I *know* what it's like to be poor, Wiggins, and now I've got so much and Charles will always give me more, so I couldn't refuse the poor devil. I handed over me necklace and ear-rings, and the jewel-box which Mary was holding — trembling all over she was — and I had a little money on me which I was glad to give as well,' she ended defiantly.

'So then he bowed politely and thanked you for your kindness and rode off without a shot fired after him? What were John and Coachman George *doing* to let the rascal escape like that?' I cried.

'John and George were sensible men and both now live to tell the tale,' snapped Nelly. 'The Sweep possessed a brace of pistols which were fully loaded, as we could hear when he fired to make us stop, and his accomplice was not far distant, also armed. I am very *glad* my men did nothing foolish, Wiggins, and I'm also glad that I helped the man. I don't suppose it's much fun doing his work in all weathers, and the highway-man's life is short, anyway.'

'Nelly, I don't know *what* will become of you, I really don't. You cannot keep handing out all your possessions to highwaymen and beggars who accost you, else you'll soon have nothing left, and neither will the King. You *know* he is always short of money, and it won't help him if you keep asking for more.'

She jerked her chin at me. 'And what would *you* have done, dear Wiggins? Would you rather have money? Or would you rather have your life?'

'If this Sweep is such a gentleman, he would not have harmed a defenceless female,' I retorted.

'Looking into the smoking mouths of them pistols I was not too sure,' she replied, 'and his hands were ever so steady. John said The Sweep is known round Marybone Fields as the most daring and dangerous of men. Anyway, I'm glad I helped him — he won't be around much longer and I hope he enjoys life while he has it.'

'Is he likely to be caught?'

'John says The Sweep is on the list of highwaymen in the Royal Proclamation and £20 is being offered for his capture.'

She cuddled little Charles closer to her breast, and her eyes were bleak.

'Ever bin to Tyburn, Wiggins? Well, all I can say is go there one day and watch an execution. Ma took me once, as a small girl, out to Tyburn Fair, and I've never forgotten it and never want to go again. They've got the triple-tree there, or the three-legged mare, some call it, and the poor prisoners are taken from Newgate Prison, riding backwards in a cart, all the way to Tyburn with ropes around their necks.

'An' the crowds gather, and people cheer and shout and laugh and it's *awful*, Wiggins, all waiting to see death. I'd rather see a play in the theatre any day. But you go to Tyburn — just *once* — then perhaps you'll better understand why I felt sorry for that man, and would never gladly see him caught and executed in such a terrible way.'

The year 1671 was another eventful one for both Nelly and me. We moved again, but only across to the other side of Pall Mall, and the house was very spacious and beautiful with a large garden adjoining the King's Garden, near St James's Palace.

It was number 79, Pall Mall and was stone-built, with long windows, and three storeys high as well as having attics for the servants. I was given my own Bedchamber across from Nelly's, and allowed to furnish it as I desired.

From my window I could look out on St James's Park, where ladies walked beneath the avenue of trees in warm weather, in their brightly coloured taffetas, and fops sauntered beside them in their periwigs and scented gloves.

It was a pretty, magical sight for me, remembering my days in the stinking Coal Yard Alley. But the gallants and courtiers still did not impress me, and I far preferred Luke Markham with his own dark brown hair and strong, suntanned face, to the numerous rakes in their silk stockings and beribboned, rosetted petticoat breeches and false curls.

Nelly and I both had Dressing-Rooms attached to our Bedchambers, though why I should have this extra chamber always puzzled me.

'You have many gowns and petticoats and much finery so you *need* space,' I said to her, 'but my wants are few and the garments I possess can be easily contained in the one oak chest.'

'But I want to spoil you, Wiggins!' she exclaimed. 'Now that I have money at last I want to share it with you. I help Ma and Rose, so why shouldn't you get some nice things for a change? You have been my best friend and companion for such a long time, and we have shared both good and bad days together, and I *couldn't* do without my Wiggins. So please take all that is given to you now.'

So the walls of my Bedchamber were hung with blue damask, and the dome and curtains of my bed were of blue velvet bordered with gold stuff. The two armchairs were covered with yellow silk, with carved gilt frames and blue fringes, and a gate-leg table of oak and pine was placed beneath my window which overlooked the Park.

A large wardrobe, set against one wall, contained all the gowns which Nelly kept insisting I should wear.

Little Peg, who had been with us since Drury Lane days, had her own room, tucked off the end of mine next to the Closet, and beside her were the back stairs which took her down to the kitchen and the servants' parlour.

Having two staircases in our new house also delighted us, and particularly little Peg.

'It's ever so nice having proper stairs for us servants, mistress,' she told me happily, 'and bein' able to carry them chamber-pots down in a more private fashion, and not meetin' Mrs Nelly's visitors coming up as we go down with them stinkin' pots.'

I nodded. Always before we had lived in abodes with but one flight of stairs. This splendid and spacious new house in Pall Mall was beautiful in every way — in the furnishings, in the many fine rooms, in the kitchen and servants' quarters below, and in the clever designing of the two staircases.

There were more Bedchambers on the floor above us, and there little Charles Beauclerk had his apartments, with further space for a visitor if Nelly had her mother, or sister Rose, to stay.

Across from my rooms, which were at the rear of the house, was Nelly's set of rooms, and they were identical to mine with her Bedchamber, Dressing-Room, servant's room and Closet, all in the front of the house overlooking Pall Mall.

She had Mary as her own maid, and poor Mary certainly had more work to do than my little Peg; with her mistress's huge amount of gowns, petticoats, ribbons, slippers and hats; and the various ways Nelly liked her red-brown hair to be arranged from day to day.

She had chosen orange and green for

the colours in her Bedchamber — 'to remind me always of me early days at the King's House,' she said, 'when I carried me basket of oranges covered with vine leaves, and shouted out me wares!'

So her wall-hangings were of brocaded satin, all orange and green with borders of gold, her bed curtains were of gold velvet, with orange cord trimmings, and her chairs, stool and firescreen were of orange and gold satin.

And the food we had to eat! Such victuals remained a surprise and joy to us for many years, and it was a constant delight not to have to consider the price of things when ordering two dozen pigeons, a stone of beef, and oysters by the barrel, for Nelly's social gatherings.

We indulged in apricots, strawberries and peaches in season, and had an excellent cook who provided us with many different vegetables like peas, asparagus and onions, and made a delicious salad in summer with lettuce, radish and cucumber all tossed with flowers and herbs.

We drank more, also, although I was never as fond of strong waters as Nelly. And it was no longer ale which wet our throats, but red and white wine, sherry, brandy and champagne.

At first Nelly was only given a lease of the new house, which angered her greatly, and she returned it to the King demanding total ownership.

'It is not fair, Wiggins,' she said, 'for he makes that Barbara Villiers into a Countess, and then into a Duchess, and he gives her a magnificent house *and* the Palace of Nonsuch. He adores her children and is already planning marriages for them, and will create a few more Dukes amongst his bastards, you mark my words.

'And what have *I* got from being a good and faithful mistress — which is more than can be said for Cleveland — what have I got? One more bastard for him, and another in me belly. A house I cannot even call me own, and no Countess, or Duchess, or even Lady to me name — just Mrs Gwyn, and be thankful.'

Fortunately for Nelly, the King was kind and eventually conveyed the house free to her, and her representatives, for ever.

'Now we are getting somewhere, Wiggins,' she told me happily once that was settled. 'And maybe titles will come next. But odd's fish! You've gotta fight for everything in this life, for nothing comes easily to the low-born creatures of the world.'

In the February of that year the King's eldest son, Duke of Monmouth, caused his father great distress.

'Trouble with that young man is that he has had everything his own way for far too long,' Luke told me. 'King Charles dotes on him, and 'tis thought by many that he will become the Prince of Wales.'

'Monmouth is most handsome and charming,' broke in Nelly, who was with us in the Common Parlour and for once not out gallivanting with her Charles the third. 'And Bucks has often told the King that he should declare him legitimate and make him his heir.'

'This latest escapade will not enhance his reputation,' said Luke grimly.

'What has Monmouth done?' I asked.

'He and a group of young noblemen went out whoring and drinking to Whetstone Park, and they were making such a noise that a beadle went to investigate.'

'Where is Whetstone Park?'

Luke smiled. 'You and your enquiring mind! You must always have everything quite clear and definite in your sweet head, must you not, my Alice?'

'Yes,' I answered.

'Whetstone Park lies between Lincoln's Inn Fields and Holborn, and is renowned for its courtesans,' he replied. 'Now then, this beadle, Peter Vernell by name, went to find out what all the commotion was about and this rowdy group of young blades attacked and murdered him, and the hand that raised the sword was Monmouth's.'

'What a bestial act! Has he been punished for such a foul deed?' I asked.

'No.' Luke raised his shoulders in a resigned shrug. 'His father granted him a Royal Pardon and all has been forgiven and forgotten.'

'But that is outrageous. Do *you* think it was fair, Nelly?' I looked across at her, with anger burning in my heart.

'No,' she answered quietly, 'but them of Royal blood can always get away with misdeeds, Wiggins, and my Charles loves that Monmouth, and had to settle this affair quickly. He couldn't have sent his own son to the Tower, now could he?'

'He could and he should,' I said. 'Royal blood, or not, if you commit a crime you should be punished for it.'

'Well, he ain't bin,' said Nelly, 'and don't go on about it, Wiggins, 'cos it's done now and Charles is King, and we must all abide by our sovereign's wishes.'

7

It was in this same year that the Court heard that Louise de Kéroualle had finally given in to His Majesty and become another Royal mistress. Arlington, whom she favoured since he had been the first to greet her on her arrival in England, had set it all up at his great mansion, Euston Hall, in Suffolk. He had invited the King and Louise to stay for a while and there, apparently, a mock marriage ceremony took place. There was a good deal of horseplay, so 'twas said, which suited Old Rowley, and Louise de Kéroualle's position at Court was assured from that day hence.

Perhaps this was the reason for Nelly's care — some called it greed — in making sure that she received everything possible for herself, and her children, from the Royal hands.

She had produced a second son for

the King that December, and this child was named James Beauclerk, after the Duke of York.

At the end of this year, also, Nelly's friend the Duke of Buckingham was once again talked about by everyone, but this time with admiration, and Nelly was overjoyed by her Bucks's success.

He had written a play entitled *The Rehearsal* and it was produced at the Theatre Royal on December 7th and the King and all the Court were present.

I remembered vaguely that Nelly had told me her friend Bucks was a very clever man, and that he wrote poetry and verse from time to time. But I had not realised that he was also a playwright. However, what apparently spurred him on to writing this master-piece was the fact that he disliked John Dryden, who had become Poet Laure-ate and Historiographer Royal in 1668.

Dryden's dramas and comedies fol-lowed one another with great speed and enormous success with the public, but his enemies were of the Court, led by Buckingham, and enforced by Rochester, Buckhurst and Sir Charles Sedley, who all considered Dryden to be an unworthy successor to the great playwrights of the past.

So Buckingham who, Nelly told me, was becoming bored with the political scene, decided to write a full-length farce in which Dryden's best effects would be brutally and cleverly caricatured.

He named his central character Mr Bayes, dressed him in black velvet (Dryden's favourite clothing) and threw in references to his mistress, his liking for stewed plums and snuff, and made him horribly complacent.

When Nelly and I went to see *The Rehearsal* we, like the entire audience present that afternoon, laughed until we wept.

Curiously enough, Mr Bayes did not cause Dryden's downfall but increased the popularity of his plays. Mr Bayes was a delightful character because he was so typical, and everyone watching him loved his air of self-delusion, and the unselfconscious excitement he portrayed about his own work. He was filled with conceit and appalling energy, and the audience went wild about him.

All seemed to be going well for Bucks at that time but, apart from political enemies such as Arlington and the Duke of York, he had made another who would prove his undoing. This was Louise de Kéroualle, or Madam Carwell as she was known by everyone, and Bucks stood for everything she most disliked about the English way of life — informality, disorderliness, eccentricity, and freedom of speech and opinion.

She would never forgive him for not bringing her safely across the Channel to England, nor did she like the great friendship between him and King Charles. Madam Carwell became stronger and stronger in her relationship with the King, and proved to be a pitiless enemy to the Duke of Buckingham.

I, meanwhile, was falling in love with Luke Markham against my will. But my heart proved stronger than my head for he was a most charming, handsome and interesting man. He began calling more frequently once we had moved to our final grand residence at 79, Pall Mall — so often, in fact, that Nelly begged him to make me his mistress.

We were in the Withdrawing-Room that day, I remember, next to the Dining Parlour, and which was also used as Nelly's Saloon where she entertained her visitors. She was very proud of this chamber with its fine plaster ceiling and gilt frieze, its marble chimneypiece, silk wall-hangings of gold and cream, and the gilded red and gold satin chairs.

'Take her to bed, Mr Markham,' she said to him, 'there's space enough for two in her apartments *and* in her great four-poster — then you can stay as long as you like. Just don't take her away from me — don't never do that!'

'I would gladly take her to bed, Nelly, but she won't agree to my advances and I am becoming greyer every day with frustration, just like the King. The grey hairs, I mean, not the frustration. There, can you see them?' And he bent his tall figure forward and showed Nelly the crown of his shining brown head.

'Sakes!' she exclaimed. 'It's easy to rectify that, sir. Get yourself a periwig like *all* the best gentlemen are wearing. His Majesty is coal-black again — haven't you noticed? Looking as he did when he was the bonny black boy of his youth.'

I had been standing listening to the pair of them twittering on like cooing doves, and it occurred to me then, as it had once or twice before, that maybe Luke was interested in Nelly and came to see me only as an excuse to talk to her.

Luke also seemed to know Nelly's Duke of Buckingham rather better than he had in the past, and they would often exchange jokes and reminiscences together about the gentleman.

'I hear Buckingham has become a proud father at last,' Luke went on speaking to Nelly, 'and he is calling the child Earl of Coventry, and has persuaded the King to stand godfather.'

'You see,' said Nelly, glancing across at me, 'mistresses can have *much* more fun than wives. I'm sorry about the Duchess, of course, and would never call that Shrew lady an ideal mistress, or mother. But I *am* glad for Bucks and he is so very proud to have a son at last.'

'You mean Duchess-Dowager,' said Luke, 'that is what we all call his wife now. Your Lady Shrew is known as Buckingham's Duchess.'

'Pah!' snapped Nelly. 'She's the Shrew lady to me and will *never* be called Duchess by my lips. *And* he's building a palace for her, ain't he, Mr Markham? Calling it Cliveden and saying it will be as fine as Windsor Castle when it's finished. Silly man.'

She shook her head fiercely. 'It's gonna cost him thousands and thousands of pounds and he ain't got that much. I believe his debts are already enormous.'

Luke nodded. 'And he keeps on spending. He's giving a water-party next week and I hoped you might agree to come with me, Alice.' He turned and looked at me for the first time, his eyes very bright. 'All the Court are invited, and you could come and gaze to your heart's content. We are to travel on gilded barges with musicians dressed as Turks, slaves and savages, and the guests will glide down the Thames in raiments of shepherds and nymphs, to the sound of flutes and violins. What say you, Alice, to an evening of pure delight?'

'You are speaking to me?' I moved a step forward, tilting my head on one side. 'You did mean me, Alice Wingard?'

'Of course.' He looked amused by my tone of voice. 'Would you not care to accompany me?'

'I am sorry. You and Nelly were talking at such length between yourselves and discussing so many matters of importance, I did not realise that I was to be included in your conversation.'

'Oops! Wiggins is affronted,' cried Nelly. 'I'd best leave you two lovers alone. Don't forget that suite of rooms,' she said to Luke as she departed, 'make a mistress of that girl and you can call this house your own.'

'Well,' I said, when she had gone, 'I have never been so insulted in all my life! There you were — talking about me as if I were invisible — saying *she* all the time, and deciding on my future as if you were God — or the Devil, more like.'

'Alice,' he said gently, coming towards me and reaching for my hands. But I snatched them from his grasp and went to sit on one of the red and gold chairs. 'Alice, I enjoy your friend Nelly, and her warmth and wit, do not be jealous, I beg. But I come here to see you, my prickly love.'

He followed to seat himself on the chair beside me.

'Now that we are alone together we can talk of matters which concern us both.'

'I do not think there is anything you can say which will interest me, Luke Markham. You know very well that I will never consent to becoming your mistress.'

'Not when Nell Gwyn approves?' he said in mock dismay. 'Not when King Charles, himself, sets the example?'

'It is immoral and you know it!' I cried, angered by his continual tone of jest on a matter which was of the utmost importance to me.

'Immoral, perhaps, but think of the wives you know, and the mistresses, and tell me from a woman's viewpoint — which of them is the happier — wife or mistress?' Luke must have understood my feelings because his voice had softened as he spoke.

Why did he always have such clever things to say? Why was his knowledge so great, his questions unanswerable? I thought inwardly. For it was true, what Luke Markham had said, of the females I knew and admittedly they were not many, but of the ones known to me there was not a single happily married woman.

Queen Catherine was the first example. Oh, 'twas said she loved the King most dearly and His Majesty always treated her with utmost respect. But was she truly happy? She had to accept her husband's licentious behaviour and make the best of a difficult life.

The Duchess of Buckingham — was she happy in her marriage? She seldom saw her husband for he was always with Lady Shrewsbury, and now this mistress had given him a son, and he was building her a magnificent palace. Not a palace for his wife — but a gift for his whore.

Had the Duchess of Orleans been happy? Married to that dreadful, perverted husband? Perhaps she had been *glad* to die at the early age of twenty-six years?

Had the Duchess of York been happy. People said she had ruled her husband, even as her father, Earl of Clarendon, had tried to rule Charles Stuart, but she had not been able to control dismal Jimmy's mistresses.

The Duchess of Cleveland had been married to Roger Palmer in her youth. Who knew if she had been happy with him? He was certainly not a contented husband now and spent his days away from England, leaving his so-called 'wife' to get on with her numerous love affairs, which seemed to be growing in number now that she was no longer with the King.

Even that Samuel Pepys, who had so admired Nelly's acting, and looked a most respectable and sober gentleman, had come frequently to the theatre to see his Mrs Knipp yes, and other actresses.

He had brought his wife with him on a few occasions, but she had not looked a contented woman to me. Maybe she did not *know* of her husband's infidelities, but she must certainly have guessed, and she did not look at ease when I saw her in the tiring-room.

'There are a great many thoughts churning in that brain of yours, Alice. I wonder what they are?' Luke's voice awoke me with a start from my day-dream. 'And have you come to any decision?'

I sighed. 'I know not what to think, for so much of what you and Nelly have said makes sense. But why are you so against marriage, Luke? We know of numerous unhappy wedded couples in Court circles, but there must be hundreds of happy families in the world. Why can we not marry and *then* share our love?'

'She speaks of sharing love — at last! My Alice has proved she has a heart. Come, kiss me, sweetheart, and make me know 'twas not a figment of my imagination and I really heard those words.'

He stood up and pulled me to my

feet, holding me close against his strong body. He was very good at kissing, my Luke, and very gentle, and very warming. I allowed him to fondle me for some time before pulling away from his embrace.

'Enough! I cannot think properly when you hold me so, and I need to think, Luke. To think and to talk sensibly, for this is important for both of us.' My lips were burning, my heart pounding, and my whole body felt as soft as melting butter. 'Leave me now and sit over there — I cannot concentrate if you are close to me.'

And, looking at him from a safer distance, I realised that his expression was the one I had longed to see — the look of love and tenderness which I had noticed before when he mentioned his beloved Thunder.

'You love me, Alice?' he asked, moving to sit on the chair beside me again, leaning forward, his eyes a very light, clear grey. 'You were made for love, dear heart, and those lips and swelling breasts are but samples of what you have to offer a starving man. How I long to see the rest of your beautiful body, hidden so demurely beneath your silken skirts.'

I was wearing a lovely gown of lavender silk that day, with a pointed bodice, round neckline with a lace collar, and full puffed sleeves caught at the elbow with lavender ribbons. I had worn it especially for Luke, as I did all the lavish garments which Nelly insisted on giving me.

'Why will you not marry me, Luke?' I asked softly. He loved me truly, I knew that now and yet, knowing my moral standards, why did he always insist on making me his mistress?

'Still that same old question?'

'Yes, I want to know.'

He sighed and leaned back in his chair, half-closing his eyes.

'You are the most persistent little witch, Alice Wingard, but if you want to know then I will have to answer,' he said slowly. 'I will not marry you because I have no home to call my own. You would have to live with Will's mother in her cottage, and I am away a great deal. You would not be happy buried on the edge of those fields, Alice, with no company or friends apart from an old woman, and I could never leave you in a state of discomfort or loneliness. Can you ride?'

'No, but I can learn.' I would do anything for him, I thought, if I could only be his wife and able to love him, and care for him, as I most desired.

'You see,' he ignored my reply, 'you cannot ride; Will's mother has no education, there are no books in that cottage, and you would not see Nelly again. How *could* you leave all that you have here, my heart, to dwell in a turnip field?'

The thought of an old woman and a turnip field was somewhat daunting, especially if Luke was not often with me.

'But we could live here,' I cried, 'in my rooms, as Nelly promised.'

'As a love-nest it would be ideal,' he agreed. 'And I would come and go as I pleased knowing that you were happy, and taken care of, and in good company. But it would not do for my *wife*, Alice. I could not leave my wife to share the house of a whore.'

'Nelly is not a whore — she is the King's mistress!' I said indignantly.

'And you shall be mine,' he answered firmly. 'A wife I am not able to keep in suitable circumstances — but dearest Alice, I most sincerely want you as my mistress. Do not wait too long in making up your mind, I beg, lest 'your quaint honour turn to dust, and into ashes all my lust: The grave's a fine and private place, but none, I think, do there embrace'. Do not wait too long, dear Alice, for life is short and who knows what the morrow may bring?'

'Whose words are those?' I shivered. 'They are very beautiful, and wise, and very sad.'

'Andrew Marvell, a fine poet and one who also writes a lot of sense. Those words were in a poem of his entitled 'To His Coy Mistress' and let us do what Marvell begs his mistress — 'let us sport us while we may — like amorous birds of prey — '.'

I needed time to consider Luke's words and to collect my thoughts and, fortunately, so much was happening at Court and in the political scene, that Luke Markham was busily engaged in other spheres and did not press for my decision.

In the March of '72 the King issued his Declaration of Indulgence, which Luke told me was a good idea.

'It is his first step in moving the country towards his Catholic design,' he informed me, 'and will mean no more penal laws against Nonconformists or Catholics. I hope you also find it reasonable, my Puritan maid? For I have long felt something like this should be introduced.'

'As I grow older, and see and hear most extraordinary things in this life on the edge of Whitehall, I am learning toleration, Luke, and can agree with you, for once.'

'If you agree on that matter there is a chance that you will agree on another subject which is closer to my heart,' he answered, smiling. 'But there is no time for love and kisses, I fear, for there will shortly be another war with the Dutch, and the King is also heading for trouble with this Declaration.'

'Not another war!' I cried. 'Have we not experienced enough battles and bloodshed? And why should the King be in trouble with such a sensible declaration?'

'Both are certainties, Alice,' he said more soberly. 'Be thankful you are a woman and can remain quietly at home with Nelly and her sons, whilst the menfolk try to sort out the country's problems. The war will be costly, as wars always are, and the King will need more money.

'Secondly, I believe he will have to avoid a meeting of Parliament for some time, as many Anglicans are infuriated by his blatant use of the Royal prerogative, and fear that Catholicism is infiltrating the Court once more. Particularly with so many rumours circulating about his brother's conversion to Rome. One of the King's present mistresses is a Catholic, as was the Duchess of Cleveland, so it is obvious his Majesty does not mind having such faith about him, and may well be influenced by them.'

'And the Queen,' I put in thoughtfully, 'although she cannot be feared by any one for her influence over her husband, poor lady.'

'But his mother was a Catholic,' answered Luke, 'as was his beloved sister, the Duchess of Orleans. The people here hate and fear the French, Alice, and that is why this Dutch war is so futile — the French can manage very well without us. But unfortunately, the King is both a lover and admirer of Catholic France and its magnificent ruler, the Sun King.'

'Why does King Charles like them so

much when his people hate them? Why can he not be friendly with the Hollanders and forget the French? I suppose it is the usual answer — money? And what the French will give him?'

Luke smiled, his light eyes shining as he looked at my indignant face.

'I love you even more when you have that wild look about you, but Charles Stuart is not totally out for wealth, Alice. He must always remember the Treaty at Dover and what he promised there. And do not forget that it was Englishmen who murdered his father and Frenchmen who supported his exiled Court.

'Charles must look across the Channel and see Louis in his Palace of Versailles, and all the very best coming from France. The sedan chairs and dainty silver brushes for cleaning our teeth; French manners, fashions, and literature; and every week perfumed gloves, pocket looking-glasses, and elegant boxes appear, all sent from Paris.'

He sighed and walked away from me to the window, where he gazed down on the garden which led towards St. James's Park.

'The French king is surrounded by nobles who do no more than help him to dress and undress each day,' he went on thoughtfully, 'and Louis had never met a Parliament. Our Charles Stuart, in this mass of intrigue and conflict, must often feel hemmed in by his rowdy Houses of Lords and Commons, and look across the water to the Sun King, wishing for his invincible armies, and his Divine Right to rule, which is supported by all his cardinals, bishops and priests.'

'How clever you are at explaining things,' I said, moving across to stand beside him. 'I can understand now why King Charles admires France, but it is a great pity about their religion. I am certain that the people of this country will never accept Popery again, Luke. Perhaps that is why the King bears such a melancholy expression, and looks older than his years, and takes so many mistresses? He should never have signed that Treaty at Dover for such a pledge is impossible to keep.'

'We can assist the French in their fight against the Dutch,' Luke said quickly.

'That part is possible, but not the secret part, Luke. The King can never make this country a follower of Rome.'

Luke shrugged and turned away from the window to face me.

'We will have to wait and see on that one,' he said. 'But it is not so splendid being the Monarch of a country which is teeming with proud, independent people, Alice, all convinced that what *they* do and think is the right solution. Charles Stuart has lived through a bloody Civil War and wants to make certain that such an evil will never happen again, and I say Amen to *that*.

'But life is difficult for him, Alice, and what he considers the best for England is not always what his subjects, nor his Parliament, want. Charles is not helped by his ministers,' he went on, and his eyes had darkened. 'Your Nelly's friend is causing trouble although still greatly loved by the King.'

'You mean the Duke of Buckingham?'

'Who else? He has made a bitter enemy of the newest Royal mistress, and she and Arlington are very firmly in control at present.'

'They are both Catholic sympathisers,' I cried, 'so no wonder they hate the Protestant Duke. What has Bucks done now?'

'He has tried to break off the marriage of Arlington's daughter, Isabella, with the Duke of Grafton. He is the King's second son by Cleveland, and the King was annoyed by this interference.'

'But that son is a child!' I exclaimed. 'I am sure Nelly told me that he was a little boy still, and she was enraged because the King created him a Duke, but has so far ignored her own two sons.'

'Yes,' he replied, 'Grafton is but nine years old and little Isabella — Arlington's only and most beloved child — is five. She is a lovely, sweet child and the Duke a handsome boy. The King's favourite bastard after Monmouth, so 'tis said. But they are to be wed this summer by the Archbishop of Canterbury, and the King refused all Buckingham's attempts to produce an heiress for the lad of *his* choosing.'

'I suppose that Bucks fears that this connection with the King's son will make Arlington even stronger in the Cabal?'

'Indeed,' Luke nodded, 'and I must say he has my support in this matter, for Arlington has a most prosy and pontifical manner and is so filled with self-importance that I would rather have Buckingham any day. Your Nelly's Bucks mimics him most excellently — his pompous way of speaking, his bowing and scraping to the King, and Buckingham has even been known to plant a black patch upon his nose to further caricature the Secretary of State.'

And his right eyebrow lifted in amusement at the thought.

'Why a black patch?' I asked, wondering why such a peculiar addition to his nose should be funny. Small, round patches upon cheek or chin I had seen on both ladies and gentlemen, and found attractive. But a patch upon one's nose would surely look ugly, unless one was the possessor of a very beautiful organ.

'Dear Alice, I forget how unaware you are of Court dignitaries. Arlington always wears a patch over his nose to show the place where he received a wound during the Civil War. It proves to all — and must never be forgotten — what a staunch Royalist he was. Now, my pretty Alice could wear a patch upon her nose,' and he bent forward and kissed mine lightly, 'or on her cheek,' and he touched my right one with his lips, 'or even on her tantalising mouth,' and he repeated his action, allowing for several moments of silence before I could remove myself from his enveloping arms and draw breath.

'An over proud man, the Earl of Arlington,' I whispered, trying to collect my wits, 'and I'm glad Bucks makes mock of him.'

Luke let go of me and stepped back, allowing his expression to become more serious as he said:

'Buckingham has his share of troubles despite his wonderful sense of humour, and a further blow to him has been the generalship of the English military contingent, which has gone to Monmouth, not to him. Apparently he protested most vigorously to His Majesty, but the King would not listen to him. He said his mind was made up, Buckingham was not fit for such a command, and in such a matter he would consider Buckingham no more than he would his dog.'

'Oh, poor Bucks!' I cried, glad to have that to think about and not the warm temptation of Luke's embrace. 'It must be due to Madam Carwell's influence on the King. What a weak man Charles Stuart is to listen to the bitter words of his mistress. But Nelly will support her Bucks — she has always been fond of him, and maybe the King will listen to *her*.'

'The King is also fond of Buckingham,' Luke replied, 'but he does some foolish things on occasion. That business of his bastard son will not stand him in good stead, either. The boy only lived for half a year and when he died, Buckingham had him buried in the Villiers sepulchre in Westminster Abbey, and registered him as the Earl of Coventry.'

'Why should he not?'

'Because, dear Alice, mistresses can be accepted, as can bastards, but what cannot be allowed is the burial of an illegitimate child in the family vault. Buckingham made a most wild and reckless gesture there, taking on himself the powers and prestige of Royalty. Such an act will be neither forgotten, nor forgiven, by his enemies, I fear.'

Of which he had many, I thought. Poor Buckingham, losing the only son, of whom he had been so proud. Yet a man who, too frequently, did the wrong thing — failing to bring the now powerful Madam Carwell across the Channel; making mock of the equally powerful Secretary of State; annoying King Charles with his interfering ways and thus losing an important military position; never attempting to hide his dislike for dismal Jimmy, brother to the King.

But, for all his reckless behaviour, I felt that the Duke of Buckingham would be around for many years to come. Nelly liked him, and she was a good and loyal friend. King Charles was said to regard him almost as a brother, despite their disagreements, so hopefully neither his new mistress's opinion, nor his Secretary of State's, would affect that warm friendship.

Buckingham was so talented, and possessed such a wonderful wit, that it seemed to me more than likely that King Charles would keep him at Court, simply to be entertained by him in the worrying days ahead.

8

That summer the Duchess of Cleveland produced another child, a daughter, whom she named Barbara.

'But it is not the King's bastard,' said Nelly pertly, 'for that whore has had so many lovers of late, I doubt if even *she* is sure who the father is.'

Nelly told me that when the King began showing *her* attention, the Duchess took many lovers for herself — 'and one was my first Charles, Charles Hart,' Nelly declared.

Cleveland had also taken one of the King's three official acrobats to be her lover, named Jacob Hall.

'He is a most handsome man,' said Nelly, 'with a fine figure and legs, and he can dance and vault on the ropes and causes great delight at Court.'

'Perhaps he is the father of her baby?' I suggested.

'I think not. She's taken up with this John Churchill now, a man she has known for some time, and we all think he must be the father. She do choose herself *handsome* lovers, Wiggins, and this young soldier is really good-looking. Not that I would change my Charles the third for anyone else,' she went on quickly, 'but Churchill is quite something.'

'Where did she meet him? And are they still together?'

Barbara Villiers-Palmer-Castlemaine-Cleveland's life was as involved as her various names, and I had great difficulty in keeping up with her history.

'This will muddle you still further, Ally-Wally,' said Nelly, laughing at my expression, ''cos Churchill's sister is a mistress of dismal Jimmy, and his aunt is in charge of Cleveland's nursery. So it was easy enough for young Churchill to move between his sister at St. James's Palace, to his aunt at Berkshire House, knowing that Cleveland liked young and handsome men.

'Now the gossip is all about the price she is paying to get her lover a place at Court. It is believed that she has already given him £5,000 and *some* say she obtained 140,000 crowns from the Privy Purse for him and now he's Groom of the Bedchamber to dismal Jimmy.'

'Clever Cleveland,' I said. 'She seems to be very friendly with the Duke of York. Has this always been so? Or only since the time she quarrelled with Buckingham? For I know he does not like York at all, and fears having him as a Catholic king when King Charles dies.'

'Is that what your friend Luke Markham has told you? Well, *I* think Cleveland and Bucks quarrelled when he found out that she had become a Catholic, and I'm sure that's what brought her closer to the Yorks. Though why my dear Bucks had to go to France and bring back a French and Catholic amour for the King, I do not know.'

'But he forgot all about her at Dieppe,' I said, 'and came home without her.'

'The only sensible thing he did do,' answered Nelly sharply, 'cept it was not all *that* sensible, 'cos Madam Carwell has hated him ever since, and gets on so well with Arlington I'm afraid those two are going to make trouble for Bucks in the future.'

'Luke thinks so, too,' I replied. Then, seeing Nelly's interested little face, and wanting to avoid questions regarding my love life, I went on hastily — 'So you think this Churchill is the father of Cleveland's latest bastard?'

Nelly nodded. 'Fairly certain. The King says he will acknowledge it in public, but declares that the child is not his in private.'

After the birth of the Duchess of Cleveland's daughter, came the announcement of a son to Madam Carwell. It was a boy, named Charles Lennox, and there was no doubt about *this* child's father.

Nelly was far more upset about the news than she had been about Cleveland's baby.

'I hate that high-nosed female!' she

snapped. 'Thinking she is the Queen, herself, most of the time. And if she is a lady of quality like she *says* she is, why does she lower herself to being another of the King's whores?'

I shrugged. Louise de Kéroualle was certainly very pretty and I had seen her properly at Whitehall now, with her round, sweet face, shiny black curls, and small, petal-lipped mouth. But although she was becoming stronger and stronger in King Charles's affections, she was not liked by anybody else — apart from Arlington.

She dressed most sumptuously in her looped gowns of satin and silk, and rustling taffeta, showing off beautiful petticoats all trimmed with the richest lace. Her jewels were many and varied, such large pearls and rubies and glistening gems of all colours and descriptions that Nelly's mouth watered when she told me what she had seen, and it was probably true that every female at Court was jealous of Madam Carwell.

But Louise was foreign and French, which the people hated; she was a Catholic, which was not popular; and she was spending huge amounts of money on her apartments at Whitehall and, 'twas said, also transferring large sums back to France.

The poor little Queen was also foreign and a Catholic, but at least she was discreet about her religion, had been King Charles's wife for many years, and the people had become used to her. Queen Catherine was also tucked away in Somerset House and in poor health, so was not seen around very often.

But Madam Carwell flaunted herself about the place behaving, as Nelly said, as if *she* were now Queen of England. Her furnishings were luxurious and believed to be ten times the richness and extravagance of Queen Catherine's.

Louise possessed new fabrics of French tapestry on the walls, with hunting scenes and exotic birds and palaces worked upon them like paintings. There were Japan cabinets, screens, tables and great vases of massive silver, and she had also taken some of His Majesty's best pictures, Nelly told me indignantly.

To make matters worse, Madam Carwell was created Duchess of Portsmouth in the summer of 1673 and Nelly remained plain Nell Gwyn.

In the spring of that year, the King asked Parliament for more funds to continue with the war against the Dutch, but he was refused any money unless he withdrew his Declaration of Indulgence.

'Poor Charles Stuart,' said Luke, 'life is treating him badly again. The Hollanders are mounting an impressive campaign against the war, and their agents are distributing pamphlets all over London. Have you not seen one, Alice?'

I shook my head. 'What do these pamphlets say?'

Once again I wished that Nelly would

take more of an interest in the political scene and tell me of important matters going on in the country. She must have heard news at Court, but people were the only things that really interested her; their love-affairs and intrigues. She always had gossip of that sort to pass on to me, but nothing of more importance.

'Tell me, Luke,' I said.

'These pamphlets are most skilfully written and suggest that our alliance with France, the Declaration of Indulgence, and the presence of so many Papists in high places at Court, are obvious signs of Charles's attempt to introduce the Catholic religion into England.'

'Which is true,' I said.

Luke smiled. 'My clever, sensible Alice, of course it is true. So now Charles has been forced to accept a Test Act by Parliament, which requires every office holder under the Crown to acknowledge the Anglican Church. Clifford has gone as Lord Treasurer, the

Queen is only allowed nine maids-of-honour, and the Duke of York has had to resign as Lord High Admiral.'

'Because they are all Catholics?'

Luke nodded.

'And what of Nelly's Froggy Madam Carwell?'

He laughed at my words.

'Madam Carwell has been saved by the Queen herself. Her maids were drawing lots to see which nine of them would be able to remain, and after the eighth had been chosen the Queen stopped the lottery and added the last name herself. Thus proving her love for her husband and allowing his beloved Louise to stay.'

'A remarkable wife,' I said softly. 'Who will be Lord Treasurer now that Clifford has gone?'

Luke was silent for a moment, then he pursed his lips together and whistled a few bars of some ditty I did not recognise, his brows drawn together in thought.

'I believe King Charles will have to

turn his sights on a very Anglican minister to appease both Parliament and people,' he answered slowly. 'If he would but control his mistresses and their numerous offspring he would not be in such dire financial straits. However, he is making Thomas Osborne his new Lord Treasurer, and as the man is a staunch Protestant and brilliant with money matters, let us hope that he can sort out England's woes. An end to the Dutch war will be his most important task, I should imagine.'

In the November of '73 Mary of Modena arrived in England to become the Duke of York's second wife.

She was an Italian Princess, very young, and closer in age to her stepdaughters, Mary and Anne, than to her husband. But despite her fifteen years she was both charming and beautiful, with a tall, graceful figure, jet-black hair which curled most lustrously on to her shoulders, and sweet, dark eyes.

There had been uproar in Parliament

against the marriage because she was a Catholic, but the new Duchess of York had been well received at Whitehall because of her grace and beauty.

I saw her once or twice at Court, accompanied by the Duke and his two daughters, and they seemed a happy and attractive family to me. The Lady Mary was more lively than her little sister, but Lady Anne was pretty enough with her brown hair and pleasant features, although somewhat plump of figure.

'Her mother, the first Duchess of York, was said to over-indulge in eating and quite ruined her figure,' said Nelly, as we watched the Yorks speaking to the King. 'And that little Anne is going the same way, I fear.'

'Perhaps food gives her courage,' I said. 'She looks a quiet little girl to me, without much confidence, whilst her older sister is fairly bouncing with high spirits. How nice for them to have a mother in St James's Palace again — although the new Duchess must seem more like a sister to them.'

'She should hold dismal Jimmy in tow for a while, at any rate,' said Nelly, with a naughty grin. 'He is almost as bad as my Charles where women are concerned, but *he* has a conscience and Charles has not. Poor dismal Jimmy, the feelings of guilt no doubt give him that miserable countenance, but at least his religion will help him to confess his sins!'

Over the years there was great rivalry between Nelly and Madam Carwell and although I think the King was fonder of Louise, she was never able to make him give up Nell Gwyn.

Fortunately, Nelly retained her sense of humour and, despite seeing Louise wearing magnificent gems, and spending money lavishly on her apartments, and on new gowns, Nelly continued to laugh at her, and make jokes about her, and the King was continually amused by his pretty, witty Nelly.

Louise was clever, I decided, and did not attempt to govern the King as

Cleveland had done. She did not have a violent temper, nor did she take other lovers hoping to make him jealous. Instead, she used her feminine wiles and studied him carefully in order to please and comfort him.

'So very French,' remarked Luke to me, once.

'But she is ever such a cry-baby,' Nelly said, 'and produces tears and sullens whenever the King refuses her anything. I call her Weeping Willow when she behaves in such a silly fashion. Or Squintabella — that really makes her furious!' Nelly let out a roar of her loud laughter.

'Why Squintabella?' I asked, thinking it was no wonder Louise de Kéroualle disliked my friend.

Nelly was ill-bred and did not possess the qualities of the ladylike Louise. But then I knew her warmth, and her big heart, even as King Charles did and he, certainly, also enjoyed her quick wit and exuberance. Neither the Duchess of Cleveland, nor Madam

Carwell, possessed Nelly's wildness, or her humour.

'I calls her Squintabella 'cos she squints, Wiggins, haven't you noticed? One eye definitely turns in — specially when she's tired, or cross about something.'

'I hadn't noticed,' I said.

But then I had never stood close enough to this Royal mistress to see exactly how she looked. My sight of her was always from afar, watching her dignified, beautifully dressed figure parade before the King and courtiers, with her rounded white arms and bosom bedecked with glittering jewels.

The more regal and stately Louise appeared, the more Nelly enjoyed insulting her and, it must be admitted, Nelly usually won each battle for everyone laughed at the naughty things she said and did. Sometimes I was surprised that King Charles did not separate them, but then he was always the first to laugh at Nelly's effrontery.

And Louise, despite the odd tear, or

231

disdainful scowl in Nelly's direction, was really in a more favourable position. For she lived in the Palace of Whitehall and kept state in twenty-four rooms. She was also given apartments at Windsor Castle for herself and her son; she was presented with a grand new coach provided for her at Royal expense, and in 1673 she was created Duchess of Portsmouth.

In 1675 her son, Charles, was created Duke of Richmond, as La Belle Stuart's husband had recently died without male heirs for the title, and the boy also became Earl of March in England, and Duke of Lennox and Earl of Darnley in Scotland.

So Louise bore all Nelly's taunts and rudeness with dignified disdain, and told her more than once to return to her dung-hill.

Nelly kept her sense of humour and her brave spirit, but her heart was saddened at times, for she was not made a duchess, neither did her sons become dukes. She was not given rooms at Whitehall or Windsor Castle, but remained apart from Court in the big house in Pall Mall.

But her courage prevailed, my dear friend Nelly, and once, when Louise went into mourning for the death of some grand relation in France, Nelly at once went into mourning for the Great Cham of Tartary, to the whole Court's amusement.

She was also delighted when she heard the words of a new ballad written about Louise once she became Duchess of Portsmouth, and Nelly would sing the words out aloud whenever she was within hearing distance of the new Duchess. I do not remember the words now, they were vulgar and cruel, but I sometimes find myself humming — 'Portsmouth, the incestuous Punk', to the tune so often repeated by Nelly.

Although Louise reigned supreme at Whitehall and became famous for her tables, instinctively knowing that King Charles and his companions enjoyed good food and agreeable surroundings, Nelly managed to keep her independence and her appeal by making her house a place of enjoyment, also.

I remember many evenings at her home, when she engaged musicians and singers and gave concerts for the King and the Duke of York. She did not forget her old friends in the theatre, and would always bring those who played, or sung, or acted well, to the attention of the Royal brothers.

It was at one of these concerts to which she had invited Henry Bowman, with the exquisite voice, that Nelly was at her best and most witty. The musical evening ended and the King was mightily pleased, so Nelly asked him to make the performers a handsome present, to show his appreciation.

King Charles said he had no money about him and asked the Duke. But he was also without money.

Then Nelly, turning to the people about her, used the King's favourite expression and cried out —

'Odds fish! What company am I got into?'

It was the droll look on her face, as well as the neat turn of words, which made everyone in the room fall about in helpless laughter.

Luke, who was always so well-read, so knowledgeable, told me of more verse by the poet he admired, Andrew Marvell. And these lines I have always remembered. They were from 'Royal Resolutions' and one verse went thus, portraying the King —

> . . . 'I'll wholly abandon all pub-
> lick affairs
> And pass all my time with buf-
> foons and players
> And saunter to Nelly when I
> should be at prayers . . . '

Dear Luke, how much he taught me over the years, and how much I enjoyed his company. Indeed, so much that when he did not appear for days on end I missed him dreadfully and wondered constantly about him, and what he was doing. I began to think about his words more and more when I did not see him, and pondered frequently on the idea of becoming his mistress.

Immorality was all around me — I was surrounded by debonair, well-dressed gentlemen who kept their mistresses in beautiful houses, dressed them in the latest fashions from Paris, and covered them with jewels; whilst I stayed chaste and pure, close to Nelly, yet not really a part of her sumptuous life. For she, too, possessed some extravagant fineries although always bemoaning the fact that she received less money from the King than her hated rival, Portsmouth.

It was in '75, I think, that she bought her own sedan-chair and a most elegant creation it was, to be sure, with fine gold carvings and lined with scarlet silk and cream-coloured velvet. Nelly, as always, was most generous in lending her chair to any friend who wished to use it, and was thus forced to hire a public chair for herself on some occasions. She engaged two more servants, whom she dressed in livery of scarlet and cream, to carry the chair on its gold-painted poles, and this air of luxury helped her to overcome her disappointment at not receiving a title from the King.

She also indulged in white satin petticoats, and white and red satin nightgowns. I saw her new scarlet satin shoes covered with silver lace, the bedstead with the silver ornaments, and the bill from the silversmith charging over £1,000 for making this bedstead with its silver ornaments of the King's head, slaves, eagles, crowns and cupids, and even Jacob Hall, dancing upon a rope.

Nelly was enchanted with shoes and possessed numerous pairs which went with her different gowns. She had silver and green slippers, sky-blue and gold, as well as her scarlet ones encrusted with silver lace.

She grumbled because she said the

King treated her more as a whore than a Royal mistress, but by the end of 1675 there were ten servants in the house, and she possessed a French coach with six horses, as well as the sedan-chair.

I remained quietly beside her, writing the letters she requested, taking all she offered, grateful for her gifts. But I had no home of my own, no children, and nobody to love and care for — nobody who cared for me and spoilt me, apart from Nelly.

Luke Markham had offered me his love and I had refused his offering. Had I been too proud, I wondered often? Was I throwing all chance of love and companionship out of our newly satin-covered windows? For there would never be another man for me except Luke — I loved him and wanted to be with him always. And if he was not prepared to make me his wife, why should I not accept him as my lover? Every other female seemed happy enough to compromise, so why should not prim and pious Alice Wingard?

Even Will, Nelly had told me with great amusement, had captured our little Peg's heart, and there was much mousing and tousing in the servants' quarters when Luke Markham visited me, and Will disappeared into the kitchen.

But there were plenty of happenings at that time to take my mind off Luke, and which prevented me from making a final decision about my future with him.

9

I remember Nelly telling me, after one of her entertainments at Pall Mall, that the King had enquired why Lady Shrewsbury had not been invited.

'And you know what I told him, Wiggins?'

I shook my head.

'I says to him — 'One whore at a time is enough for you, Your Majesty!''

'Oh, Nelly you didn't!' I exclaimed. 'What did the King say to that?'

'He just smiled, Wiggins, and I was being honest, wasn't I? After all, Punky Portsmouth ain't invited, so why should I have that Shrew lady in my home? And I likes my Bucks and can have much more fun with him if the Shrew ain't around. And with Charles and dismal Jimmy, and the merry gang, we can all enjoy ourselves and have fun together. Mind you, I have to watch

Bucks at times 'cos he really don't like dismal Jimmy, and I'm never sure what he's going to say next. I won't have no squabbling or getting cross in *my* house, Wiggins, and I tells them so.'

I also remember Nelly being annoyed about the news of her Bucks's disgrace in the House of Commons, which must have happened soon afterwards.

'Parliament is blaming him for the alliance with France, the un-Christian war with Holland, for speaking treasonably against the King, and they're even going on about the murder of Lord Shrewsbury which was years and years ago, and it's all most *unfair*, Wiggins,' she cried.

'Wars are always costly,' I answered, thinking of what Luke had once told me, 'and I suppose a scapegoat must be found for the latest waste of money and life. Like the Earl of Clarendon last time, they will use Buckingham now, and he is not the most tactful of men, so how has he answered his accusers?'

Nelly placed her hands over her

mouth for a moment, and her eyes shone with merriment before she cleared her throat and looked more demure.

'It is not really funny, and I am worried about the dear man, but he always makes me laugh, Wiggins. This time, in the House of Commons, Bucks blamed those in authority over him and said that he could always hunt the hare with a pack of hounds, but *not* with a brace of lobsters!'

And she threw back her head and let out her roaring laugh.

'A brace of lobsters?' I smiled, despite my shock at what the words envisaged. 'Did he go on to say who he meant by that awful description?'

'No.' Nelly wiped away the tears of laughter from her cheeks. 'He did not *name* the King and the Duke of York, but it was obvious to all who he meant by that remark. And Charles,' she went on soberly, 'Charles is not at all pleased. Bucks is to be deprived of the Mastership of the Horse and it is going to the Duke of Monmouth instead.'

'I should think the King was annoyed, but is being Master of the Horse an important position? It does not seem very special to me,' I said.

'Oh, it is!' cried Nelly, her eyes big and round in her pink face. 'It brings with it a splendid yearly allowance, and I remember Bucks telling me that one of his many duties was to charter hackney coaches with six horses each, and arrange for all the Royal servants to travel in them and go wherever the King went; from Whitehall to Hampton Court, or to Windsor Castle, or Newmarket — in fact, to any Royal residence. It was an awful lot to arrange, Wiggins, on time, and with all the right numbers accounted for — but Bucks enjoyed it hugely. I don't believe Prince Perkin will be half as good.'

'Prince Perkin!' I exclaimed.

Nelly grinned her impudent little smile. 'I calls him that when he does things wot annoy me. He *thinks* he's a Prince, Wiggins, and acts like one some of the time. And my Charles goes on giving him important tasks, and heaping titles and rewards on his handsome head, so it's no *wonder* he believes he'll take the Crown one day,' she ended indignantly.

'Your Bucks used to think that Monmouth would make a better king than the Duke of York,' I said thoughtfully, 'and Monmouth *is* a Protestant, after all. Would you like to see him as the next King of England, Nelly?'

'No.' She shook her head determinedly. 'I like dismal Jimmy, even if he is a Catholic, and the throne is his by right, Wiggins. Although my Charles adores his son and spoils him dreadfully, I'm sure he won't make him legitimate. After all, his brother is legitimate and the rightful heir, so a bastard son should *never* be allowed to stand in his way.

'But let's not talk of who is next,' she said quickly, 'cos that makes me think of Charles dying and he's got years and years ahead of him still. He's a most vigorous and healthy man, Wiggins,' and she smiled again, no doubt remembering nights spent in the Royal bed, so I changed the subject with haste.

'Tell me more about your friend Bucks's dilemma,' I said.

'The one good thing in all this is that the House of Lords has made him promise never to cohabit with that Lady Shrew again,' she answered, 'and both of them had to sign bonds of £10,000 each, declaring this. *She* is weary of him, anyway, thank the Lord, and all his friends are glad that their affair is over.'

'What has happened to Buckingham now?'

'He has returned to the country, which is the best place for him until the King has regained his humour. You know, Wiggins, if Bucks had said something like that in the privacy of His Majesty's Bedchamber, the King would probably only have laughed. He usually enjoys a joke, even at his own expense, and Rochester has already written his epitaph *and* told him,' she said. 'Have you heard it?'

I shook my head.

'It goes thus.' She cleared her throat.

''Here lies a great and mighty
    king,
Whose promise none relies on.
He never said a Foolish thing,
Nor ever did a wise one.'

Now *that* was wicked, Wiggins, but my Charles the third only smiled when he heard it, and replied that his words were his own but his deeds were his ministers.'

'What a pity he did not react in such a calm way to Buckingham's words,' I said.

'Course, dismal Jimmy and Punky Portsmouth are overjoyed at his departure,' went on Nelly, 'but Bucks still has friends here, and the merry gang will wait and work patiently for him, putting in a good word with His Majesty whenever we can.'

Nelly was not the only person to miss the Duke of Buckingham, for Luke also told me that he had liked the man and enjoyed playing him at the basset tables.

'But we will see him again, I have no doubt,' he said, 'for there is a new party forming as Opposition, led by Shaftesbury, and they will need Buckingham's mockery and magnificence to support them.'

'Now you are muddling me again,' I said. 'Who is this Shaftesbury?'

Luke smiled. 'Forgive me, Alice, but I thought you would have known that with your clever, seeking brain. Shaftesbury is the gentleman we have spoken about before — the Lord Ashley of the Cabal. He is a minister I have long regarded with respect, but no love. He was Chancellor of the Exchequer from 1661 to 1672 and — '

'But that was Clarendon!' I cried.

'Clarendon was *Lord* Chancellor, Alice, do please pay attention. And this Ashley became the Earl of Shaftesbury in 1672. He and Buckingham work together hand in glove, and the little man is a most relentless politician.'

'What is this new party called? And what does it hope to do?'

'It is the Country Party, and the leader is pale-eyed Shaftesbury with the venomous tongue. I do not trust him, and neither does the King, for he is a fanatic and would, I believe, like to see the monarchy destroyed.'

'Then how *can* the Duke of Buckingham support him? Bucks is like a brother to the King and would never want to stand by a man like Shaftesbury.'

'Buckingham is a law unto himself,' said Luke, 'and not easily understood. He enjoys the company of Monmouth, and agrees with some of Shaftesbury's ideas and, as you know, they all dislike the Duke of York and dread Catholicism taking over in England. Meetings of this new party are held in the King's Head Tavern at the corner of Chancery Lane and Fleet Street, and I feel sure Buckingham will soon return and join the members there, with their bottles of claret and sherry, and with their smoking of long clay pipes.'

'Have you been to this Club, then?' I asked.

Luke shook his head. 'I am not a member, Alice, but I have stood with the crowd below in the street and watched the various gentlemen appear on the balcony above, and heard them exchanging jokes and slogans with the admiring mob.

'The people love Buckingham because of his good humour and gaiety, and he will come back to add zest to this party, and to join the other idol of the crowds — the Duke of Monmouth.'

'Is Monmouth still popular? Even after that terrible murder of the beadle?'

Luke sighed. 'That was soon forgotten, Alice, and Monmouth is adored by both King Charles and his people. He is warm-hearted and beautiful but not clever, and gets by with his graceful bearing and engaging manners. He is, of course, the Protestant hero, which puts him way above his Catholic uncle, York, and even his uncertain and devious father, the King.'

'Why does King Charles not make Monmouth his legitimate heir and then everyone will be happy?'

'Because Charles is adamant in his defence of Royal prerogatives, and his brother is next in line to the throne and Charles Stuart will never swerve from that belief,' answered Luke. 'But Monmouth is loved for his generosity, his enjoyment of music and sport and pretty women, and he possesses a natural ease, like Buckingham, with the common folk.'

'And like his father,' I put in quickly.

'Yes, the King is also good with the people, but there is always that fear about his religion, and whether he will publicly announce his Catholic faith. Monmouth is a staunch Protestant and attends service regularly at St Martins-in-the-Fields, thus he is loved and trusted the more.'

'And you?' I said quietly. 'What is

your faith, Luke? You have never told me. Are you still working as an agent for the French? It seems a dangerous business at present with so much dislike in the country for King Louis of France.'

Luke smiled as he took hold of my hand. 'Always my questioning, intelligent, wanting-to-know Alice. No, my sweet, I am no longer sending information across the water because King Louis has his own agent now, who is very much closer to the King of England than I am.'

'The Duchess of Portsmouth?'

'Portsmouth, indeed, the King's beloved Fubbs, so called because of her chubby cheeks, and without whom he would be very distressed, I fear. She is good for him as he grows older, and brings much comfort and serenity into his troubled life. But it is unfortunate that she is so hated by the people. Your Nelly is by far the most popular of the King's mistresses.'

'I know. But then Nelly has never put

on airs and graces — she is common and lowly-born and one of them. She never forgets her background and has such a happy disposition, it is no wonder everybody loves *her*. But how do you manage for money, Luke?' I went on, returning to my earlier thoughts. 'How do you still manage to live in style if you no longer receive amounts of money from France?'

I was thankful that he was no longer in the employ of a foreign court but his elegant appearance surprised me. How could he afford his large feathered hats, his lace cravats, and his splendid velvet jackets now?

Luke did not answer for a while and once again I heard the short, lilting notes of the song he had whistled once before when deep in thought.

'I spend a great deal of my time at the gaming tables,' he answered eventually, 'and manage to win large amounts without much difficulty. That is another reason for missing Buckingham — his debts are enormous but he always had money with which to play the tables.'

I frowned. Gaming was another pastime which disturbed my Puritanical mind.

'Is that the only source of income you have?'

It was surely not the right way to get money? But then most gentlemen of breeding owned estates and possessed inherited fortunes, so if they gambled away some of their family wealth, there was always more at hand. But Luke had nothing. He had told me that everything had been lost during the Civil War and he had been left penniless, and homeless. And what if he should lose one day, instead of winning at cards? What would he do then?

'Such a precarious existence worries me,' I said quietly.

'Alice, there is another string to my bow which brings me gold on which to live,' he replied gently, 'pays all my expenses and those of Will, and which I have been engaged on for many years — before I was an agent for the French, in fact. But if I tell you about it you will never speak to me again. And I could not endure life without my prim, pure and adorable Alice.'

He lifted my hand as he spoke and caressed my fingers with his lips.

I was unsure if he were jesting, or not. His voice was sober, but his light eyes were sparking like Nelly's when she was excited about some devilish trick she had played upon the disdainful Portsmouth.

'You had better tell me and then *I* can decide how best to react.'

'Very well.' He held my hand very firmly in both his warm ones. 'But will you promise not to shriek in terror and have me thrown out of the door?' he said, both eyebrows lifting in mock concern as he gazed down at me.

'Oh, Luke, stop annoying me with such foolish notions! Tell me, please, what you do to dress with such elegance, and how you can afford your seats at the theatre, and all those gold pieces to use at the gaming tables.'

He sighed and let go of my hand,

placing his arms firmly across his broad chest.

'Very well, Mistress Wingard. I shall tell you the terrible truth about Luke Markham and trust in your complete discretion. For nobody, apart from Will and his mother, knows the true history of the man you see before you. I am, dear heart,' and he gave a graceful bow, 'a gentleman of the road.'

'What do you mean?' I gasped, my heart starting to beat like my Lord Craven's drums.

'I mean, my love, that when I am bored with Court life and the sordid gossip and scandals at Whitehall, and when I no longer have money for the gaming tables, and am filled with dislike for the continual company of dissolute rakes like Rochester and Sedley, I take to the road, Alice, with Will and my beloved Thunder. We go off to the country and to the fields beyond these walls, and play Robin Hood to our hearts' content.

'I am a highwayman, dear heart,

known as The Sweep.' And he bowed again before my horrified eyes.

'Do not sit there gulping like one of His Majesty's odd fish,' said Luke after a while, when I had still not spoken, 'say something, I beg, even if it is to scold.'

His words had in very truth struck me dumb, and all I could see before my eyes was the gallows, as Nelly had once described to me; all I could hear in my ringing ears was the excited, laughing crowd, jeering as the carts brought their victims to Tyburn.

'Oh, Luke,' I whispered at last, 'how can you be so foolhardy, so insane to act in such a way?' And I placed my hands tightly over my bosom to try and still my drumming heart.

He moved forward and sat down beside me.

'Calm yourself, Alice. I realise my news has been a shock but you asked me to tell you, and I have been truthful. Thank heavens you know, my love, for it has not been easy trying to deceive my sweet Puritan maid.'

'But why?' I stared up into his handsome face, into the light grey eyes which were unrepentant beneath their dark brows. 'Why do you face death so readily? For the gallows await you, you must know that. You cannot get away with this highway robbery for much longer.'

'I have managed very well for these past years and believe Fortune will continue to smile upon me.' He reached for my hands again and held them against his chest. 'Thunder is the fastest steed in England, and nobody can catch me on him.'

'But the pistols!' I cried. 'They have only to shoot your horse beneath you and *then* you'll be caught. Or maybe they will shoot you.' I hesitated. 'You were out as The Sweep that night you were wounded — when Will came to me in Drury Lane and asked me to take you in because you had been hurt in a duel? It was not a duel, was it, Luke? You had been shot then for robbing a coach, but that time you got away.'

He nodded, lowering his head to kiss my trembling fingers.

'With my Alice's help I was soon mended and able to go on my way again.'

'That time! But how many more times will you be so lucky, Luke? I remember Nelly saying that a Royal Proclamation was offering £20 for capture of The Sweep. Oh, do stop this dangerous life, I beseech you!'

I leaned forward, clutching at his big hands which held my own.

Luke smiled most tenderly, his eyes darkening as he saw my distress.

'I knew it was wrong to tell you, Alice, and I was a fool to burden you with my secret,' he said softly. 'But in a way I wanted you to know, wanted you to understand the other reason for not marrying you. How can I take a good, gentle girl as my wife when I rob for a living? When I never know when I'll long for the fresh air and the wild gallops across the heath, with the wind in my face and the moon smiling down at me, and Thunder, keen and powerful, carrying me into the night?

'Don't you see, my love? There is a freedom, an ecstasy, about those rides which I can never find amongst the perfumed gallants at Whitehall, or in the crowded, stinking streets of the City. And such a way of life, dear heart, can never be shared with a wife.'

'But what of your crime?' I asked, anger giving me the strength to pull my hands away from his warm grasp. 'What of the men and women you plunder? The fear you instil into innocent hearts? Don't speak to me of ecstasy, Luke Markham, for what you do is wicked and I can never understand it.'

'Innocent?' He repeated the word with a surprised laugh. 'You call them innocent, those people I meet travelling in their splendid coaches, clutching their ill-gotten gains? No, Alice, I do not rob innocent folk, but take from those who have more than their share of worldly goods. I take from the whores of rich men, from wealthy landowners who have bet and won at the races. I never take from those who cannot afford to give, nor do I rape, or murder, as some so-called gentlemen are known to do.'

'But how do you know who your victims are? Of course you will hurt an innocent one day. You cannot always know who is travelling at that hour of the night,' I argued.

'I can, and I do,' he said firmly. 'Why do you suppose I spend so much of my time at Court? Gaming and drinking with courtiers and rakes? It is not solely for their company, Alice, for many of them are boring and unintelligent fools. But they are all wealthy, dear heart, so I spend my time in learning who is going where, and storing up all the information which interests me.

'I would never halt a group of travellers, and they are getting very careful about how they travel now. But there is often a single man anxious to leave ahead of the party, to visit his mistress, perhaps. Or a lady, with her maid, like your Nelly, who has some reason for wanting to hurry in one direction, or the other.'

Of course he would know everything. With his numerous contacts, and knowledge of all that was going on in Court circles, Luke would be very well informed. But it was a highly dangerous occupation and one day he would be caught.

'Does nobody suspect when you are away from London so often?'

'Why should they, Alice? There are always hundreds of people swarming around Whitehall — like a mass of bees — I have no close friends, or companions, who wish to know my business, and there are agents and spies, soldiers of fortune and criminals, all around the King. They whisper and listen, glean what information they can, just like me, and many hope to catch the King's ear and plead for money, or position, or to be invited into the

Withdrawing-Room.

'Others spend their days at the card tables, eager for the gold pieces which change hands with remarkable speed. So no,' he went on soberly, 'nobody suspects Luke Markham, nor asks his business, and if I feel like a gallop out on the heath, I state merely that I am off to attend to my estates in Hertfordshire, and that is accepted readily enough by the few who listen.'

'Do you not fear death, Luke?' I asked huskily, my throat very dry as I fought back the tears of misery at this unexpected, unwanted knowledge.

He shrugged at my question, but I could see that he was not afraid. I do not believe Luke feared anything at all.

'Death comes to us all, Alice, sooner or later, and at least I will have experienced great joy in my life. 'The highway is my hope, his heart's not great that fears a little rope'.'

'Not another Andrew Marvell! I cannot bear clever words at this time.'

'Not Marvell, dear love. I do not

know the name of that poet, nor where I first learned his verse. But those words stay with me always and there is no fear of death in my heart. I have even set the words to music and Will and I often sing, or whistle, as we ride. Shall I give you a few bars of the refrain?'

And he pursed his lips, about to whistle the tune I had heard several times before, without knowing its dreadful meaning.

'No!' I cried out. 'I could not bear it! You have given fear to me now, and know not how I shall sleep at night, or pass the hours until we next meet, living always in dread of your capture. Oh, Luke, how can you do this to me?' And I buried my face in my hands and wept.

'Gracious, what a to do!' Nelly had arrived, sweeping into the room in her new gown of orange satin, with bodice and sleeves decorated with green bows. 'I was wanting to show you this and ask whether my green shoes, or the scarlet ones, would go best. But what ails you, Wiggins? Dearest friend, what is wrong?'

She came to me and knelt on the floor in all her finery, pulling my hands away, peering into my tear-stained face.

'If you have hurt my Wiggins,' she snapped, turning her head to look up at Luke, 'if you have done anything to alarm or sadden my best friend, I'll have you in the Tower — just see if I don't!'

Her words brought me to my senses and I choked back my tears, leaning over to touch her satin-clad shoulder.

'No, no, it was not Luke. He told me some upsetting news about Will's mother,' I said desperately. 'Will is so fond of her, and now she is very ill and it is sad for all of us.'

It was not a good excuse but it was all I could think of in my troubled state; that, and the fact that Nelly must never learn the truth.

'Will's mother?' Nelly looked surprised, then gathered up her skirts and rose slowly to her feet. 'I have never seen you cry before, Ally-Wally, and am still not certain that Will's mother could have caused such grief on your face. But there — ' she paused and looked fiercely across at Luke again — 'as long as it is not this handsome gentleman causing you trouble, I shall let things be.'

'You are very gracious, Madam Gwyn.' Luke had risen to his feet, and gave her his most courteous bow.

'Then kiss her quickly and wipe her tears away,' she went on sharply, 'and if you haven't taken her to bed yet — the more fool you!'

She left the room, her gown unnoticed, and I never did learn what shoes she chose to wear that night.

Luke attempted to take me in his arms once we were alone, but I pulled away from him.

'Leave me now,' I said. 'I need time to compose myself and to consider all that you have told me. It has been a dreadful evening and I need time to think.'

He nodded in understanding, but my heart wrenched at the look of unexpected sadness on his face.

'But you will come again?' I called out as he walked away from me, suddenly terrified that I might never see him again. 'You will come — in a day, or so? And we can discuss this matter further.'

'I will come again, Alice.' He stopped and looked back at me, his eyes very tender. 'I'll never leave you — you should know that by now. Despite your puritanical mind and daunting morals, I won't give you up, nor swerve from my attempts at seduction.'

I smiled at his words, despite my tearful countenance.

'I love you, too, Luke Markham, though Heaven alone knows why.'

10

Fortunately for my piece of mind, although still worrying about Luke, there was so much going on around us, both in the political scene and in Court gossip, that I was not able to think about him constantly, in every hour of every day, as my aching heart longed to do.

There was the household to attend to, for though Nelly had a proper housekeeper now, I, as her amanuensis and closest friend, had the responsibility of her home; making lists of all visitors and social occasions; what she would wear and what we should eat each day; what time the coach, or the sedan-chair, should be ready for her use; and I always helped her to dress and watched the maid attending to her hair — 'for my Wiggins is the only one who knows if I look me best' she would say.

The Duchess of Portsmouth had introduced a new hair arrangement at Court, brought with her from Paris, and for a long time Nelly had refused to copy it. But eventually she gave way to feminine vanity and had her maid, Mary, dress her hair in the new mode. We all agreed that she looked even lovelier in this fashion.

It took a long time to arrange, however, and sometimes Mary and I would spend hours curling and puffing and brushing a mass of small ringlets out to both sides of Nelly's enchanting little face. The top of her head remained centre-parted and very flat in contrast, and her shining red-brown tresses at the back were left long, and drawn over one shoulder in several loose ringlets.

Old Madam Gwyn came and stayed many times during those years, which was not a pleasure for me, but she was old and ailing and Nelly was a most considerate and caring daughter.

I often felt that the old woman would have fared better in health if she had not been so fond of brandy. But she was far too old to change her ways, and her drink was more important to her than the food she put into her mouth. I can remember even now the amount of the apothecary's bills which came to the house in Pall Mall whenever old Madam Gwyn stayed, and they contained charges for plasters, glysters and many cordial juleps. Fortunately, they were all paid for with money from the King.

At last, in the July of 1679, old Madam Gwyn died — certainly to my relief, possibly to her own, and probably to Nelly's, although she never once spoke a bad word about her mother.

She ordered black-bordered broadsheets to be circulated on her mother's death, entitled 'An Elegy upon that never-to-be-forgotten Matron, Old Maddam

Gwinn, who was unfortunately drown'd in her own Fishpond on the 29th of July, 1679.'

But George Etherege, in his 'The Lady of Pleasure, a Satyr' was less kind to both mother and daughter.

'I sing the song of a Scoundrel
    Lass
Raised from a dung-hill to a
    King's embrace — '

and he referred to old Madam Gwyn as —

'Maid, Punk and Bawd fully sixty
    years and more,
Dy'd drunk with brandy in a
    common-shore — '

But Nelly did not mind.
'Ma always drank too much,' she told me, 'even when Rosie and me was little. It was her one solace, she used to say. And being so fat and all, no wonder she fell into the pond. Good way to die, I

say. After all, we've all gotta go *some* way in the end.'

But not at the end of a rope, I thought desperately. Not that way, please God.

Old Madam Gwyn had been living at the Neat Houses in Chelsea when she met her death, but Nelly gave her a magnificent funeral, also paid for by the King, and she was buried at St Martins-in-the-Fields.

'Where I want to go when me time comes, Wiggins,' said Nelly firmly. 'If it be before you — you make sure that your Nelly is put away nice and proper, next to her old Ma.'

I frowned. 'Don't talk of death, Nelly. We both have years and years ahead of us so I'm not going to listen to your funeral plans.'

'Very well, I'll say no more. But don't *forget*, Wiggins, that's where I want to be.'

Apart from Nelly's mother during those years, there was also her Duke of Bucks, and she never ceased pestering the King for his return to Court.

'He has friends amongst the wits at Whitehall who are also begging for his return, so I'm certain His Majesty will give in to our pleas eventually,' she said.

She mentioned the names of Rochester, Sir Charles Sedley, and Dorset, as being Buckingham's closest friends and companions.

'Dorset?' I queried. 'Who is that? It is a new name for me although I know the other two gentlemen.'

Nelly laughed. 'Sorry, Wiggins, that's Lord Buckhurst, really. Only he's succeeded to the Earldom since his father died and is now a grand Earl of Dorset.'

'Do you still see him?' I asked in some surprise. 'I thought you could not abide him after the way he and Sedley treated you at Epsom?'

'Oh, I don't mind old Buckhurst now,' she declared, 'and I *must* remember to call him Dorset. I see him quite often at Court 'cos he's a close companion to my Charles, and has long been one of his Grooms of the Bedchamber. I've got over my dislike of him, Wiggins, 'cos once I became the King's mistress, I was *important*.' And she let out a spurt of raucous laughter. 'All them wits and rakes treat me with more respect now in case I can put in a good word for them in my Charles's ear.'

I smiled. 'I'm glad to hear that your Duke of Bucks may soon be returning to Court, but let us hope he behaves himself and is careful about what he says in future.'

'The King misses him,' said Nelly more quietly. 'Bucks is by far the wittiest and liveliest member of his Court, and I do not believe they will be parted for long. He has promised to come here and stay awhile, when he's allowed back, so you will get to know him better, Wiggins.'

The Duke of Buckingham's visit to Pall Mall was another thing which kept me busy, although I was saddened by the sight of the gentleman I had not seen for a long time.

It looked to me as if Buckingham was becoming more and more careless about his appearance for he was no longer the graceful, beautifully attired courtier I had once known. There seemed to be little gaiety in his coarsened face, with its swollen nose and double chins. His one-time beauty had disappeared, leaving him bruised and despoiled, and his teeth seemed very false to my searching eyes.

Even Nelly begged him to buy new shoes that he might not dirty her rooms, and a new periwig that he might not stink so much.

I felt sorry for the man, despite my shock at his changed appearance, and when I told Nelly, she said it was little wonder that he had sunk so low.

'For he has now separated permanently from his wife,' she remarked sadly, 'and it is, of course, all due to the Shrew lady and what she made him suffer over the years with her wicked influence. But he still makes me laugh,' she went on more brightly, 'for Bucks has not lost his conversation and merriment, and he has even reduced the King to tears of laughter by his imitation of Lady Danby.'

The Duke of Buckingham was not yet allowed back at Court, but he had seen the King privately and kissed hands, and had returned to his duties in Parliament.

The Earl of Danby was an industrious and brilliant man with his management of money, and married to the large lady whom Nelly's Bucks mimicked so cleverly. His loyalty was to the King and the Anglican Church, and he cared not a fig for France, so Luke had told me. His greatest enemies were Lord Shaftesbury and, naturally, the Duke of Buckingham.

'I see England as a battleground once again,' Luke said with a wry smile, 'with the war waged by four antagonists — Charles Stuart, Danby, Louis of France, and Shaftesbury.'

'Go on,' I said, glad to have him

safely with me for a while and enjoying, as always, his knowledge of politics. I loved the way in which he taught me things about my country, things which would be impossible for me to learn without his keen mind and intelligence.

'Luke Markham, you should be a tutor in some nobleman's household, teaching the sons of the family. That is what you should be doing with your life — not this dangerous riding about the countryside, with a price on your head, stealing from people,' I cried.

'What? And give up my freedom?' He raised his dark brows and looked at me in mock amazement. 'I can take so long at Whitehall, visiting the coffee-shops and the theatres, gleaning all the information I need, but never will I be pinned down to one place, at one time. I am not an animal to be caged behind bars, my love, and must always have my independence and my pride in doing what I want, when I want.'

His lips pursed as he finished talking,

and he began to whistle the infuriating song again.

'Don't do that!' I said sharply, knowing the meaning of that refrain now. My Luke was a wild, untamed spirit who could never accept imprisonment — except against his will. The thought of that made me feel sick at heart, so I changed the subject quickly.

'Go on about Danby and the others, please. I like hearing you speak about sensible things.'

'Very well, Mistress Wingard,' replied Luke, clearing his throat and bracing his shoulders in judicial fashion. 'Lesson two for today. Charles Stuart had to end the war against the Dutch because neither country was winning, and both loss of life and money was becoming enormous. He dismissed Shaftesbury from his ministerial post and made Thomas Osborne the Earl of Danby and Lord Treasurer. This Danby is a brilliant financier, Alice, and he pleases King Charles because he is gradually restoring some order to the chaos we were in.'

He paused, his brows furrowed in thought for a moment.

'I see Charles as deceiving and cajoling King Louis in order to obtain the money that makes him independent from Parliament,' he went on slowly, 'and I think he wants religious tolerance in England, but at the same time wants to link this country to Louis' policy of European conquest. Charles desires absolute monarchy, which is what the Sun King enjoys, and then he would be the proud possessor of unlimited wealth, idleness, and a firm seat on the throne of England.'

'And what about the Earl of Danby?'

'Oh, he represents Church and State,' replied Luke easily. 'He wants the Dutch to help him overpower France, and a submissive peasant class here with an enormously wealthy landowning lot to do whatever he decides is best for the future of England. Most surprisingly, he has formed a friendship with the Duchess of Portsmouth, Catholic though she be, and both are working against Buckingham. Your Nelly may well plead for her Buck's return to Court, but I feel the King will heed the words of his Lord Treasurer and his favourite mistress, more than he will those of pretty little Nelly.'

'Will Danby and the King succeed in their ideas?'

'They have King Louis and Shaftesbury to reckon with,' answered Luke, 'and Shaftesbury is to be particularly feared. When Charles dismissed him from office, the little man said that it was only a laying down of his gown and a girding up of his sword. I can see him building up a very strong Opposition from now on.'

'A dangerous man,' I said.

'I am talking too much and these are only the feelings I have from information gleaned in Whitehall from day to day,' Luke replied quickly, 'but it makes a delightful change for me to talk to you and not bore Will with my prattle.'

'And I love listening, so please give Will a welcome break and go on telling me,' I answered.

He smiled at my words and reached for my hand, which he folded warmly in his own.

'I think Louis must fear Danby very much, for he knows that Danby wants war with France and friendship with the Hollanders. And Louis' grasp on Europe is beginning to slip away as his expenses grow.

'Shaftesbury, with his warped body and agile mind, is against France, against Catholicism, against the Duke of York. He would like to see himself governing England, with Monmouth as the puppet ruler. He does not want a monarch with too much power and he *says* he is for religious tolerance — but I fear the Papists are not to be included in his tolerance.'

'Oh, Luke, you always leave me in such a muddle! Although I do understand what you have tried to tell me,' I added hastily. 'But what is the future for this poor country? Where will it all end? And what will happen when the King dies?'

'Who knows?' He shrugged. 'Not The Sweep, that is for sure. I am thankful to be clear of Parliament, Alice, and all the intrigue and mishandling of State affairs. I like to hear what is going on around me and then to be off with the wind, doing what pleases me most, grateful for my freedom and for not having to make decisions for anyone else. Or perhaps visiting my dear love and endeavouring to take her to bed — which seems an even more difficult task. But no,' he went on swiftly, seeing my expression, 'I must not tease you or I'll not be welcomed here again.

'Seriously, Alice, there is one thing of which I am certain — you will hear two new names shortly which will come into many conversations, so mark them well. Danby is building up the Court Party among members of Parliament, and gaining support for his ideas. His enemies are calling his group 'Tories', which is an insulting name given to Irish thieves and rebels.

'Opposing him is Shaftesbury, with his Country Party, and they are growing against the followers of the Court and known as 'Whigs', which is the name for Scottish outlaws. The Duke of Buckingham is known to be giving them his support, and so is the Duke of Monmouth.'

'Tories and Whigs,' I repeated thoughtfully.

'Yes, dear heart, those words will come to have more and more meaning in the months ahead, you wait and see.'

Then he lifted my hand to his lips and the rest of that evening was spent in pleasant dalliance, although not in my bed, which was where Luke most wanted to be.

★ ★ ★

My new Bedchamber pleased me mightily for Nelly was generous in the way she spent her money — or the

King's, as Luke would have said — on me. She was always wanting me to have new gowns and petticoats, and my wardrobe became gradually filled with garments.

'It is so foolish!' I protested. 'For I do not lead the busy social life which you enjoy, and three or four gowns would easily take care of my needs.'

'A fresh gown every day, Wiggins, and a special one on Sundays and Feast days,' she answered firmly. 'And you must come down and attend *some* of my evening entertainments, even though you dislike my visitors. You must also come to Whitehall with me on occasion, and beautiful gowns are essential, I do assure you, my friend.'

She was always giving me presents of sweet-smelling perfumes, but these were more for Luke Markham's enjoyment than for my own. I received lemon water to whiten my already pale skin, damask perfume, rose water, and a delightful combination of violets, gilly-flowers, and pinks which she assured me would smell fragrant and also cleanse and brighten the skin.

To hold all the perfumes and salves, the kohl for my eyes and the belladonna drops, Nelly gave me a sweet coffer, which was a lovely box of alabaster.

Luke, also was most generous with presents, although at first I was unwilling to accept them once I knew about The Sweep.

'These are not your ill-gotten gains, are they?' I asked, gazing down at the necklace of pearls which he had placed in my hands one day.

'Dear heart, would I give you thieves' bounty?' he replied in a hurt voice.

'Yes, I rather believe you would. If you can rob so easily from one lady, why not hand the expensive trophy to another?'

He advanced on me, his eyes very dark as he placed his hands around my neck.

'If I did not love you so much, I would gladly throttle you, Alice Wingard, for your evil thoughts!'

'Oh, the pearls!' I cried, trying to lift my arms to thrust his hands away, yet hampered by the string of milky loveliness which was slipping between my fingers.

'You do not want them,' he answered, his eyes glinting dangerously, 'and regard them as stolen property. Let them fall, Alice, and I will grind them to dust for your satisfaction.'

'You shall not destroy my pearls,' I said in sudden fear, lifting them to hold against my bosom.

'Cold, lifeless stones are held against my beloved's breast, yet her warm-hearted and passionate lover is denied such bliss.'

Luke's hands slid down my neck, on to my shoulders, and then he pulled my hands away from my body and tucked them behind my back, the necklace slithering to the ground out of my reach.

'Proud, beautiful Alice, how I adore you,' he whispered, bending his head so low that my mouth was against his shiny smooth hair, and his warm lips travelled gently, caressingly over my bosom.

The neckline was far too low, but it had been Nelly's choice. The lace trim scarcely covered my nipples and with Luke's insistent, tantalising kisses, I feared that at any moment they would break free from the tight bodice.

'I believe you about the pearls, so do not tread on them,' I said breathlessly, 'but let go of me, please, for I cannot breathe and shall faint unless I sit down.'

'If you faint I shall carry you up the stairs and put you to bed myself,' he murmured against my thudding heart. Then he loosened his hold on me, allowing me to step back and move to the nearest chair.

'I feel so weak when you touch me,' I whispered, trying to breathe normally and regain my composure. 'Do you feel that same weakness — like butter melting in the warmth of the sun?'

'No, dear heart,' he replied, half-smiling, 'we males are built somewhat differently, and tend to feel stronger and harder the more we touch and kiss and love.'

I thought for a moment about what he had said then, as realisation dawned, I blushed violently and fixed my eyes on the pearls which he had placed on my lap.

'Allow me to put the necklace on you,' Luke said gently, changing the subject. 'They will look splendid with that gown, Alice. A new one, is it not?'

'Yes,' I said softly, 'you and Nelly spoil me dreadfully and I do not deserve half of what you give me.'

'Nelly has her reward in your loyal friendship and companionship,' he answered, fastening the necklace behind me, beneath my hair. 'And I live in the hope of rewards to come. Not that presents such as this are any form of a bribe,' he went on hastily, moving round to study my appearance, 'but a hope of future ecstasy with my sweet Alice.'

Another time Luke gave me a tall-crowned hat, made of deep blue velvet which darkened the blue of my eyes. He liked me best in that colour and wanted me to wear it constantly, although Nelly was all for variety in the colours she gave me to wear.

This hat was beautiful, the tall crown making me look more regal and dignified, I thought, and the wide brim trimmed with pale blue ribbons and two glorious ostrich feathers.

I felt like a duchess when I wore it, or a countess, at least, and with my blue velvet gown, looped at each side to show my white petticoat, and the full sleeves with the fine lace cuffs — yes, and Luke's pearls at my throat — I was grand enough to take my place at Whitehall, amongst the many elegantly attired females there, and be proud.

11

In the winter of 1676 a new lady appeared at Court and Nelly was very excited about her arrival.

'This will *really* upset the Weeping Willow,' she said, with a look of devilry in her eyes, 'for I can see that Charles is interested and although I can understand Old Rowley and his naughty ways, the Weeping Willow can't!'

'Who is this newcomer?'

'Her name is Hortense Mancini Duchess of Mazarin, and she is cousin to the Duchess of York. She is *supposed* to have come to England to visit her cousin, but *I* think she has come specially to capture the King.'

'What makes you think that?'

'Because she has left her husband, she is very beautiful, and my Charles is known throughout Europe for his interest in lovely women. You must come with me to Whitehall, Wiggins — I know you don't like it there — but come just once and see this Hortense for yourself.'

I did go with Nelly on one occasion and saw the 'Roman Eagle' as she was called, with my own eyes. Once again I was surprised at Nelly's calm behaviour, and admired her self-control, for the King was obviously infatuated with this Italian beauty and could keep neither his eyes, nor his hands, off her.

But Nelly remained her usual bright, happy self — smiling at King Charles when he looked in her direction, nodding graciously at the Duchess of Mazarin, and chatting and joking with her many friends and acquaintances at Court as if she had not a care in the world.

What probably gave her confidence was the fact that the King still needed her; her wit and her joyful temperament, as much as her bodily comforts. For, despite his beloved Fubbs, and the many nocturnal visitors who, we were informed, still trailed frequently up and down the Privy Stairs, Charles Stuart enjoyed Nelly's company and often came to visit her and his two Beauclerk sons in Pall Mall.

However, as I watched the Royal hands fumbling with the Duchess of Mazarin's bosom, and saw his lips nibbling at her ear, and her neck, and any other part of her body he could reach, I turned my eyes away with a feeling of disgust. King he may be, charming and generous also, but I knew that *I* could never see the man I loved behaving with such lechery in public, and still love him. Yet Nelly did love her Charles the third. She remained totally faithful to him always, and her devotion was remarkable when one considered how often *he* divided his attentions between his many mistresses.

If I ever saw Luke Markham behaving in such a debauched fashion, I thought angrily, I would never see him, or speak to him, again. Then I felt myself blushing at the very thought for, after all, I was not Luke's mistress and he had every right to love another female, if he so desired. But then Luke Markham was not the sort of man to indulge in various sexual activities; he was a good and moral man apart, of course, from his thieving.

I sighed, wondering for how long I could hold out against his warm embraces and whether, in fact, it was sensible to do so. He was living a dangerous life, my Luke, playing an exciting but foolhardy game against authority, and one day I dreaded his being caught and sent to his death at Tyburn.

'Wiggins, you are looking very sour,' said Nelly's voice beside me. 'I know you do not like it at Whitehall, but you must agree that the Duchess is a very beautiful woman. My Charles has taste, has he not?'

I looked again at the King and his companion, and had to agree with Nelly. The lady was not young, about thirty years of age, I estimated, glad to have something else to occupy my mind and take my thoughts away from The Sweep. Hortense Mancini possessed a mass of black wavy hair and large violet eyes. She was dressed in the deepest midnight blue satin, a colour which enhanced her eyes, and the lace on her sleeves and petticoat was embroidered with silver and pearl drops. She looked like a lady born to rank, power and wealth. Her manner was both careless and languid, and I could see that not only King Charles was captivated. Courtiers all around were watching her with fascination.

'That lady is a law unto herself,' said a voice behind us, and we turned to see the Earl of Rochester, friend of both Nelly and the Duke of Buckingham, and one of the merry gang. 'She came here for the King and 'tis obvious her conquest will be swift. A dangerous creature, Nelly, so be careful in your dealings with Hortense Mancini.'

I studied Rochester carefully as he spoke to Nelly, admiring his slender figure in its buff velvet jacket and breeches, all decorated with gold trim, and his lace cravat which was pinned with a gold and ruby brooch at his throat.

He was a very handsome man yet possibly as dangerous as the 'Roman Eagle' in his way. For I remembered Luke telling me of how this young lord was drunk most of the time, and knew also that he had seduced and married an heiress, Elizabeth Malet by name, and had been imprisoned in the Tower for six weeks for this offence.

But handsome and charming Rochester certainly was, as well as being a fine poet, and although renowned for his wild behaviour and seduction of women, King Charles had him frequently by his side and obviously enjoyed his company.

'Why is she dangerous?' asked Nelly, and my ears pricked for although I seldom went to Court, I could not resist listening to the gossip and chat which was spawned there.

'She loves to swim,' replied Rochester in his easy drawl, 'so that will please Charles. She adores all kinds of animals and birds, so will enjoy visiting Newmarket with him and sauntering in the park to see his wildfowl there. She is an excellent shot and can bring down quail as well as the best man, and she is also a compulsive gambler.'

'Good,' said Nelly, 'for I have a basset table at my house and delight in the game. I must see that the Duchess is invited to my home for an evening's entertainment.'

'Then be sure that you keep your faithful Wiggins by you,' went on Rochester, with a swift glance at me, 'for the 'Roman Eagle' is also renowned for her passionate friendships with both sexes, and I do not believe you are that way inclined, are you, Nelly?'

'Gracious, no!' exclaimed Nelly, glancing across the room at Hortense again. 'My Charles is *quite* enough for me, thank you very much. But I wonder how he will accept the news of his latest amour's escapades?'

The Duchess of Mazarin was to cause quite a stir in our lives, one way or another. By August of the following year Portsmouth was weeping all over the place, as Nelly had predicted, and Hortense was installed in Cleveland's old apartments above the Holbein Gate in Whitehall.

One interesting fact was that the Duchess of Cleveland left for France soon after Hortense Mancini arrived in England.

Nelly told me that she set off in style with two coaches and a string of horses, taking four of her children with her. Her eldest son, Charles Duke of Southampton, was left to study at Oxford, and her eldest daughter, Anne, remained with her husband, the Earl of Sussex.

'Does Cleveland fear this 'Roman Eagle'?' I asked, smiling.

'There is much gossip about her departure,' answered Nelly, 'and nobody really knows the truth except Cleveland herself. But *I* believe she has been forced to go abroad because of her creditors, and 'tis said by many that her lover, that John Churchill I told you about, has taken more than £100,000 off the lady.'

'Dear me!' I cried, shocked by the huge amount. But Nelly looked neither shocked nor surprised.

'Serve her right,' she said tartly. 'And I'm glad she's gone for whatever reason. Now we shall see how this Hortense affects silly old Portsmouth!'

To help matters along, Nelly ordered both her sedan-chair and her coach to be bedecked in mourning, and insisted on wearing a black gown and veil whenever she was going to, or anywhere near, Whitehall.

'Nelly, why?' I asked her. 'What is in that scheming little brain of yours?'

Her hazel eyes gleamed as she gave me her most impudent smile.

'I am only showing concern for Portsmouth, and letting everyone know that I mourn for the miserable creature now that her supremacy at Court has been taken over by the Duchess of Mazarin.'

There was trouble when Hortense became involved with the Countess of Sussex, eldest daughter of the King and Cleveland.

I remembered Nelly telling me about the girl's wedding some years earlier, and what a magnificent affair it had been. Anne Fitzroy had married Lord Dacre at Hampton Court amidst glittering ceremony, with the King giving his daughter a dowry of £20,000 much to Nelly's annoyance.

'Fancy giving all that to Cleveland's bastard and not even sure if the girl is *his*,' she said angrily. 'Poor Roger Palmer still thinks she's his daughter. And my sons, which Charles must know for sure are his own, get nothing from their father — absolutely nothing!'

'But they are young yet,' I had answered, trying to calm her unusual display of temper. 'And you have a fine house, Nelly, and an annual allowance from His Majesty.'

'But no *titles* for my boys, nor one for me, for that matter, and only a measly £1,000 from the Secret Service whilst Punky Portsmouth gets double that amount *and* a title,' she snapped. 'Cleveland's bastards are always getting things — that Charles Fitzroy has been created Duke of Southampton, Henry Fitzroy is Duke of Grafton, and Portsmouth's bastard is Duke of Richmond. Now this Anne marries a Lord and gets £20,000 for doing it. It's not *fair*, Wiggins, and I am sick of being treated like a common whore — just because I was once an actress — instead of a Royal Mistress.'

When Nelly heard that Lord Dacre had been given the title of Earl of Sussex after his marriage to Anne, her fury knew no bounds, and she showed her wrath when King Charles came to visit her and her sons.

'Come,' she said to Charles Beauclerk, 'come, my little bastard, and greet the man who is your father.'

'Now, Nelly,' said the King gently,

'that is not a pleasant thing to call our son.'

'But what else can I call him?' she answered tartly. 'He *is* a bastard and I have no better name for him. He must get used to being Charles Beauclerk Bastard from now on.'

I was always amazed at the way in which Nelly spoke to her sovereign but he never seemed angered by her impudence. Maybe the violent rages of his long-time mistress, Barbara Villiers-Palmer-Castlemaine-Cleveland, had taught him to accept another female's short bursts of temper. Certainly, Nelly was never vindictive when she was cross.

'What is happening about this affair between Hortense Mancini and the Countess of Sussex?' I asked her later, when she came from Whitehall fresh with the news. 'Does the King know?'

'Yes,' said Nelly, grinning all over her bright little face, 'and his daughter has been sent away to Paris to join her mother. But odd's fish, there was a lovely lot of gossip whilst it lasted!

Didn't I tell you, Wiggins? You *must* have heard.'

I shook my head. I knew that Cleveland had departed for France taking some of her children with her, but I had not heard the drama of the King's eldest daughter, who had been given that splendid wedding at Hampton Court, until now.

'Tell me,' I said.

'Well, you know Rochester warned us that Hortense was a dangerous woman and attracted both males and females to her charms? First she caught the Duchess of York in her web, and the Duke gave her a house nearby in St James's Park and she and the young Duchess used to romp together a great deal of the time. Then the Countess of Sussex became involved with her, and every afternoon they would play battledore and shuttlecock, or have fencing lessons, and in the evenings they would retire to Cleveland's old apartments above the Holbein Gate, and make sport with dogs and sparrows and other creatures.'

'And the King?' I asked. 'What did he think of these goings-on?'

'Oh, Charles used to visit them and spend hours upstairs, so Will Chiffinch has informed me, giving orders that they should not be disturbed.'

'How very strange.'

'The Countess was expecting a baby,' went on Nelly, 'and one evening she and Hortense went down to the Park with swords hidden beneath their nightgowns, and they had a mock duel, Wiggins, in front of several passing gentlemen. It was an admirable performance, so I've been told, but when the Earl of Sussex heard about such happenings he was simply furious, and came up to Whitehall to drag his wife home to the family castle at Herstmonceux.'

'And quite right too!' I exclaimed. 'Their behaviour was scandalous.'

'Anne lost the baby,' said Nelly, 'which was not surprising considering the circumstances, but she still pined for Hortense, and spent so much time hugging and kissing her portrait that there were fears for her sanity. So she has been packed off to Paris to join Cleveland. But *I* say like begets like, and that Anne, Countess of Sussex, is growing up exactly like her mother and will no doubt have countless lovers before she is through.

'I have told Charles that the girl should not be with her mother, but he will never hear a word against Cleveland, or her numerous bastards. And he gave Anne a necklace of matching pearls before she left, worth £800,' she added indignantly.

However, Nelly, herself, was to have a reward after years of waiting. I do not know if it was because of her sharp words on the subject of her bastards but that winter, in December, the King created Charles Beauclerk Earl of Burford, and gave Nelly her lovely Burford House at Windsor.

'It's not as good as Punky Portsmouth — 'cos she's a Duchess and her bastard's a Duke,' she said, but I could see that she was well-pleased, nonetheless. '*And* she's got apartments in the Castle itself for herself and her son. But Burford House will do very nicely for us, won't it, Wiggins? And Charles says it is mine for life and in trust for my Earl of Burford and his heirs.'

'Oh, Nelly, I'm delighted for you!' I threw my arms about her and gave her a hug. 'When can we go and see it?'

'Soon,' she said, her hazel eyes sparkling. 'We'll travel to Windsor when the King next goes there for I do not want to be caught again by The Sweep, and 'tis said he is often on the road to Windsor and becoming more and more daring. That Frenchman, Claud Duval, has been caught and executed but The Sweep is still at large, so I've heard tell. Mind you,' she went on thoughtfully, 'I liked the man and would not enjoy hearing of his hanging. But his days are numbered, if you ask me.'

Her words caught at my heart and I thought again about Luke and his devilish occupation. Perhaps if I bargained with him he would give it up? If I offered to be his mistress, would that entice him to lead an honest life? But deep down I knew it would not. Much as Luke desired me, much as he cared for me and would do almost anything for my happiness and contentment, I knew that Luke Markham would never make me his wife, and would never give up his life on the open road until *he* decided to, or unless, God forbid, he was made to give it up by the law.

'Wiggins, you are not listening.' Nelly's voice broke into my thoughts. 'Charles says he will pay for all the furnishings and anything else I need at Burford House, so you see, a bit of shoving and squawking did the trick in the end, didn't it?'

I nodded, trying to smile at her exuberance, and wishing that the man I loved could be manipulated by some shoving and squawking, also.

★　★　★

Although the Duke of Buckingham had returned to Parliament, and to White-hall, thanks to Nelly and her merry gang, as Rochester, Dorset and Sedley were called, he was not to stay around for long. Such a reckless man would always cause trouble in Parliament, Luke told me, because he cared not what he said, and both he, and Lord Shaftesbury, were determined to get rid of Danby and his growing Court Party.

'The Whigs against the Tories,' I said knowingly.

'You have remembered!' exclaimed Luke, his grey eyes sparkling with delight. 'Would that I could teach you in other matters — but, no, do not tighten those sweet lips and look affronted, dear love, listen to this.'

And he went on to tell me that Bucks and Shaftesbury had clashed with Danby in the House of Lords, and Bucks had surpassed himself with an over-vigorous speech, demanding that Parliament be dissolved.

'Why should he want that?' I asked.

'Because the King has prorogued both Houses for fifteen months now, and both Buckingham and Shaftesbury declare that it is high time Parliament was dissolved.'

'Thus leading to new elections and more hope for the Country Party which they both support?'

'Exactly that — well done, my clever Alice.' Luke gave me his warmest smile, filled with both affection and pride. 'Unfortunately,' he went on, 'the House of Lords decided that both Buckingham and Shaftesbury had made most defiant speeches and should apologise. When they both refused they were sent to the Tower for high contempt — so your Nelly's Bucks is once again in disgrace.'

'Oh, no!' I cried. 'Will that man never learn to hold his tongue and remain safely in one place for any length of time?'

'I do not believe the Duke will have to remain imprisoned for long,' Luke answered gently, 'for King Charles still enjoys his wit and his companionship, and no doubt Nelly and her friends will be pestering for his freedom again. Shaftesbury is another matter, however, because Charles has no liking for 'Little Sincerity', as he calls him, and looks upon him as a most dangerous rebel.'

'He probably is. I remember you telling me that Shaftesbury would like to rule this land with Monmouth as the puppet monarch.'

Luke nodded. 'I have been told that once, when Shaftesbury was Lord Chancellor, before the King dismissed him from office, Charles called him to his face — the greatest rogue in England. And Shaftesbury answered — 'Of a subject, Sire, perhaps I am'.'

My hands flew up to my mouth and I let out a gasp. 'But that is most insolent! Much worse than the things Nelly says — for he was implying that Charles, as *King*, was the greater rogue?'

Luke smiled at my expression. 'There is no love lost between those two, Alice, and it will not be long before one is total victor. I think and *hope*,' he went on more soberly, 'that it will be Charles Stuart for with him, at least, we are faced with reasonable sanity. The little man, brilliant though he may be, is a most scheming fanatic.'

Another matter which intrigued us about this time was the wedding of Lady Mary, the Duke of York's eldest daughter, to her cousin, William of Orange.

'She is much against the marriage and I cannot blame her, Wiggins,' Nelly said to me, 'for 'tis said he is a most cold and solemn man, many years older than she is and several inches smaller.'

'Can she not refuse the match?' I asked, feeling sorry for the young girl who I remembered as being most bright and vivacious, and still only fifteen years of age, but now, according to Nelly — 'crying all over the place.'

'No, dear Wiggins, she cannot refuse if the King has decided. And he has made his decision so she must obey. The Queen was more sympathetic, I heard, and told Mary that *she* had not even seen the King when she came to England as a bride. But Mary answered that Queen Catherine *came* to England and she is being forced to leave it.'

Luke, too, spoke about the compulsory marriage.

'It is a strange fact that nobody was pleased about this girl's birth, for she was female and the granddaughter of the hated Earl of Clarendon,' he told me. 'But now, for her wedding, the excitement is intense with much rejoicing, and bells being rung, and bonfires lit — like the Restoration all over again.'

'Why is there so much jubilation when she is leaving this country, marrying a foreigner, and desperately unhappy about the whole affair?' I said indignantly.

'Because, my sweet, King Charles is for once doing something sensible, something his people like. His niece is a Protestant and marrying a Protestant. William of Orange is also regarded as a brave soldier king, since he ordered the dykes to be opened and his land was flooded in the face of the approaching French army — making them depart in a hurry.'

'The people like William because he is against the Catholics and against the French?' I said thoughtfully.

'Exactly. They love and admire the Princess of Orange, as Mary is now called, and her new husband, whereas they have nothing but dislike for her father, the Duke of York.'

'It may be sensible of King Charles,' I said, 'but I think it is most hypocritical of him because you told me once that His Majesty disliked the Hollanders and had no affection for Orange William, either. Yet now he is *forcing* his niece into a marriage she does not want for his *own* reasons.'

'It is politics, Alice. Individuals and their private thoughts and emotions do not matter. King Charles has to rule this land as best he can and keep his people happy. And having lived through a bloody Civil War, he has to make sure that such a tragedy never happens again. With the mounting antagonism to Popery, and his brother's now acknowledged conversion to the Church of Rome, Charles has to act most carefully. So, a popular marriage within his family, between two staunch Protestants, is a decisive and important move on his part.'

12

Whilst Luke kept me informed on political matters, Nelly always excelled with Court gossip and the doings of the amusing and immoral folk around her Charles.

She was tending to ignore the Duchess of Portsmouth of late, I was glad to notice, and when that lady caught the pox from King Charles and went off to take the waters at Bath to improve her physical state, Nelly just shrugged and looked complacent. She, thank God, remained in good health.

She was also spending more time in the King's company, which pleased her mightily, for Hortense Mancini Duchess of Mazarin had flirted outrageously with the Prince of Monaco, and been told to leave Court. So, with Portsmouth also away for a while, Nelly reigned supreme as Royal Mistress.

She was very interested in the Duke of York's new mistress, which must have been early in 1678, I think, and told me many stories about Catherine Sedley, who was the only daughter of Sir Charles Sedley, long-time friend of Buckingham and one of the merry gang. He was also the gentleman who had been at Epsom with Nelly and Lord Buckhurst so many years before.

'Poor girl, this Catherine really is extremely plain,' said Nelly, 'but makes up for her lack of beauty by her wit and intelligence.'

'Inherited from both her parents, or just her father?' I asked, knowing that Sir Charles Sedley had long been acknowledged as one of the great wits at Court.

'Oh, not her mother,' answered Nelly, 'for she went mad soon after Catherine's birth and is now hidden away in some convent place abroad.'

'How sad for Catherine and her father.'

'They seem to have managed all right

without her,' said Nelly calmly. 'Sir Charles has had many mistresses but has now taken up, some believe permanently, with Ann Ayscough. She is quite penniless, Wiggins, and comes from somewhere up in Yorkshire, but if she makes old Sir Charles happy, who cares?'

'And his daughter?'

'Daughter Catherine has done very well for herself, first becoming Maid of Honour to the Duchess of York, and then catching dismal Jimmy's eye.'

'Even though she is not beautiful?'

'Oh, Wiggins — haven't you heard my Charles on that subject? No, obviously not! It is *so* funny — listen to this. Charles says that he believes his brother is given his mistresses by his priests for penance — because they are all so ugly!' And Nelly let out one of her loud laughs.

'How cruel,' I said, 'for the ladies cannot help how they look.'

'But Catherine Sedley is *particularly* plain, Wiggins, with a long nose, a very large mouth, and so thin she is like a beanpole. The King is often moaning at me because he says I am too slender, and he admires his plump Fubbs. But I call Punky Portsmouth *fat*, Wiggins, and am quite content the way I am.

'It is a bit surprising about dismal Jimmy, though, 'cos I remember a time when he did not even admire *my* legs and said they should be short, plump, and best covered with green stockings. Maybe Catherine encases her skeleton limbs in green silk.' And she let out another burst of laughter.

'You always look nice, but especially when you wear the Rhine-graves His Majesty bought for you.'

These were theatrical garments, which had short, wide, divided skirts and when Nelly danced her favourite jig, which she did whenever the music was right and she was in the mood, her Rhine-graves flew up, to everyone's delight, showing her excellent legs to advantage.

'You are also fortunate in the fact that the King still admires you after so many years. But I do not understand the Duke of York, for I have seen his new Duchess a few times, and she is such a beautiful lady, why should he be wanting mistresses, and plain ones, at that?'

Nelly shrugged. 'Men always *do*, Wiggins, and I, for one, am thankful.' She gave me her impish smile. 'Now, now, wipe that prim look off your face, *please*. This Catherine Sedley is ugly and skinny but she has great wit, Wiggins, so perhaps that's why dismal Jimmy chose her. But no,' she went on thoughtfully, 'that can't be so for this lady has said herself of the Duke's mistresses that none of them is handsome, and if they possess wit, he does not have enough to discover it.'

I had to smile at her words, despite myself.

'She is nicknamed 'Dorinda' at Court,' went on Nelly, 'and I'm afraid Dorset — that's Lord Buckhurst, remember? I'm afraid he does not like her at *all*, even though he is such a friend of her father's. He has written some wicked verse about her, Wiggins; let's see if I can remember some of it.' She cleared her throat.

    ' "Tell me, Dorinda, why so gay
    Why such Embroidery, Fringe and
      Lace
    Can any Dresser find a way
    To stop th' approaches of Decay
    And mend a Ruin'd Face!" '

My smile faded. 'Hurtful words, Nelly. But perhaps Dorset is frightened by the lady's wit? A sharp tongue used by a female is probably never appreciated by a witty man.'

'Maybe.' She shrugged. 'But I'm glad my Charles appreciates *me* and does not make cruel remarks about his Nelly. He has an awful lot of things on his mind now and worries dreadfully about James,' she went on. 'He often says that when he is dead and gone he knows not what his brother will do. He said to me once,

Wiggins, that he is very much afraid that when James comes to the throne he will be obliged to leave England again.'

'Because he does not feel the people will accept a Catholic king?'

Nelly nodded. 'I like dismal Jimmy,' she said staunchly, 'and can understand him and his rigid ideas. But you see, my Charles knows how to bend with the wind, Wiggins, but the Duke will *never* bend to anything, or anyone, once his mind is made up.'

'Stubborn?'

'Stubborn and brave,' said Nelly, 'cos he will not give up his faith and so makes enemies of my naughty Duke of Bucks and that foolish young Duke of Monmouth. Dearie me, I feel we are going to see changes in our lives, Wiggins, and I just hope nobody gets hurt. Not like the last time when poor Charles the First had his head chopped off.' And she gave a little shudder.

So did I, in my heart, thinking of Luke Markham and what lay in store for him if he was not very careful.

In 1678 also, we heard the first rumblings of what came to be known as the Popish Plot. It really did not mean a great deal to either me, or Nelly, but against our wills we were dragged into the tension and fear of that disturbing time.

It was all caused by two wicked men named Israel Tonge and Titus Oates, who were both liars, and determined to discover any Jesuit plots they could, by fair means or by foul.

'What surprises me,' said Luke, from whom I gleaned all the information, 'is that everybody is willing to believe these dangerous men. Tonge is but a cleric and spends most of his life nosing about for non-existent conspiracies, and squat, bull-necked, big-jawed Oates is a professional perjurer.'

'But are they telling the truth this time?' I asked.

He shook his head. 'It is impossible to believe all the things they say and I think they have invented the whole affair, and made up evidence to support it.'

'Tell me the whole story, Luke — you always make things so clear and easy to understand. All I know is what I have heard by way of servants' gossip, but Nelly admits that all this agitation has affected Court life. The Duke of York is most restless and unhappy and her Charles is irritable and given to sudden rages, and that is not like King Charles at *all*.'

'I feel sorry for the King,' said Luke, 'for he is sensible enough to see that all this cannot be true, yet at a Privy Council meeting he listened to Oates and Tonge being examined, and they were apparently faultless in their full details of this Popish Plot.

'Oates has compiled a pamphlet of sixty-eight pages, which is entitled — 'His True and Exact narrative of the Horrid Plot and Conspiracy of the Popish Party against the life of His Sacred Majesty, the Government, and the Protestant Religion'.

'This conspiracy is said to be led by five Catholic peers, aided by the Pope himself, the King of France, and the Archbishop of Dublin. At a given signal, it says, thousands of Catholic fanatics will rise and murder all the honest Protestant citizens of London. The City will be burned to the ground and the King assassinated. The Duke of York will then take the throne, and England will be saved for the Papists.'

'What nonsense!' I cried. 'It cannot be true. Does Parliament believe all that?'

'Yes, Alice, I'm afraid it does. So do the people. Mobs march through the streets shouting 'No Popery!' and Shaftesbury and other members of the Country Party are delighting in this opportunity to attack the Duke of York and the Popish policies of the King.'

'I am a firm believer in the Protestant faith and have no love for the Church of Rome,' I said hotly, 'but this so-called conspiracy is quite ridiculous and must be yet another worry for King Charles and the poor Duke of York. No wonder Nelly says the Court is an unhappy place at present. But it is all wrong, Luke — can nothing be done to ease the situation?'

'It is very bad at present,' Luke said soberly, 'and Catholic peers in Parliament have been deprived of their places in the Upper House, and all over the country a witch-hunt is going on to find and imprison Catholics. The best thing would be for King Charles to dissolve Parliament to try and cool the political fever.'

In fact, this was exactly what happened and writs were issued for new elections. The Country Party, led by Shaftesbury, was jubilant and determined to get rid of Danby and his Court Party.

'Charles has begged his brother to give up his faith,' Nelly informed me, her eyes very round in her bright face. It was the first time I had seen her so excited by a political crisis. 'Of course James has refused, so he is being sent off to Brussels for his own safety. But my Charles is being very firm about Queen Catherine,' she went on breathlessly, 'and when that nasty Oates man accused Her Majesty of being in this silly plot, 'tis said the look on Charles's face was so terrible it completely silenced the man. He has summoned her back from Somerset House, Wiggins, and has installed her, and her household, in Whitehall again.'

'Luke says that Oates has become a national saviour,' I said. 'He has been installed in guarded apartments in Whitehall and given a State pension, and he is causing hundreds of innocent people to be imprisoned every day.'

'Even my old admirer Samuel Pepys has been taken,' Nelly cried indignantly, 'and just because he worked at the Navy Board under the Duke of York, isn't that too stupid? But the crowds are getting worse and worse, Wiggins, like — like packs of starving wolves.'

Her manner of speech and choice of words was growing better with every year, I thought, smiling to myself despite our serious discussion. For Nelly had painted an excellent mind picture for me, of the throng eager for blood, yet Nelly had never seen a wolf and I doubted whether she knew what such an animal looked like.

'I was stopped in my coach yesterday and really thought my end was near,' she went on, 'such ugly faces thrusting in at the window, Wiggins, and such cruel jibes and insults were shouted at me.'

'What did you do?' I asked, thinking how frightening it must have been for her, although Nelly was usually admired and loved by the people.

'I plucked up my courage and leaned out of the window and shouted back at them,' she said, 'realising that they had mistaken me for Punky Portsmouth. And I called out in my best actress voice — as loud as loud could be — 'Let me pass, good people, for I am the *Protestant* whore!' And they laughed then, and the coach was allowed through with much cheering and clapping and I *was* relieved, I can tell you!'

After the elections which brought in the Whigs, as Luke expected would happen, there were bonfires all over London to celebrate their victory, and Shaftesbury was made Lord President.

But in Parliament, agitation still continued with fears of Popery and the Commons now wanted an Act of Exclusion. But the King made it clear that on succession he was adamant — his brother was not to be excluded from the throne.

Unfortunately, fanned by the flames of Titus Oates, there was more and more gossip and evil talk, and suddenly we began hearing about a mysterious Black Box, which was said to hold the certificate of marriage between Charles Stuart and the mother of the Duke of Monmouth, Lucy Walter.

'She is long since dead so cannot be asked the truth,' Luke told me, 'and as this box has been seen by many — yet remains strangely unobtainable — it is difficult to know what to believe. Shaftesbury is pleased, of course, for it makes Monmouth legitimate and the heir to the throne, and a Protestant heir, at that.'

'What does the King say?'

'He denies all knowledge of the Black Box and all rumours of a previous marriage,' answered Luke, 'but Charles Stuart tells many lies so his words are being doubted now.'

In the May of '79 King Charles dissolved the short-lived Parliament, and in the August he became suddenly ill, having caught a chill after walking by the river after a hard game of tennis.

That, perhaps, was a good thing for the country because everybody suddenly realised how frightening it would be if the King died when England was in such a sorry state. The Duke of York was hurriedly summoned from Brussels, and Nelly went about with a face as white as a sheet.

'What will become of us, Wiggins, if

my Charles leaves us all alone?' she asked piteously.

I did not know, and Luke was away from London so I could not ask his advice.

Fortunately the King recovered, and for a time everything returned to normal, though still with that strange feeling of tension and panic in the air.

In November Luke called and asked me to go with him to the City, to see the Pope-Burning there.

'Pope-Burnings are not for the weak-minded, Alice, but I think you should see the Procession once, it will be good for your education,' he said. 'You will not like it, I think, and need never go again, but as the presentation is being arranged by the Duke of Buckingham this year, and you know the gentleman, it might interest you to see yet another display of his talents.'

'Pope-Burning? That sounds horrible. Is it like a play, and does Buckingham have a part in it?'

'It is a pageant rather than a play, and

no, Buckingham does not take part in it for he has presented it for our entertainment. With his knowledge of dramatic display at the theatre, he has used both real actors and puppets made of wax for this spectacle, so I have heard.

'Horrible it is sure to be, but the sight may interest your Puritan mind. At least you can be certain that Mr Titus Oates will never point a finger at *you*, Alice. Come with me now, and we will venture forth to Temple Bar, as all good Protestants do, and watch the scenes which take place on the anniversary of Queen Elizabeth's Accession. Now *she* was a good queen, was she not?'

I knew that he was teasing me again but I nodded, remembering how my father had always spoken of the Tudor Queen with pride and respect, whilst continually condemning the Stuarts.

'Catholics say that their enemies prefer Bess, Queen of England to Mary, Queen of Heaven,' he remarked, as we made our way towards the Strand.

Nelly had kindly allowed us to use her coach, but after a while the crowds were so great that Luke asked Coachman George to stop and wait for us at the church of St Clement Danes, as we would do better on foot.

There were people everywhere, coming out from all the joining lanes and alleys, all intent on going in the one direction towards Temple Bar.

'Luke, are you a Catholic? You have never answered me when I ask you that.'

He smiled and took my hand, tucking it under his arm as we made our way slowly forward into the City.

'You seem able to force the truth out of me these days, sweet Alice, whether I like it, or not. No, Luke Markham is not a Papist, nor yet a Protestant. I have my own God, in my heart and in my mind, and confer with Him often. My God is in the trees and fields, Alice; in the wind and the stars, in everything that is Nature. I bow to no carved idol in the Catholic church, nor yet to the boring, self-righteous preachers in the Anglican pulpits. Now, do not look so offended, and I will tell you an amusing tale about Buckingham.'

He was holding my arm so tightly that I was unable to withdraw it from his grasp.

'Maybe that is why I like your Nelly's Bucks. For I do not believe that he has a faith, although often, as you will see this night, aligning himself with the Protestant religion.'

'Then what is this amusing tale?' I asked sharply.

'Some years ago, when Buckingham had joined the King at chapel, there was a young preacher who had chosen for his sermon the text — 'I am fearfully and wonderfully made.' Buckingham found all sermons long and tedious, and took great delight in fixing the preacher with his eyes in a most penetrating and disturbing way. This poor young chaplain became so unnerved by Buckingham's fixed stare, that he began stroking his sweating face with his hands, as he tried to deliver his sermon. But his black gloves had been imperfectly dyed, and soon his face was streaked with black paint making the entire congregation, led by the King and Buckingham, burst into uncontrolled laughter.'

I lowered my chin into the velvet of my dark blue cloak and began to giggle, visualising the scene, and the hilarity caused by the young chaplain's appearance and unfortunate choice of opening words. Then laughter overcame me, and I threw back my head and laughed almost as loudly as Nelly.

'There — that is better,' said Luke with satisfaction. 'Now we can go on and see what your friends the Protestants, organised by our mutual acquaintance, Buckingham, have in store for us. The Procession will come towards us from Aldgate, and if we make our way as far as Ludgate Hill, you will be able to see it before it reaches Fleet Street.'

It was a good thing I had laughed then, because before the night was out I was to be both upset and disgusted, filled with deep hatred for people who could behave with such savagery.

It was dark when we reached Ludgate Hill and the street was packed tight with bodies, as were all the windows and balconies in view. The torch-lit Procession would move down to Temple Bar, Luke told me, and claret would be distributed to the crowd by stewards of the Green Ribbon Club.

'That is the club I told you about, Alice,' he said, holding me close to his side as men and women pushed and shoved and shouted all around us. 'The Procession will end there, at the King's Head Tavern, and beyond in Temple Bar you will see the huge bonfire. That will be where the climax of this evening's entertainment takes place.'

He pointed out Lord Shaftesbury to me as we passed the tavern, who was standing quite alone in one corner of the balcony, apart from the group of men who were at the other end. They were all gazing down at the seething mass beneath them.

'That little frail man with the huge fair periwig and elegant dress, is a very rich man and a very able one,' Luke said, bending his head close to mine so that I could hear him through the din. 'He is also the most unscrupulous and merciless of men, and has but two objects in life.'

'And they are?' I said, looking up at the tiny creature above me and wondering how such a little person could have such power.

'They are the liberty of the English people, and his own direction of that liberty. He wants to be all-powerful, Alice, and with Monmouth in his hands as King, he could achieve that aim quite easily. Good heavens!'

I turned my head to look up at him, surprised by his sudden exclamation. 'What is it? What have you seen?'

'There is Monmouth — look, Alice, look quickly to the right of the balcony, about to speak to Shaftesbury. He was sent to Holland by his father, for he was considered too dangerous to have in this country whilst everyone was clamouring for a Protestant heir to the throne. Now he has returned for the Accession Day celebrations of a Protestant Queen. I wonder if the King knows he is here?'

I looked up at the tall young man standing beside the small one, and as the torches and lanterns lit up the balcony scene, I could see how handsome he was. The crowd saw him too, and there was increasing uproar as cheers, raised hands and hats waved in welcome. 'God bless the Duke of Monmouth!' came the roar from a thousand throats.

James, Duke of Monmouth, leaned forward over the rail and acknowledged the jubilation. His hair was wonderfully long and curled and shiny, his cravat frothed with lace below his smiling face, and his body was slim, and gracefully encased in breeches and a long jacket of yellow satin. Over his shoulders hung a black travelling cape, lined with gold silk, and his hands, holding the balcony rails, were heavily encrusted with jewelled rings which glinted and sparkled in the hundreds of lights.

'He has a fine house in Hedge Lane, near to Charing Cross,' muttered Luke, somewhere above my head, 'and no doubt Buckingham and Shaftesbury will accompany the Protestant hero back there to celebrate this night.'

'You do not like him?'

'I do not know him, but hear that he is very charming, very reasonable. I fear only Shaftesbury and his hold over a young and willing puppet. He offers Monmouth the hope of kingship, and 'tis said the Duke is already omitting the bar sinister from his coat-of-arms. The talk about that wretched Black Box has fully convinced him that he is the legitimate heir.'

'Yet the King denies it?'

'He does. And, knowing King Charles, can you imagine that he will put aside his brother — who is the rightful heir to the throne — and allow his bastard son to wear the crown?'

'No,' I said, 'for King Charles will always stand by the Royal Prerogative and the right of succession for James, Duke of York.'

'Well said, Alice!' And he gave me a hug. 'You have learned your lesson well.'

'With an excellent tutor,' I managed to gasp, before his mouth closed on mine and he kissed me long and hard amidst the swirling crowd.

'Don't *do* that in such a public place,' I cried, when I could remove myself a few inches from his embrace. 'It is not seemly.'

Luke lifted his head and laughed aloud into the fire-lit sky.

'Dear, sweet Alice, who cares!' he shouted. 'There are thousands of people in the streets tonight and not one of them is interested in us, believe me.'

It was true, for nobody looked at us, nobody cared. They were all looking upwards at the balcony and I heard around me the shouts of 'A Shaftesbury!' and 'A Buckingham!' and 'Long live the Protestant Duke!'

Suddenly I shivered, despite the warmth from my cloak, and the enveloping throng, and the burning torches.

'Why are they shouting so much?' I asked.

'Protestant slogans,' answered Luke, smiling slightly. 'They are building up their passion and fervour for this evening's glorious bonfire.'

My heart was filled with dread as I realised for the first time the strength and ferocity of a London mob. And I heard Nelly's voice telling me of the same kind of cheering, excited crowd who watched the executions at Tyburn.

'I want to go home,' I said, pressing my face against his arm. 'This was a foolish idea — take me back, Luke, away from here.'

'Now, Alice Wingard, no hysterics, I beg. And there is no way we can force our way back at present. Be brave, dear heart, for I am with you and will see that you come to no harm. When you have seen all that we came to see I will take you safely back to the coach and deliver you to Nelly.'

Memories of that awful night will stay with me until I die; memories of that, and of one more dreadful still. Both return to me in my dreams filling my silent chamber with the very smell of death.

But first the 17th November, Accession Day of Queen Elizabeth, when all London, it seemed, gathered together to applaud a display of bestial and revolting cruelty.

The first figure to appear, leading the Procession down Ludgate Hill, was a bell-man, dressed all in black. Behind him came a great white horse on which was mounted an actor, dressed like a Jesuit, with a crucifix in one hand and a bloody dagger in the other. Then followed a group of actors as cardinals, monks and friars, and another group of nuns, followed by two priests — one of whom distributed pardons, and the other who carried a phial of poison labelled 'Jesuit powder.'

Behind these was the climax of the show, a sledge drawn by four singing boys. On it sat the Pope, a wax figure, dressed all in white, wearing his triple crown and carrying a blood-stained sceptre. Behind him on the sledge crouched the Devil, an actor, who was robed in scarlet and black and had both horns and tail. He was continually whispering into the ear of the Pope, as they progressed forward through the crowd.

We followed as the Procession moved slowly on to the huge bonfire which lit up the sky above Temple Bar, and the mob around us shouted, jeered, and screamed out insults and abuse until the sledge stopped in front of the flames. There the Devil leapt away and the frenzied people rushed forward to assist in flinging the wax effigy of the Pope on to the fire.

Up until that moment I had been interested enough, protected by Luke's tall figure and his firm arm around my body, and in the shelter of a doorway in which we had managed to squeeze ourselves. But as the Pope's figure was thrust into the flames a most terrible shrieking rent the air, shriller, more ear-piercing, more unforgettable than the raging of the mob. And the sound went on in the most hideous agony.

'Luke!' I shouted. 'What is happening? You said the man was made of wax?'

But it was a living sound which cut the air, making my flesh creep and my heart pound wildly against my bodice.

'Stop them, Luke — he is alive!'

I tried to rush forward, push through the laughing madmen, do anything to try and stop that piteous dreadful screaming.

'Alice, it is all right — he was not living.' Luke's arms held my trembling body, pulling me closer to him, one hand gently stroking my cheek. 'That figure was made of wax, I do assure you.'

'But the noise?' I felt tears stinging

my eyes as the dreadful sound dwindled, and then ceased in the roar of the flames.

His fingers gently wiped away my tears. 'I fear it was cats, Alice. Live cats stuffed into the belly of the Pope. It was them you heard, burning to death.'

From that day until I heard of his own death, in the April of 1687, I hated the Duke of Buckingham. It was no good Nelly reminding me of his good qualities, of his wit and wonderful talent for mimicry; of his play which had entertained us so long ago. I could think only of the terrible night in November, when I was a witness to his mastery of drama and his hatred of the Roman Church, both portrayed with such ferocity in the agonised screaming of those cats.

13

During the rest of that year and into the next, I was to see more of the Duke of Monmouth, for he began calling frequently on Nelly, hoping that she would use her friendship with the King on his behalf.

He excelled at dancing, and he and Nelly made an attractive pair in the sumptuous elegance of her Withdrawing-Room, with its silk wall-hangings and satin-covered chairs — all in shades of cream, gold and red.

Monmouth was one year older than Nelly, and with his dark chestnut hair, delicate features and light hazel eyes, he could well have been taken for her brother. Although he, like most fashionable gentlemen at that time, usually wore a periwig, Nelly always asked him to appear with his own hair when he visited her. As with me and my Luke, she far preferred her Prince Perkin with his own gleaming locks, which were cut short to his ears.

The Duke of Monmouth was a tall young man, though not as tall as his father, and most lithe and graceful in movement. Nelly told me many times that he was an excellent sportsman, and loved running and leaping and, best of all, hunting.

'It is such a pity that Charles is cross with him, Wiggins, for he is truly a son to be proud of, and the two of them have much in common. Still, I shall keep on worrying Charles until he agrees to *talk* to Monmouth, at least.'

King Charles had been very angry at his son's return to England when he had been sent away to the Continent, and refused to allow him to Court, or into his presence, Nelly informed me.

'I have begged my Charles to show forgiveness and to see Monmouth,' she said, 'for the young Duke is really miserable about this separation from the father who has always adored him,

344

and is growing quite thin and pale in his face.'

'Why is the King so determined?' I asked. 'The Duke of Monmouth has always been regarded as his favourite bastard.'

'He shouldn't have taken up with that evil Shaftesbury — my Charles really detests that little man,' she answered fiercely. 'And he should forget all about the Crown and his mother's so-called marriage to Charles Stuart.'

'Is there still talk of that marriage between the King and Lucy Walter?'

She nodded. 'Charles has stated most firmly that he has *never* been married to any female except Queen Catherine. And I believe him, Wiggins. But you *know* how rumours fly, and Monmouth has got it into his handsome head that his father and mother were married years ago, and Shaftesbury keeps telling him that he is really legitimate and should be the next King of England. Poor Prince Perkin is in a dreadful state — believing Shaftesbury, knowing how the people adore him — wanting to be accepted as the next king — yet his father refuses to see him, and keeps saying he is a bastard with no right to the throne.'

'*I* feel sorry for King Charles,' I said firmly. 'Gracious me, Nelly, he must be the one who really knows, and he would certainly tell the truth on this matter, for he sees how unpopular his brother is, and how the people hate the idea of a Catholic successor to the throne. I am *sure* he would accept his beloved son as the rightful heir if that son were truly legitimate.'

Nelly nodded her red-brown head but looked worried.

'Course,' she said, 'if Charles and that Lucy Walter really had taken part in some sort of marriage ceremony when he was much younger, he would have to explain that now to his present Queen and his brother, wouldn't he? And that might be difficult. Anyway, I feel ever so sorry for my Prince Perkin, who doesn't know who he is any more

— and he dances superbly, Wiggins, and is *such* a graceful and charming young man.'

'But scarcely the right temperament for a *king*,' I answered stoically. 'Monmouth must abide by the rules, Nelly, and to my mind he is behaving like a spoilt child — wanting something which he is not allowed to have.'

'Well, I blame that wicked Shaftesbury,' she cried passionately. 'If he didn't keep whispering in Prince Perkin's ear, the young man wouldn't *hope* so much. I'll keep on pestering my Charles 'cos it ain't right that father and son should be separated, and have bad feeling between them.'

* * *

The year 1680 was one of sadness for Nelly and one of total despair for me. But with her help and companionship, and our mutual affection for each other, we got through those dreadful days and tried to look ahead to a better future.

Easier for Nelly, perhaps, because she lost her youngest son. I lost the man I loved.

James Beauclerk had been sent to Paris early in the year to visit an oculist, who was supposed to be very clever in the knowledge of eye infections. For some time little James had been suffering from a watering of his eyes, and when Nelly spoke of the trouble to the Duke of York, he had advised a visit to France.

His youngest daughter, the Lady Anne, had suffered from the same trouble, he told Nelly, and the French oculist had been able to help her.

So Nelly sent her young son off to the Continent in that fateful year, with two servants to accompany him, but James Beauclerk and one of his attendants caught the smallpox whilst on their visit, and never returned to England.

When Nelly heard of his death she was grief-stricken. But she, at least, had another son to love and cherish, and spent much of her time planning for his future with renewed vigour.

I, in my distress, had nothing to cling to, no hope of a future, no plans for my lonely life ahead. But Nelly comforted me, as did dear, kind Will, who was almost as upset as I was, and we got through that year somehow.

I shall never forget the day Nelly came to me, early in the morning and still in her night-smock. I was dressed and pinning up my hair, very surprised to see her at such an hour.

But one look at her white, strained face told me that something was drastically wrong.

'Charles?' I questioned immediately. 'Has something happened to young Charles?'

For since the death of little James, her eldest son had become increasingly important to her.

'No, Ally-Wally, not Charles.' And she came to me as I stood up from my stool, and took my rigid body in her arms, her hands stroking my back with trembling fingers. 'It is bad news for you, dearest Wiggins, and I do not know how to tell you.'

Her face was pressed to my shoulder and even as she spoke I guessed the truth.

'Will called for me just now — he is so upset and does not know how to see you. They have caught The Sweep, Wiggins, and it is — ' she faltered — 'it is your darling Luke and he has been deceiving us all these years. But I don't care, Wiggins, I really love that gentleman, an' I know you do, too — and oh, what are we going to do?'

She was sobbing, her body heaving in its satin night-smock against mine, but my eyes were dry — so was my throat.

'Where is he?' I whispered, finding the words with difficulty. 'Where is he? And what will they do with him?'

I knew, of course, before she answered, knew that the thing I had been dreading for so long had come to pass. There was no looking back now — no wishing — no wanting to be his mistress. It was all too late and pure, chaste Alice Wingard would go to her grave a virgin. For the man she loved had left her forever.

'Newgate,' Nelly moaned, 'and they will hang him at Tyburn.'

Suddenly I knew what to do — the idea came to me with a rush of hope.

'The King!' I cried. 'I will see the King and beg for mercy. He has a kind heart — you are always telling me that — and Luke has friends at Court who will surely plead for him. Quickly, send for the sedan-chair, Nelly, and I'll go to Whitehall at once. Who do I ask for there? Who will take me to His Majesty? Who will listen to me at this hour?'

'Will Chiffinch,' she said quietly, biting back her tears. 'Will is Keeper of the King's Private Closet. Make for the Privy Stairs and ask for him. But wait!' she screamed, as I made for the door. 'Wait, Wiggins — you must prepare yourself before seeing the King.'

'What do you mean?' I stopped for a moment and looked back at her, frowning. This was not the time for more talk, more discussion, more deciding what to do, and say. I would *know* what to say the minute I saw King Charles. 'Oh, Nelly, do not delay me!' I cried, as she came rushing towards me, her eyes wide, her night-smock flapping against her legs as she ran to grasp my arm.

'Wiggins, listen to me. You must go properly clad, you — '

'I am dressed and my hair is done. Let me *go*, Nelly!' I struck at her clinging hands with one fist and tried once more to leave.

'Alice Wingard, you listen to *me*!' she shouted, and I was so surprised at her use of my real name, and the anger in her eyes, that I hesitated, allowing myself to be pulled back into the room.

'I know Charles better than you do,' she said fiercely, 'and this visit is important to Luke Markham, to you, and yes — to me, also. So sit down there, Wiggins, and do as I tell you, for a change.'

She shoved me back onto the stool and stood before me, her arms akimbo.

'Now, you are going to Whitehall in your finest gown, Wiggins, with your hair most beautifully dressed, and with all the jewels and finery I can give you. You *know* the King is entranced by beautiful women, and he has only seen you as my secretary, my serving-girl, if you like. *This* time you are going to Whitehall as a lady of breeding and of beauty, for you will need to stun him with your magnificence, Wiggins, and appeal to his masculine heart with all the grace and loveliness you possess.

'Now sit there whilst I call Mary and Peg, and we will do our utmost to make you so enchanting that my Charles will be able to deny you nothing.'

They worked, Nelly, Mary and my little Peg, how they worked. Striving for the impossible whilst I moaned and groaned, helping them not at all in my desperate wish to be at Whitehall as quickly as possible.

My newest gown of strawberry silk

was taken from the wardrobe, to be worn over a heavily embroidered smock, which had puffed sleeves and lace cuffs. My petticoats were also trimmed with lace, and the strawberry silk of the overskirt was looped up with pink satin bows at the sides.

The tight satin bodice was also decorated with stiff bows, and when Nelly and the maids had finished with my closely curled hair, with its massive fringe over my forehead, and the back hair drawn up and tied in a bundle of curls, ribbons, and pearl-studded pins, a fine lace veil was placed carefully over my head, falling just to the edge of my scooped neckline.

Luke's pearls were placed beneath the veil and fastened at the back of my neck, and I wore Nelly's pearl drops in my ears and a splendid ruby and pearl ring on my right hand, which she said King Charles had given her many years ago, and she didn't believe he would remember it.

'Anyway, it goes beautifully with your

strawberry gown, and you look real fine now, Wiggins. Take my sedan-chair, which is waiting for you, and go to the King. We will be waiting and praying for you till you return.'

I did as Nelly bade me and asked for Will Chiffinch, but it took a great deal of time for me to gain admittance to the Privy Chamber. However, I saw King Charles before midday, and he listened to my tale above the grunting and snuffling of numerous dogs.

But he would not do as I begged.

'Mistress Wingard,' he said, lifting one of the spaniels in his arms and gently fondling its ears, 'this man has terrorised the highways for many years, and has robbed innocent people of their most precious possessions. If I show mercy to The Sweep, for how many others must I also show clemency? How many weeping wives and sisters and sweethearts will come knocking at my door begging for mercy?'

'But he has never murdered, Sire. Never raped or mutilated his victims as *some* grand gentlemen have been known to do. Surely robbery is less of a crime than those wicked deeds?' I cried, forgetting my finery and falling on my knees at his feet. 'Send The Sweep to America, if he must be punished, but not to Tyburn, I beg you.'

King Charles shook his head in its heavy black periwig, and his eyes were sad, but kind.

'As you are a friend of Nelly's, and a most beautiful one at that, Mistress Wingard, I shall make sure that you receive a pension for life, so that you need not fear poverty when your lover has gone. But I cannot save him from the gallows, me dear, so do not ask further.'

'Nelly said you could save him, Sire. She loves Mr Markham — The Sweep — also, and she would have come with me today, only she was in such distress at hearing of his capture that she could not leave the house. Please, please listen to the women who love him.'

Tears were running down my cheeks

although I strove for self-control, knowing that only this man before me, this great and majestic figure, could save my love from death.

But King Charles had seen too many women crying and my misery failed to change his mind.

'Up, Mistress Wingard, and do not spoil that fine lace veil with your tears,' he said, and his voice had hardened. 'I have entirely made up my mind on this matter and nothing will alter my decision. The Sweep must die — but I will make sure that he is saved from the gibbet. Now, let me tell you of my escape from Worcester,' he went on lightly, 'and all the adventures that befell me before I reached the safety of France.'

He lifted me to my feet with one hand and gave me a handkerchief, before propelling me firmly towards the door by which I had entered, the dog tucked beneath his other arm.

'I was dressed as a servant, with my face blackened in disguise, and my poor feet were ill-shod and bleeding. There were posters everywhere, Mistress Wingard, describing me as — '

'Yes,' I said, 'yes,' as his voice droned on, telling me the same old story which we had all heard many times before.

It was a foolish idea of mine, I thought dully, as I travelled back to Nelly's house in all my useless finery. The King had seen death many times in his own family, and the loss of dear ones had to be borne with courage. His father had been executed when Charles was but eighteen years old, and his favourite sister had died at the age of twenty-six. And we had always known, Luke and I, that he played a dangerous game and faced death every time he took to the road. But knowing this did not make the acceptance of his capture, and certain hanging, any easier to bear.

'I must go to him,' I said, after telling Nelly of my hopeless venture. 'I must go to Newgate and see him one last time.'

I thought of handsome, elegant Luke

Markham, penned in with motley rabble, knowing that the fresh air and the wind on his face was denied him forever.

At least I could go to him, tell him I loved him, hold him in my arms for a final embrace.

God give me courage, I prayed, taking the sedan-chair once again, and the gold crowns which Nelly had pressed into my hand.

'Take them,' she said, weeping again, 'for you will have to bribe the gaoler to let you in, and Luke will need money for the little luxuries he might want.'

Twice I visited Newgate, once before Luke's trial and again when he had been convicted and was in the condemned cell.

Our first meeting was held amidst a throng of miserable, wailing unfortunates, women and children amongst them, and I could scarcely speak to Luke, or hear him, in the uproar. He held me close, thanked me for going to see him, and asked that Will might take him fresh linen, and his finest breeches and jacket of mulberry velvet with the gold trimmings, in readiness for his trial.

'You are a brave, beautiful girl, my Alice,' he whispered, as I clung to him, 'coming to see me at such a time, in such a place. But the waiting will not be long, and then I shall have my freedom and you will be able to concentrate all your kindness and goodness on Nelly.'

'Your freedom?' I lifted my face and stared up at him. 'I begged the King for mercy but he would not agree to your release. Has someone spoken on your behalf, Luke? Has Buckingham, or another of your acquaintances at Whitehall spoken for you?'

He laughed, a happy sound amidst so much misery, and his eyes were as clear and light as crystal.

'The Sweep has taken from too many of those gentlemen, Alice. In fact, there are not many courtiers from whom he has not indulged in pillage at one time, or another. No, dear heart, not the freedom you have in mind.'

He bent his dark head and kissed me most tenderly.

'But the freedom to fly with the wind,' he went on, 'to gallop across the heavens until my love comes to join me. Do not fret for me, my Alice. I'll be there, waiting for you to join me in the glory of all Eternity. Now, go back to Nelly, sweet.'

Gently he brushed away the tears which were rolling uncontrollably down my cheeks.

'Come once more, after the trial, if you can bear it. I should like to see you one last time.'

I went again, as he asked, and this meeting in the condemned cell was easier for us both, with no other prisoners to disturb the quiet. He looked well, my Luke, and said he had been eating like a prince with bribes for good food from the money I had left him, and also able to pay for the privacy of one of the condemned cells.

'Now that it is finally over I am quite

composed, my love, and want only to know that you, too, have found tranquillity of mind for your life ahead.'

'I cannot think very far into the future,' I said huskily, 'for you will take all hope, and all happiness, from me when you go.'

'Alice, dear heart, do not weep.' His arms held me close against his chest and one hand gently touched my hair. 'Remember the good times and do not fear the future, for Nelly will be with you, and she will look after you.'

'There is no future without you,' I whispered, 'and Nelly is a good friend but she has the King, and I have no one without you.'

'You must care for Will,' he answered firmly, 'for he has been a part of my life for longer than you have. He will need you, Alice. His mother is no longer alive so take care of him, I beg. There is money put by — Will knows where to find it — it is to be halved between you.'

'I do not want money.' I sniffed and

drew away from him. 'King Charles also offered me money — a pension to save me from poverty once you had gone.' I tried to smile. 'But I want *you*, Luke Markham — not your ill-gotten gains.'

'Proud, honest Alice, do not refuse my gains, for who knows what Fate has in store for you and Nelly? And independence is a very pleasant thing, especially as one gets older,' he added gently.

'What of Thunder?' I asked, suddenly remembering the horse which Luke had loved so much. 'Is Will to have him?'

Luke's eyes darkened. 'Thunder has gone,' he said, sitting back on his wooden stool and making the chains clink around his ankles. 'Will knew what to do — the moment I was captured he went to find my horse and he shot him. Nobody,' he went on quietly, 'nobody was going to ride Thunder apart from me.'

'Oh, Luke.' I ran forward and knelt at his feet, burying my face in his cold hands.

'Do not grieve, Alice, 'tis done now and for the good of both master and steed. One of the best things about my capture,' he said in a more cheerful voice, 'is the fact that I will never grow old. I often thought about it, you know, when I was out on the road with Thunder beneath me, and the stars shining above. And I dreaded the idea of old age; of Luke Markham shrunk into a chair, toothless and irritable and pained with gout. But such an end is not for me, thank God, and I shall die whilst still fit and strong.'

'I would have looked after you,' I said, rising to my feet and wiping my face with my hands. 'We could have grown old together, slowly and gracefully.'

'But I would not marry you, dear heart, and you would not consent to becoming my mistress. So this is a better way, is it not? You will remember me as being reasonably young and handsome, and do not ever forget that I am there — somewhere above — waiting for you to join me.' He leaned

364

forward and took my hands in his. 'Promise me, Alice, promise that you will not forget your Luke.'

'I promise.'

'And that you will try not to mourn, or be too sad about my death?'

'I cannot promise that!' I cried, lowering my head so that he could not see my face.

'Then say only that you will try,' he went on softly, 'that you will try to find some happiness in your life with Nelly and with Will, until we meet again.'

I nodded, unable to speak for a moment.

'But what about that horrid poem,' I managed at last, 'that one by Andrew Marvell, about the grave and nobody embracing there? How can I *know* that we'll meet again to enjoy the freedom you speak about? What if it is only damp earth, and worms, and rotting bodies? Oh, Luke — I cannot bear to think of it!'

And I moved towards him once more and wrapped my arms around his warm body, holding his face close against my breast.

'Alice,' his voice was muffled. 'Alice, I cannot breathe.'

Hastily I let go of him and saw that he was smiling.

'Do be serious,' I implored, wondering how he could face death and still be amused. 'How can I know that we will meet again, Luke?'

'By your faith, Alice Wingard,' he said sternly, although his eyes remained bright. 'You believe in Heaven, do you not? Then think of me up there, amongst the stars, waiting for your arrival. And Marvell's poem was only about our earthly bodies, dear love. Rest assured that our spirits break loose after death and float in glorious freedom.'

'You are sure?' I asked tentatively, longing for something to cling to, some hope to hold in my heart during the long and lonely years ahead. 'You will be there waiting to greet me?'

'I will be there,' he answered firmly.

'Now, I have one last request for my Alice, and you must answer truthfully, as you have always done in the past.'

I nodded, wondering what was to come.

'I would like to leave this world looking at your dear face. I know that Tyburn is not a pleasant place, despite the Fair and the gloating of the mob at such a spectacle. Remembering your dismay at the Accession Day pageant, I can well understand that Tyburn is not for you. But would you feel able to come there, my heart, and let me see you before I swing?'

My whole body tensed at his words and my stomach heaved with the thought of what he had asked.

'You need not come,' he went on quickly, 'I only ask if you feel able to face the horror?'

'I will be there, Luke,' I answered, looking him straight in the eyes. If he could be brave and have no fear of death, then I would find courage from him.

'A dying man's last wish?' And he looked back at me, humour glinting in his eyes again.

'His last wish, and also that of his Alice,' I replied, then went to him and we held each other very close for the last time.

Will came with me to Tyburn but Nelly begged forgiveness.

'I *cannot*, dear Wiggins,' she said, 'please forgive me and you are most wonderfully brave, but I just can't see that lovely man — '

'That is understood, Nelly,' I broke in hastily, not wanting to discuss the matter further. 'Will and I will have each other so neither of us need face it alone.'

He was dreadfully upset, poor Will, so it made things easier for me in trying to comfort him.

'If you are going to weep at the gallows, you must turn your face away,' I said, as we forced our way through the excited crowd.

And I must be brave, I thought

silently, praying for strength. When Luke sees me he must see only a calm and loving countenance. His last sight of Alice must give him peaceful, tender thoughts at the end.

We saw the gallows, as Nelly had described them so long ago, calling them the triple tree, or the three-legged mare, because they were a triangular structure of three upright posts topped by cross beams.

And we saw the cart come slowly along the Tyburn Road, filled with three figures. My Luke was the most handsome, best-dressed occupant in his mulberry velvet. The other man was poorly clad and looked so thin and dejected it seemed that he was ready for death. But the third figure on the cart shocked me for a moment, taking my thoughts away from Luke.

It was the figure of a boy, perhaps ten, or eleven years of age, and in such black and sooty clothing it was clear that he had been a chimney sweep. Luke had taken hold of the lad's hand

and so they rode, close together, and it appeared that they were talking, for every now and again Luke bent his dark head, taking the loose rope with him, and the boy would look up at him, smiling through the grime on his young face.

Then I had eyes only for Luke, and the rope around his neck.

When the cart stopped beneath the gallows and the executioner began fastening the ends of the three ropes around one of the beams, I saw Luke lift his head, straining his eyes into the mob around him. I was not sure that he would see me for there was so much noise, so many cries and shouts and screeches of laughter. So I took off my high-crowned hat, the one he had bought for me, trimmed with the ostrich plumes and the pale blue ribbons, always his favourite, and waved it high above my head.

He looked and saw and he smiled, then I held the hat against my heart and looked straight at him — at his dear face, his fine dark hair, his beloved eyes.

So we remained, quite still and strong, and although Will's head came down upon my shoulder and I heard his sobs, I held mine back until it was all over — until the cart was driven away at speed and Luke Markham swung to his death, still holding the little lad's hand until the final moment, with my face before his eyes — exactly as he had asked.

14

Something within me died with Luke that day at Tyburn. I still lived — breathing and talking, eating and sleeping. Slumber came to me, much to my surprise, but dreams were bad and often I would put off going to bed until the early hours of the morning, fearful lest I should see the gallows again and the hopeless, dangling body of my love.

I dreamed often of Tyburn, and also of the ghastly screaming of Buckingham's cats as they were burnt to death, sewn into the belly of the waxen Pope.

Nelly and I had not shared a bed, or a chamber, since our days at Lincoln's Inn Fields, but our rooms were opposite each other across the central hallway in the Pall Mall residence, and many a night she would come to me and I would awaken from nightmares to find her arms around me, and her gentle voice soothing me back to sanity, with little Peg's anxious face peering through the doorway behind.

'You does shout loud, dear Wiggins,' she would say, smoothing back my hair and using her night-smock to mop my sweating face. 'I reckon *you* should have been on the stage, not me.'

She made me smile and her easy chatter helped me to forget my dreams. Dear Nelly, what a comfort she was to me in those weeks of misery, and how hard she tried to draw me into her social life. She was also good to Will, and took him on in her household as a footman, and very smart he looked in the livery of scarlet and cream.

Nelly made me travel with her whenever she visited Burford House in Windsor, and constantly asked my advice on new hangings and new furnishings for the place. It was a fine red-brick house, with spacious gardens which included an orangery and bowling-alleys.

She insisted on teaching me the game of basset, which I hated, and was always begging me to go down and join the company around the basset table in her Withdrawing-Room. Sometimes I went, simply to ease her mind, and one night I saw Nelly lose 1,400 guineas to Hortense Mancini. This lady had been reinstated at Court once she had tired of the Prince of Monaco.

Nelly swamped me with new gowns and ribbons and petticoats, which I did not need, and asked the Rector of St Martins-in-the-Fields to visit me.

'Ain't he a really good man, that Dr Tenison?' she said to me after one such visit. 'I want him to preach the sermon at my funeral, Wiggins, 'cos I like him ever so much.'

'You are always going on about your funeral arrangements,' I answered crossly, turning away from her. 'Haven't we had enough death in our lives this year?'

'Sorry, Wiggins.' She came swiftly across to me and patted my tense shoulder. 'Silly of me, but the words ran out of me mouth before I could stop 'em. But Dr Tenison *is* good,' she insisted, 'and is building a large house near St Martins Churchyard, and is going to make the upper part into a public library so *any* person who can read will be allowed to borrow books. And the bottom part is to be a workroom for the poor.'

I nodded. Dr Tenison was a man of God, and a pious and caring rector. I listened when he came to the house in Pall Mall and I agreed with everything he said. But when I asked him for reassurance that I would see Luke again, he could not give me a definite answer.

Dr Tenison made me pray with him for some time, but all I could think of was Luke and wishing, oh wishing, that I had 'let us sport us while we may — like amorous birds of prey'.

Still, I tried to enjoy life, as Luke had wanted me to do; I put on Nelly's lavish gowns, accompanied her to Windsor, to Whitehall, to the theatre, wherever she wanted to go.

I also taught her to write the letters

of her name, for she now decided that she wanted an attorney for herself, and intended making a will.

'Now, don't go shouting at me, Wiggins,' she cried, 'that's not talk of death — that is *sense*. And I want it all done proper like, so teach me to put down EG.'

'Why EG?' I asked. 'You have been Nelly for as long as I have known you.'

'E is for Elinor, ain't it? That's like Ma, and is my given name. Nelly ain't got no ring to it, but Elinor Gwyn sounds real fine and I've got to think of me son now, and the fact that I'm mother to the Earl of Burford.'

So, any documents or letters which required her signature, now passed through her hands with an EG upon them, written with some difficulty.

She also kept me informed of the Duke of Monmouth's behaviour, which seemed to be growing in stupidity and ambition.

'He wrote to my Charles begging for forgiveness, and wanting to be allowed back at Court again, Wiggins. But the King was quite firm and said *only* if he obeyed orders and gave up that Country Party, and friendship with Shaftesbury.'

'Did Monmouth agree to that?'

I was not really interested, not caring whether the Duke was legitimate or not, whether he and the King made up their quarrel or not. Nothing really mattered to me once Luke had gone, and human life was so unimportant. What did it *matter* who was King of this realm? Death and imprisonment and hatred were all around us, and I had been punished for falling in love with a criminal. How could I be expected to care now what happened to another man and his bastard son?

'No,' said Nelly soberly, in answer to my question, 'Prince Perkin has gone off to the West Country, visiting all the estates which belong to members of the Country Party, and he told me he was going to places like Devon and Somerset and Dorset, to gain support for his cause.'

'So, disobeying orders once again. The King must be furious.'

'He is,' replied Nelly, 'and so is dismal Jimmy.'

In the July of 1683 the Duke of York's youngest daughter, the Princess Anne, was married to another satisfactory suitor, a Protestant like Orange William, but this George of Denmark was of the Lutheran faith, not an Anglican.

'Poor lady,' said Nelly, 'I hope she is happy with him, for once again this marriage has been arranged between Charles and dismal Jimmy, and the Princess was simply told that her future husband would arrive for the wedding in a couple of months time.'

'Have you seen this man, and is he of Royal blood?' I asked, trying to show interest in affairs which no longer mattered to me.

'Prince George is brother to the King of Denmark,' answered Nelly, 'so quite suitable for the King of England's niece. And they will make their home

378

here, so she was not crying all over the place like her sister was when she had to leave for Holland.

'Charles is ever so funny about him,' she went on, lowering her voice and trying not to laugh. 'He says George is both stupid and dull and has a remarkable fondness for food and drink. My Charles says he has tried him drunk and tried him sober but there's nothing in him!' She could not control her merriment then, and let out one of her raucous shrieks.

'What does he look like?' I was interested despite my initial lethargy.

'George is big and blond and some twelve years older than his wife. But he will put on more weight with his great appetite, Charles says. There are ever so many jests about poor George at Court, Wiggins, and as he suffers from asthma, some wit has said that George is forced to breathe hard lest he be taken for dead and removed for burial!' And she shrieked again.

'Oh, Nelly,' I said, smiling against my

will. So many of the witty sayings at Court were cruel and hurtful to somebody, yet so clever that it was difficult to hide one's amusement.

'There — I've made you smile, Wiggins, and that's the only thing that matters at present. But one other thing may interest you, and that is the Princess Anne's first Lady of the Bedchamber.'

'Yes?' I queried.

'The lady in question *was* Sarah Jennings, a great friend of Anne's in her youth, and now married to a certain John Churchill. Remember his name, Wiggins?'

I frowned. So much had happened over the past few years that I could not remember all that I had been told.

'The name is familiar — who is he?'

'John Churchill was one of Cleveland's lovers. The one she was believed to have given £100,000 to — then she had to escape to France to avoid her creditors. She wanted him back, 'twas said, but he had met this Sarah

Jennings and fallen totally in love with her. And she *is* very lovely,' went on Nelly, 'with a fine brow, fair hair and blue eyes. Anyway, she's married her soldier Churchill now, and as they are supposed to be much in love with each other, that has put old Cleveland nicely out of the way.'

We travelled frequently to Windsor at this time, I remember, and always admired the decorative wall-paintings at Burford House, which Nelly had commissioned the Italian artist, Antonio Verrio, to paint all the way up her staircase and along the ceiling above.

She had asked for her Charles the third to be shown taking part in his favourite pursuits, and there were glorious scenes of the monarch on horseback, hunting and racing; on board one of his beautiful yachts, *The Cleveland*; and playing his favourite game of pell-mell.

'Good thing I didn't ask to have him painted in the Royal Bedchamber, with me or Punky Portsmouth in his arms,' she said roguishly, and then looked at my face and changed the subject quickly.

Nelly had recently purchased a limewood mirror for her Bedchamber at Burford House, carved by Grinling Gibbons with great care and beauty, depicting fruit, flowers and birds. And in her Withdrawing-Room were installed two lacquer cabinets on giltwood stands. Everything was paid for by the King, and the expense must have been enormous for he had also commissioned alterations for himself and the Queen at Windsor Castle, and the Duchess of Portsmouth, as Nelly never ceased reminding me, was continually making changes to her own apartments.

Although she and Portsmouth were managing to accept each other's presence both at Court, and in the company of King Charles wherever he happened to be, Nelly was still outraged when she heard that Portsmouth's son, the Duke of Richmond, had been made

Master of the Horse, and Cleveland's Duke of Grafton created a Vice-Admiral.

'My Charles has taken the Master of Horse away from Prince Perkin because he is so angry with him,' she told me, 'and given it to his darlin' Fubbs's son. And he is only nine years old, Wiggins! Isn't that silly?'

'Seems foolish to me,' I agreed, 'but it just shows how the King feels about Monmouth.'

She shrugged. 'I remember Prince Perkin telling me how much he enjoyed doing it — just like Bucks used to, and I can't see a nine-year-old boy making all them travel arrangements, can you?'

I shook my head. 'How old is Grafton now? He was the one who married Arlington's only daughter, wasn't he? And they were wed at the extraordinary ages of nine and five. Perhaps the King has some special admiration for nine-year-olds!'

'Who knows what is going on in my Charles's clever mind.' And she smiled.

'The Duke of Grafton is about twenty now, so being a Vice-Admiral is quite all right, I suppose, but *not* that important position for Portsmouth's little bastard!'

Fortunately for Nelly, if she waited patiently — as she had done in the past — rewards eventually came her way. King Charles became increasingly fond of her son, Charles Earl of Burford, and in the January of 1684 created him Duke of St Albans.

'Wiggins, I shall now die happy!' Nelly exclaimed, coming to tell me the great news, then lifting her skirts to attempt her famous jig. But Nelly was older now, less agile than in former years, and her heavy breathing showed that her jig would have to give way to more stately dances.

'Never mind,' she panted, when I told her to sit down and calm herself. 'I do not care about my dancing any more, but oh, Wiggins, I care *so* much about this. It is the thing I have longed for over the years and now you see before you Elinor Gwyn, proud mother of a *Duke*, Wiggins. Just think of that!'

I smiled at her joy and thought that it really was a wonder — little Nelly, raised in a bawdy-house, or on a dung-hill — as the Duchess of Portsmouth delighted in reminding us — now the mother of a Duke, sired by the King of England.

'And he is also to become Registrar of the High Court of Chancery, and Master Falconer of England,' she went on, 'and I need never fear poverty for him again. With these titles and positions, my young Charles will be safe for his lifetime, *and* his heirs after him.'

'You have done well, Nell Gwyn,' I answered soberly, 'for you have had nobody to help you, but have raised yourself to present glory by your own wit and intelligence, and most brave spirit.'

'Oh, Ally-Wally, do not speak in such a vein or I shall weep from embarrassment,' she replied, her eyes glistening with unshed tears. Then she came to me and put her arms around me, and we stood silently for some moments, hugging each other in mutual pride and affection.

I remember the coldest winter we had ever known that year, and how a Frost Fair was created on the Thames, and tents and booths were set up on the hard ice. I went there with Nelly, and we were amazed to see horses and coaches riding all over the river, and so many people and stalls, children and dogs, walking on the water — it was an unbelievable sight.

In the November of that year the Queen's birthday was celebrated with a firework display, followed by a ball in the Palace of Whitehall.

Nelly begged me to accompany her, so I agreed, and we both wore sumptuous and extravagant gowns. Although everyone there was very gay, very elegantly and richly clad, the scene depressed me. So many folk I had once known were either old, or absent.

Nelly's first Charles, Charles Hart,

had died and so, too, had the clever, hard-drinking, immoral Rochester. And my Luke was also dead. King Charles looked older than ever, despite his black periwig, and the Duke of York was no longer the handsome man he had been, having grown stout, and red-faced, and less attractive in his fifty-first year.

To my surprise and disgust, the Duke of Buckingham had been restored to the King's favour and was seen frequently at Court. Nelly told me with delight that Bucks and her Charles went sailing together at Portsmouth, and he seemed in good health.

'The only thing that still worries him is that if Charles should die, he will be in great trouble,' she said. ''Cos dismal Jimmy dislikes him, and he won't be accepted at Whitehall no more when James is king. But that won't be for years yet,' she went on happily, 'for my Charles is not an old man by any means, and it is ever so funny, Wiggins, hearing the two of them chat away about the good old days, and the women, and the horses, and the politicians they have known.'

'Is Buckingham still involved with the Country Party, or the Whigs, as they are known?' I asked. Yet again thinking of Luke, and how much I missed him — for his companionship, for his love, and for his knowledge of political intrigue.

'Oh, I don't know about *that*,' said Nelly carelessly, 'but I don't think he has anything to do with Parliament any more, or things like that. His physicians have told him to lead a gentler life, and he's dreadfully in debt — which ain't new — so he spends his time in Yorkshire, and visiting friends, and coming to Court — so *most* of his food and wine is free.' She giggled. 'He is naughty, but I still like old Bucks, and the King is always pleased to see him.'

More than I am, I thought bitterly. But Buckingham, renowned for his talents and audacity, removed himself from trouble just in time, by having no more connection with the Whigs.

Somehow, and I was never sure how he managed it, the King had got rid of most of the Whigs so the Tories were now in control. When the Rye House Plot was discovered, the government managed to smash the Whigs completely, and Shaftesbury, so I heard, fled to Holland.

Again and again I wanted to ask Luke questions about the conspiracy, find out the truth from him, listen to his dear voice telling me what I yearned to know, what *really* happened. But I had to be content with gleaning what I could from Nelly, and how correct her version was I shall never know.

It must have begun in the spring of 1683, when the King and the Duke of York went up to Newmarket to visit the races. They both took a party of friends with them, so Nelly was amongst the group, but she returned earlier than I expected saying that there had been a fire which destroyed many of the buildings, including the King's house there.

'So we all came back sooner than we wanted,' she said.

However, during the following months news and gossip raged in Whitehall, and when I finally got the story from Nelly, it was a frightening tale of treason against both the King and his brother.

'They was going to ambush our party on the Newmarket Road, Wiggins,' she told me, her eyes nearly popping out of her head with rage and shock, 'and both Charles and dismal Jimmy was to be assassinated, and Monmouth made king!'

'Who are 'they', Nelly?'

'They was fanatics,' she spat, 'and it was all planned in that Rye House on the Newmarket Road, and was that evil Shaftesbury's idea with those other Whigs of his, like Russell and Sidney and Essex. Beastly men!' she cried. 'Wanting my Charles to die, just like them that cut off his father's head. Well, it didn't work, Wiggins, and you know why?'

I shook my head, trying to work out

all that she had said in my puzzled mind, and wishing that I knew more about the men she had mentioned.

''Cos of that fire, see? We came back earlier than expected so their nasty plot failed.'

'Then how has the news leaked out? Who said anything about it? As it never happened, who was foolish enough to speak of it?'

She looked at me with anger. 'You mean it should all have been hidden, Wiggins? This terrible conspiracy should never have been told? Well, I think that's a wicked thing to say and anyway,' she went on more cheerfully, 'tongues always do wag and some of the plotters were so scared of being found out that they turned informer's and *that*'s how we all know, and a good job, too.'

'And the punishment?'

'Monmouth has rushed away to Holland, and most of the Whigs have gone to the block for treason. Essex, I think, has taken his own life in the Tower.'

'A fortunate ending,' I said slowly, 'and let us pray that it is also the end of these savage plots. But what is going to happen to Monmouth? As long as he lives there will always be trouble with him, will there not?'

Nelly shrugged. 'I don't trust him no more, really, and he wants the throne. A reward of £500 has been offered for his capture, but I don't think my Charles wants his son brought to justice.'

In fact, Nelly was to tell me later that year that Monmouth came to see his father in great secrecy, and the King begged him to make a written confession about his involvement in the Rye House Plot, then he would pardon him and all would be forgiven. This Monmouth agreed to do and was received at Whitehall that autumn with obvious delight by the King.

But Monmouth still had Protestant friends to whom he listened, and when they persuaded him to demand his confession back, saying that he still had a chance of being King of England, the foolish young man did so.

'Charles was furious,' said Nelly, 'and told his son to go to Hell. So Monmouth has gone into exile yet *again*, and we shall just have to wait, and hope that nothing dreadful happens.'

'Kings!' I remarked scornfully. 'What does it matter which king we have on the throne? Not one of them can be trusted — we cannot put our faith in any of them — so who *cares* whether it is Charles, James, or Monmouth wearing the crown?'

'Why, Wiggins, what has got into you?' she asked in surprise, and came closer to me and peered into my hot face. 'What is it, Wiggins?'

'I am filled with wrath and resentment,' I said bitterly, 'for I begged for Luke's life from that Charles of yours, yet my plea was refused. Now Monmouth seeks pardon and is graciously given it by his doting father. And he and his friends plotted *murder*, Nelly, and my Luke never killed, or hurt, anyone.'

'There, there,' she said softly, 'I understand how you feel but you see, Wiggins, we are not of Royal blood — not your Luke, nor me, nor you. And I've told you before, dear friend, that they is different to us. Something *special*, like.'

'Special?' I snapped. 'Oh, yes, they can condemn people to death, sending them to the gallows, or to the block, and call that punishment. But I call that murder, Nelly. Perhaps Monmouth will return — perhaps he will be made king. I don't *care*! They are all out for their own pleasure and give not one thought for anyone but themselves. They are all rotten — your lazy, dishonest, licentious Charles Stuart; stupid James of York, with his mistresses and his confessions; and that spoilt, ambitious bastard Monmouth!' And I burst into a wild storm of weeping.

It was the first time I had really cried since Luke's death, and Nelly understood my misery and allowed me to sob, sitting quietly beside me, not speaking, until my rage and sorrow had been spent, until I felt ashamed of my outburst but considerably easier in my heart.

'That has done you the world of good, dearest Wiggins,' she said, when I had wiped my eyes and gained control of my emotions. 'Now, you are to come with me on the morrow, and we will all go down to Winchester to stay there awhile. You have not been before, Wiggins, and the journey to the countryside will do you the power of good. You have been living too long in this house, with all its memories, and a change of scenery will be the best thing for you.'

'Why Winchester, Nelly? Has the King a palace there?'

'He will have,' she answered. 'Mr Christopher Wren, who is so clever with churches and is organising the rebuilding of St Paul's Cathedral after the Great Fire, you know?'

I nodded.

'Well, he is building Charles a palace

on the hill above the town of Winchester, and there are to be tall windows looking down an avenue of trees, with the lovely cathedral and the Downs in the distance. It is going to be the most beautiful of *all* the Royal Palaces, and my Charles is quite delighted with it already, and says he will spend his last years there, watching his fleet sailing below at Spithead, and thinking of the joy his new palace will bring to the future Kings of England.'

15

I think it was probably in that fateful year of 1685 that Nelly began to lose her excellent health. She had been putting on weight for some time before, and although she told me that the King liked her bones well covered, I had visions of her mother waddling all over the place, and I worried about Nelly. She was not so inordinately fond of brandy as old Madam Gwyn had been, but she ate well, loving all kinds of food, and drank large amounts of wine and absinthe.

As Nelly put on extra flesh, her breathing became heavier and even the new French dances, more sedate than her wonderful jig, became too much for her.

Then, with the King's death in the February of that year, Nelly was grief-stricken for weeks, and I believe it was then that she ceased to care very much about life. Her Charles the third had been a part of her existence for seventeen years, and although they had not lived in the same building, he had visited her frequently, taken her with him on many of his journeyings round the country, and had always enjoyed her companionship and sparkling wit, as well as her bodily love.

Old Rowley had loved many women and had remained faithful to none; but there had been something about Charles Stuart which had endeared him to many different people, despite his grievous faults.

Even Queen Catherine, the little foreign bat, whom he had mistreated more than any of the others, adored her husband, and was so overcome by his death that she had to be carried back to her own apartments, almost senseless with misery.

'I was not there when he died,' said Nelly, when informing me of that black Friday, 'and the first I knew was when the bells began tolling. Portsmouth was not allowed in, either,' she went on, ''cos it would not have been decent to have his mistresses weeping beside his Queen. But my son was there and received his father's blessing, along with his other bastards — all except Monmouth, that is. And he spoke of me at the last, Wiggins.'

She lifted her tear-streaked face with a look of pride.

'His brother told me that Charles asked him to look after Portsmouth and all his children, and then he mentioned me. 'Let not poor Nelly starve,' he said. Was that not wonderful kind of him? I shall never, never forget my dearest Charles.'

And I took her into my arms and allowed her to weep.

So, our lives had gone full circle, Nelly's and mine. From poverty-stricken youth to our great love for two very different men; both of us unmarried, although Nelly bore her lover two children and I was never to know that joy. Then to the death of our loves, and the loneliness of having to manage without their affection and comfort in our empty lives.

But at least we still had each other, and could face the aching sorrow of bereavement together.

'Life must go on,' I said quietly, as her sobs lessened, 'and you have a son, Nelly, a Duke of the Royal blood. Think of your St Albans, and pray for his future now.'

'I nearly was a countess,' she replied, sniffing, and drawing away from my embrace. 'My son *nearly* had a mother to be proud of, but my darling Charles passed away before he could make it proper.'

'A countess?' I asked in surprise. 'I did not know that. Why didn't you tell me?'

'It was only a short time ago — just after Christmas — and he told me that he was thinking of doing it. We decided on the name together, Wiggins, and it was to have been the Countess of

Greenwich. Just think of that! But I didn't say nothing to you 'cos I wanted it to be a surprise.'

'The Countess of Greenwich,' I repeated slowly, 'that would have been perfect for you. But never mind,' I went on quickly after seeing the look on her face, 'it was in his mind and you both knew it was what he intended. So hold that knowledge close to your heart, Nelly.'

She also told me that her Charles had died a Catholic.

'It was ever so secret, Wiggins, and not many people know, but Will Chiffinch told me that Father Huddleston was smuggled in at the last minute, up them Privy Stairs, and heard his confession then gave him absolution and the sacrament of extreme unction. Lovely words, ain't they? I learnt them from Will and it made me feel like I was on the stage again.'

'Father Huddleston?' I queried. 'Was he not the priest who helped with King Charles's escape from Worcester all those years ago?'

She nodded. 'Will Chiffinch said it was ever so hard finding a priest who was not known by the folk at Whitehall 'cos none of the Queen's priests would have done.'

'Then it seems that Father Huddleston was an act of God,' I said, wondering why I was no longer filled with hatred for the Papists, and did not mind at all that the late King had found solace at the last.

'This father was visiting the Queen, quite by chance, and Charles was so glad to see him even though he was a-dying, and said how right and proper it was that the man who had saved his body should now come to save his soul.'

She blinked, and I could see tears welling beneath her lashes again.

'What happened to all the people in the Bed-chamber?' I asked quickly. 'I remember you saying that it was always difficult to see the King on his own, and at his death-bed I should imagine the room would have been filled with his relations, and friends, and loving servants.'

'It was.' She sniffed back her tears. 'But Will Chiffinch said the Duke of York — I hope I remember to call him King from now on, Wiggins — it'll be ever so hard at first, and dismal Jimmy won't do at *all* now!' She smiled, and I was thankful to see her more composed. 'Well, the Duke of York, as he was *then*, was marvellous, Will said, so brisk and soldier-like, and he managed to get rid of them people, Wiggins, keeping only two Protestants in there with him and his brother. But them two most trustworthy attendants and they will never speak of what they saw and heard. But having them there made sure that all the bishops and clergy were not worried by the sudden emptying of the chamber.'

'I am glad he died content,' I said softly.

At least King Charles would have no regrets — not like Alice Wingard, with her prim morality and haunting sense of loss: 'the grave's a fine and private place, but none, I think, do there embrace'. Charles Stuart would never have those words embedded in his heart through all Eternity. He had loved frequently, and possessed numerous bastards to prove it.

Alice Wingard had nothing.

Unfortunately, with the death of King Charles came further sorrow for Nelly when her great friend the Duke of Buckingham left London for good. The new King James held no love for that once beloved and witty courtier, and he was deprived of all his places and most of his privileges; his debts were said to be more than £141,000, and he retired to Yorkshire for good, to live in the once great stronghold of Helmsley Castle. His father-in-law, General Fairfax, had by Cromwell's order destroyed the castle, but a little wing remained almost untouched, next to the tower. So the famous George Villiers, 2nd Duke of Buckingham, ended his days surrounded by shattered stonework.

Before he died he wrote several times to Nelly, knowing that I would read aloud to her his letters, which still showed him as being both intelligent and amusing with his use of words. And he spent the rest of his time drinking and fox-hunting with his Yorkshire neighbours.

In his last letter to Nelly he wrote some lines which have remained in my mind ever since, and helped me to feel some kindness towards the man who had so disturbed me with his cruel Pope-Burning Pageant. He wrote — 'In all those mighty volumes of the stars, there's writ no sadder story than my fate.'

Nelly also had trouble with her debts which were becoming ever more numerous and, having lived so well for so long, she had no idea how to curb her extravagances. It was almost as if the ordering of new gowns and jewellery helped her to forget her grief.

I tried to reason with her, tried to make her see that money was no longer available and she could not always have what she wanted. But she took no notice of my advice and continued to order the velvets, the satins, and the shoes which she loved, and the jewels and furnishings she craved.

The Duchess of Portsmouth, however, fared worse, for King James had never liked her because of the influence she had had over his brother; she was always regarded as a foreigner, and her debts were greater than Nelly's. She took refuge with the French Ambassador after King Charles's death, but King James would not allow her to leave for France until she had paid off all her debts, and returned some of the Crown Jewels which were in her possession.

The Duchess of Cleveland was better off, having long been friendly with James and his wife, so she returned to England and took her place in the Coronation Procession, in April. King James was also fond of her children and her son, Henry Duke of Grafton, also took part in the Coronation as Lord High Constable of England.

Hortense Mancini, Duchess of Mazarin, was safe because she was related to the new Queen Mary. Once she had finished with her Prince of Monaco, King Charles had allowed her back at Whitehall, and she had continued seeing both him, and the Yorks, during the following years.

Fortunately for Nelly, she and James had always got on well, despite the fact that she remained a Protestant, and the new King did not forget his brother's dying wish. When Nelly was outlawed for non-payment of bills, King James came to her aid and paid over £700 to tradesmen to clear her debts. He relieved her of outlawry, and made two additional payments of £500 each in that same year.

'It was ever so good of King James to remember me and my problems, when he has enough of his own,' she said to me.

I nodded, for Monmouth was back

and causing trouble.

If only that handsome, charming young man could have accepted his father's wish, realised that he had no claim to the throne of England, and settled quietly in the country as his other half-brothers were doing, he would have had a secure future. But Monmouth had been too long under the influence of the fanatical Shaftesbury and clever Buckingham, and although one of those men was dead and the other had retired to faraway Yorkshire, Monmouth believed he had a right to the throne, and thought he also had the allegiance of the people.

At first I scarcely bothered to listen to Nelly as she chattered on about the Duke of Monmouth this, and her Prince Perkin that. I had never seen much of the man, and when he began visiting Nelly more and more frequently, hoping for her influence with King Charles, my mind had been totally taken up with Luke Markham and his tragic death, so I had not been interested in the King's bastard son.

But then the King died, his brother, James, took the throne, and Monmouth suddenly invaded England with a small fleet, landing at the port of Lyme in Dorset on 11th June, 1685.

Nelly was still friendly with Will Chiffinch, who remained at Whitehall under King James II, and she gleaned all her news from him. Against my will, life became exciting again and I was caught up in the unexpected and stupendous happenings of the following weeks.

Nelly, too, became highly involved in the drama, for it was not the political scenes which caught at her attention, but the people involved in those scenes — many of whom were known to her.

I remember her coming to me in great agitation after hearing from Will Chiffinch that Monmouth had been attainted of High Treason in the House of Commons.

'He is such a *foolish* man,' she cried, her eyes dark with worry. 'He is being proclaimed King Monmouth at Taunton, a town in Somerset, and his declaration is being read out in the Market Place for all to hear.'

'What is this declaration? Does he intend marching on London?' I was enthralled, despite my earlier lack of interest.

'He is saying that he has invaded England to free it from the usurpation and tyranny of James Duke of York, and he accuses King James of poisoning and murdering his brother, Charles. He says he has come to revenge his father's death. Now isn't that all too *stupid*, Wiggins? And I can't blame Shaftesbury this time, 'cos Will Chiffinch says he died two years ago.'

'What *is* going to happen?' My heart had begun to beat more rapidly as I listened to Nelly's words. 'And what will King James do about this invasion?'

'He is sending Lord Churchill with troops from London,' Nelly answered. 'Remember that John Churchill who was a lover of Cleveland, and now married to Sarah Jennings? Well, it's him going and the Duke of Grafton, also, one of Cleveland's sons. That's a sad thing, isn't it, Wiggins? To think if there is a battle one half-brother will be fighting against another.'

'Not more death!' I cried. 'If Monmouth is victorious he will march on London, and the crowds here have always favoured him. Then what will happen to King James?'

'I don't know,' said Nelly quietly. 'Only God knows how all this will end.'

We heard that Monmouth marched towards Bristol, gathering more and more enthusiastic volunteers as he went, and I remembered how Shaftesbury had advised him to tour the West Country years before, and how he had gathered a great deal of support at that time. Now, those travels were standing him in good stead, it seemed.

But then the Duke of Beaufort, who lived in a place called Badminton, and was the Lord-Lieutenant of Gloucestershire, proved loyal to King James and

411

went with twenty-eight companies of foot to defend the city, declaring that if Monmouth entered Bristol he would burn it about his ears.

So Monmouth turned towards Bath.

On the 26th June we heard that the Duke of Grafton, at the head of the Life Guard Dragoons, had met Monmouth at Norton St Philip, and they had fought in the fields and lanes around that village. It had poured with rain during this encounter and Monmouth had proved victorious, leaving more than eighty of the Royalist troops dead, and many others wounded. Grafton and his men retreated to Bradford-on-Avon and Monmouth marched on to Frome.

The final battle was at Sedgemoor.

'A dreadful low-lying peat moor covered with deep ditches which have been built to stop floods in rainy seasons,' said Nelly. 'And there Churchill and his troops beat Monmouth, and he has escaped towards the New Forest, so

Will Chiffinch says. Oh, Wiggins, if he could only flee to France, or to Holland, like my dear Charles the third did so long ago, that would end all this horrid bloodshed, and King James could remain on the throne, and Prince Perkin would be able to settle down to a quiet life on the Continent, harming nobody.'

'Will he get away?' I said. 'And even if he does — will King James ever be able to trust him? He will surely live in dread of another invasion and another attempt at the throne by his ambitious nephew?'

'I don't know!' cried Nelly, clasping her hands to her breast. 'Oh, I wish I did not like them both so much. How *can* I take sides when they are like family to me?'

On the 13th July we heard that Monmouth had been captured at Holt Lodge in Dorset, and brought to London.

Nelly hurried across to Whitehall in her sedan-chair, and waited many hours to see Will Chiffinch. When she returned to Pall Mall she was quite exhausted, and her face was bleak.

'It will soon be over,' she said, coming to me and burying her head on my shoulder. 'Oh, Wiggins, we have had enough death and disaster in our lives, you and me, and 'tis terrible hard to have to take more.'

I stroked her hair, which was greying now, despite the fact that she was only in her thirty-fifth year, and the tresses were lacking the richness and lustre which had once made them so beautiful.

'Tell me,' I said gently.

'He asked to see King James when he arrived here and the King was good, I must say, and agreed to see him in Will Chiffinch's lodgings. They spoke for half an hour,' she went on huskily, her voice muffled against my gown, 'and Monmouth blamed all those Whigs exiled in Holland for encouraging him in his invasion of England. James listened and was very calm and not at all *bestial*, Wiggins, but he could not forgive him.'

She sniffed and lifted her face to look up at me, misery in her hazel eyes. 'He could not forgive my Prince Perkin for assuming sovereignty and for calling himself King. Nor could he forgive those terrible accusations that he had killed his own brother, my beloved Charles.

'Of *course* it was wicked of Monmouth — of *course* he behaved appallingly. But oh, Wiggins, I wish he did not have to die!'

And her head fell on to my breast as she broke into a torrent of sobs.

I held her, rocking the small, plump little figure in my arms, murmuring soothing sounds but no words. For what could be said at this tragic moment?

It was so sad that the late King's oldest and best loved son should be put to death by order of his uncle; it was such a waste of a young, vital life. And Monmouth had possessed some excellent qualities — else why had so many followed him — faced death for him? It could not only have been because of his Protestant faith. He had been a most graceful, charming, and fascinating hero to many, with enough of the Stuart blood to catch men's eyes, as well as females', and to grip their hearts.

But the Duke of Monmouth had also been weak, I decided, to listen to words of the wrong advisers, and he had been wilful, too, and unable, or unwilling, to accept the decision of his father, Charles II, King of England.

Much of this tragedy had been brought upon himself, and he had now to pay the cost.

Monmouth was taken by Royal barge to the Tower and executed on St Swithin's Day, 15 July, 1685.

Neither Nelly nor I went to the scene of his execution, and for that I was always thankful. But we heard the news later from Nelly's faithful confidant, Will Chiffinch.

There had been a vast crowd surrounding the scaffold and soldiers were brought in, some armed with pistols, for fear of a rescue attempt.

'Monmouth dressed very carefully for his last day on earth, Will said, and looked most beautiful and composed in his grey suit with black linings, and a dark periwig,' Nelly informed me. 'He asked for Dr Tenison to attend him — you remember him, Wiggins? He's the person I want to take my funeral and he's from St Martins-in-the Fields.'

'I remember.'

'Jack Ketch was the executioner, and Will says he was a bad choice 'cos he had bungled jobs before and was ever so nervous, whilst Monmouth remained calm.'

She began to weep then and I begged her to stop telling me the dreadful details.

'Wait until more time has passed and you are more composed,' I begged.

'I have to tell you — I will say it all now and then put the whole miserable scene out of my mind. If I can,' she whispered.

417

'Will Chiffinch said that Monmouth refused to be blindfolded, or bound, and after he had removed his coat and cravat and periwig, he lay down and placed his head on the block. But the first blow from the axe only wounded his neck. Oh, it was terrible — so terrible!'

But she would not remain silent.

'Then Jack Ketch struck again and after this second blow Monmouth crossed his legs. So calm still — but the fear and agony must have been quite awful!'

Holding my hands tighter and tighter, and with tears coursing down her white face, she went on —

'The third blow *still* did not sever his head from his body, so Jack Ketch had to finish the job with his knife.'

'Oh, God.' I clung to her then, both of us weeping without restraint, and we remained for some time in that gracious Withdrawing-Room, the room with the silk wall-hangings of gold and cream, and the gilded red and gold satin chairs, where I had once seen Nelly in flirtatious conversation with her handsome Prince Perkin.

Those last few years were filled with tragedy and sadness for Nelly, and I believe it was then that she lost interest in life and wanted to die herself.

First it had been her youngest son, James Beauclerk, then my Luke, of whom she had been genuinely fond. Then her beloved Charles the third died, followed by his handsome, reckless son. Lastly, in the April of 1687, we heard of Buckingham's death. Nelly did not say much to me about the news. She knew I disliked the man and could not have shown true regret, although I did feel sorry for Nelly and longed to cheer her. But she had become ill herself by then, sending often for the doctor, and beginning to take as many juleps and cordials as her mother had done.

'What ails you, Nelly?' I asked her, for she no longer seemed to care about life and began rising later and later each day. 'Are you in pain? What does the doctor think is wrong?'

'He does not know.' She shook her head slowly, closing her eyes, and I saw tears seeping from beneath her eyelids and trickling down her puffy cheeks.

'Nelly, take heart and get out of bed, and let me dress you in your prettiest gown. Do not give way to ill health, I beg you.'

'I have no heart left.' She opened her eyes and looked at me without emotion. 'There is no *reason* for me to live now, Wiggins. Can't you see that? I am fat and ugly and the time has come to join my Charles in Heaven. If I am quick about it, I'll get there before Punky Portsmouth and Cleveland, and even his little bat wife!'

It was a joy to see the flash of humour in her bloated face.

'Nelly, you are too young to die!' I cried, wondering what I should do without her. 'And what about me? Have you no love left for Alice Wingard — who has been a part of your life longer than any of the others? Why can we not grow old together, you and me?'

She smiled and stretched out her hand to touch mine. But it was very swollen now, and the rings she wore would soon have to be sawn off, so embedded were they in her waxen flesh.

'Wiggins, I promised always to take care of you and so I shall. Write to my lawyer, and the trustees, and ask them to call on me. 'Tis time I made my will and set my house in order.'

She also asked for her son to visit her, and he came with the trustees of her Burford House estate, who were none other than the Earl of Dorset (once Buckhurst) and her good friend, Will Chiffinch.

The Duke of St Albans was fond of his mother, but it had been apparent to me for some time that he had outgrown her, and was a little ashamed. The late King had loved him, as he had all his children, and after his visit to France, the lad had gradually drifted away from Nelly, to his friends and companions at

Whitehall. They were all better educated than the illiterate Nell Gwyn, who had been brought up in a bawdy-house, had earned her living as an orange-girl and then as an actress, and had not even been given a title to wear with pride.

The King, I think, had been worried about this son's future, believing, perhaps, that Nelly would not be able to see to his education as best befitted a Royal bastard. And young Charles Beauclerk Earl of Burford was growing up a most high-spirited lad; pretty as his mother, with red-gold hair and light hazel eyes, and possessing none of his father's dark swarthiness.

So, in the year 1682, I think it was, King Charles had arranged for the boy to go to France to receive military and mathematical training, and telling him to learn all he could from the magnificent Sun King, Louis of France.

Nelly was upset by her son's departure, but I had to admit that since her little James had died, Charles

Beauclerk had become increasingly spoilt by his adoring mother.

'It will do young Charles the world of good,' I had told her, 'and a stay in France will give him more experience and knowledge for the years ahead.'

'But my little James died there, Wiggins,' she had said piteously. 'What if I should lose my remaining son?'

'The King is very fond of Charles,' I had said firmly, 'and will make sure that he is well cared for and protected. Do not fight against this chance for your boy, Nelly.'

In fact, Charles Earl of Burford was to benefit greatly from his French stay, returning to London from time to time, and looking more mature and more handsome on every visit. When King Charles created him Duke of St Albans, it was obvious that he, too, was well pleased with Nelly's attractive and graceful son.

Nelly had very little money now, although she was out of debt thanks to King James, and the pension she received. But her son and the trustees agreed to do all that she requested and Nelly, in her warm-hearted way, thought of me, and Will Brown, and many others besides.

She asked to be buried in St Martins-in-the-Fields, and that Dr Tenison should preach her funeral sermon.

That £100 should be given to Dr Tenison to spend on the poor of St Martins and St James, Westminster, and to buy them clothes in winter.

She also asked that her son should spend £20 each year for releasing poor debtors from prison every Christmas Day.

Also that Dr Tenison should be given £50 to give to any two poor people of the Roman religion, who inhabited the parish of St James.

'I want to make sure that the people who do not have my faith, should also receive some charity from me,' she said.

And she made her son promise that both Will and I would be allowed to stay either in Pall Mall, or the house in Windsor, for as long as we lived, and continue to receive the food and the comforts to which we had grown accustomed with her.

When all these requests had been written down and her lawyer, and the trustees, and her son had departed, Nelly smiled happily and lay back upon her pillows, clasping her hands together over her large belly.

'Now I can die at ease,' she said, 'knowing that I have done everything right and proper.'

'You will not die,' I said, wishing that she would not keep talking about her death as if it were imminent. 'If you would only get up and dressed, and lead a more vigorous life, you could live for years and years, Nell Gwyn. Why, your own mother lived past her sixtieth year, so there is no reason for you not to do even better. Pull yourself together, I beg, and take an interest in life once more.'

She looked across at me most tenderly.

'Poor Wiggins, my dearest friend and companion for so many years. I have left you alone a great deal, and have not always been as thoughtful as I should. But we have had fun together, haven't we? Fun and sorrow — both shared, and now that I am satisfied about your future, I can leave this life without care. No,' she went on sharply as I was about to speak, 'I mean it this time, Wiggins. I am very unwell and do not believe there are many days left for me. Do not forget, dear friend, those words I spoke as Florimel in Dryden's *Secret Love*.'

She leaned her grey head back against the pillows and closed her eyes again. But this time she did not weep.

'"I am resolved to grow fat and look young till forty" — remember, Wiggins? "And then slip out of the world with the first wrinkle." Well, I am not yet forty, nor has a wrinkle appeared — unless it be hidden beneath so much flesh! But I am going soon and cannot say that I am sorry. Forgive me, if the truth hurts, but Will is nearby with his Peg, and my son will abide by his promises and see that you do not starve.'

Nelly died of apoplexy in her thirty-eighth year, and was buried on the 17th November, 1687 at St Martins-in-the-Fields. Dr Tenison preached the sermon as she had requested.

I shall end the tale now, in this year of 1690, for it is her story, written by me, as she once asked many, many years ago.

I still remain in good health, as do Will Brown and his little Peg, and their two children look upon me as their grandmother.

In some ways I am glad that Nelly died when she did, for there has been more tumult over the past few years, which would have distressed her. Poor King James has gone to France with his wife and baby son, but strangely enough it is his daughter, Mary, who has returned to take the throne, in partnership with her Orange William.

The people are happy because they now have a Protestant King and Queen, and as there are no children by that marriage, the crown will next go to Princess Anne, who is Mary's youngest sister.

It is all rather puzzling to me, but I find one does not worry so much about things as one grows older, and without my dearest Luke to converse with, my brain is becoming steadily slower and emptier of thoughts. I think of him frequently, of course, and remain true to my promise believing that we *will* meet again, despite the good Dr Tenison's uncertainty on the matter, when the Lord decides it is time for me to leave this earth. I never forget my Luke, and remember both him and my friend Nelly, with love.

Sometimes, when I am feeling mentally agile and content with my own memories, I wonder how the old King feels — Nelly's once 'dismal Jimmy' — having to live in exile because of his faith, knowing that his own daughter

428

bears the crown of England, because of hers. And what emotions does the Earl of Clarendon have, looking down from Heaven, seeing his granddaughters become Queens of this realm, when he was forced into exile — not for his faith, but for his ideas?

Memory also returns to me of Luke's words, spoken so long ago. I hear him saying that he saw England as a battle-ground, with a war waged between four antagonists — King Charles, Shaftes-bury, Danby and Louis of France. I also remember my shock when first hearing him speak of the secret Treaty of Dover.

Yet now, twenty years on, what does all that worry and intrigue matter? England still remains in one piece with no bloody Civil War, and no Catholi-cism has been thrust upon us against our wills.

Shaftesbury is dead, so is Charles Stuart, and Danby is of little impor-tance any more. Orange William and his Mary reign over us, a good, Protestant King and Queen. And that magnificent

Sun King, Louis of France, has not gained control of either Holland or England, despite his efforts.

It seems to me that Charles Stuart did very well for himself in the end. Despite the Treaty of Dover, he did not force the Roman Church upon us, nor did he shock his adoring people by changing his religion whilst he reigned. He left his poor brother James to bear the brunt of trying to rule a land which hated both him, and the faith he believed in.

Yet Charles Stuart managed to get his own way at the very end, and die in the faith which had always appealed to his heart, and so few people knew the truth, that he will always be remembered with affection as the Protestant King Charles II.

Now I shall finish writing and put all these pages carefully away until such a time as the Duke of St Albans should wish to read them. I hope that his mother has been portrayed both kindly and fairly, and that one day he will feel proud of the knowledge that his mother was the most popular of Old Rowley's mistresses. Her name may even go down in history as being that of King Charles's pretty, witty Nelly.

Bibliography

The Life and Times of Queen Anne, Gila Curtis. Weidenfeld and Nicolson.

Charles II, Antonia Fraser. Weidenfeld and Nicolson.

The Life and Times of Charles II, Christopher Falkus. Weidenfeld and Nicolson.

Costume 1066–1966, John Peacock. Thames and Hudson.

English Costume of the Seventeenth Century, Iris Brooke. Adam and Charles Black.

Lives of the Duchesses of Portsmouth and Cleveland, Mrs Jameson. Grolier Society.

A History of Everyday Things in England 1500–1799, Marjorie and CHB Quennell. BT Batsford.

Life in the English Country House, Mark Girouard. Yale University Press.

The Story of the English Stage,

Alison Taylor. Pergamon Press.

Book of English Poetry, G.B Harrison. Penguin Books.

Great Villiers, Hester W Chapman. Secker and Warburg.

Crimson Book of Highwaymen, Peter Newark. Jupiter Books.

The Illustrious Lady, Elizabeth Hamilton. Hamish Hamilton.

Ladies-in-Waiting, Anne Somerset. Weidenfeld and Nicolson.

James Duke of Monmouth, Bryan Bevan. Robert Hale.

Nell Gwyn, Bryan Bevan. Robert Hale. *The Story of Nell Gwyn*, Peter Cunningham. Grolier Society.

The Illustrated Pepys, ed. Robert Latham. Bell and Hyman.

Royal Children, Dulcie M Ashdown. Robert Hale.

Penguin Book of Restoration Verse, ed. Harold Love.

Stuart England, ed. Blair Worden. Phaidon Press.

The Stuarts, JP Kenyon. Collins Fontana Library.

The Stuarts in Love, Maurice Ashley. Hodder and Stoughton.
The Weaker Vessel, Antonia Fraser. Weidenfeld and Nicolson.

We do hope that you have enjoyed reading this large print book.

Did you know that all of our titles are available for purchase?

We publish a wide range of high quality large print books including:
Romances, Mysteries, Classics
General Fiction
Non Fiction and Westerns

Special interest titles available in large print are:
The Little Oxford Dictionary
Music Book, Song Book
Hymn Book, Service Book

Also available from us courtesy of Oxford University Press:
Young Readers' Dictionary
(large print edition)
Young Readers' Thesaurus
(large print edition)

For further information or a free brochure, please contact us at:
Ulverscroft Large Print Books Ltd.,
The Green, Bradgate Road, Anstey,
Leicester, LE7 7FU, England.
Tel: (00 44) **0116 236 4325**
Fax: (00 44) **0116 234 0205**

ONCE UPON A TIME

Zelma Falkiner

City girl Meredith plans to write a novel in the peace and quiet of the country, but finds her chosen retreat is over-run by a film production company. Despite her best intentions, she is soon lured from her story-telling into a make-believe world of early Australia, with handsome, bearded bush-rangers on horseback, and women in long skirts, boots and gingham bonnets. But in the real world, a little girl is in danger . . .

A TOUCH OF MAGIC

June Gadsby

Lorna is trying to rebuild her life after the war that robbed her of her husband and her son of a father he never knew. However, eleven-year-old Simon refuses to accept that Max is dead. Lorna does not believe in miracles, but it is Christmas and all Simon asks is the chance to see the place where his father's plane crashed. In the dense Basque forest, a man called Olentzero brings a touch of magic back into their lives . . .

A DREAM COME TRUE

Chrissie Loveday

Jess inherits an idyllic cottage in Cornwall and is determined to begin a new life. But there are surprises waiting. Someone is entering the cottage each time she goes out. Are they hoping to drive her away? If so, why? Can she risk abandoning everything she knows to move away from her parents? Dan, her new neighbour, and his family are persuasive — and she could see a future for herself in Cornwall . . . if she can get over the problems.

A NEW BEGINNING

Miranda Barnes

When Kirsty Johnston visits Fells Inn it's no longer the happy place of her childhood memories, but run-down and up for sale. The only other guest is the mysterious Bob, who keeps to himself. Despite this a friendship develops between them, but Bob proves to be a difficult man to know. And when Kirsty decides to make an offer for the inn and start a new life, it brings them into direct competition. Will they ever resolve their differences?